Rosalind

Rosalind

A Family Romance

A NOVEL BY

Myra Goldberg

𝒵

ZOLAND BOOKS

Cambridge, Massachusetts

First edition published in 1996 by
Zoland Books, Inc.
384 Huron Avenue
Cambridge, Massachusetts 02138

Copyright © 1996 by Myra Goldberg

FIRST EDITION

Book design by Boskydell Studio

Printed in the United States of America

02 01 00 99 98 97 96 8 7 6 5 4 3 2

This book is printed on acid-free paper, and its binding
materials have been chosen for strength and durability.

Library of Congress Cataloging-in-Publication Data
Goldberg, Myra, 1943–
Rosalind: a family romance: a novel /
by Myra Goldberg — 1st ed.
p.   cm.
ISBN 0-944072-59-3 (alk. paper)
1. Family — Massachusetts — Boston — Fiction.
2. Women — Massachusetts — Boston — Fiction.
3. Heart — Surgery — Patients — Fiction.
I. Title
PS3557.03582R67   1996
813'.54 — dc20   95-43973
CIP

TO MY MOTHER
Ruth Kronman Goldberg
AND MY DAUGHTER
Anna Resnikoff

ACKNOWLEDGMENTS

Parts of *Rosalind* appeared in slightly different form
in *Representations of Motherhood*, edited by Donna Bassin,
Margaret Honey, and Meryle Mahrer Kaplan
(Yale University Press, New Haven, 1994).

I would like to thank all of the people who helped me with
this book, including the staff at Dorell Casuals
and at Dr. Thaler's office, Dr. David Zimmerman,
Bill Sokol, and Constance Bloomfield. My
thanks to Sarah Lawrence College, which continues
to provide a community of writers
to work within.

Run, run, Orlando, carve on every tree
the fair, the chaste, and inexpressive she.

As You Like It, III.ii.10

Rosalind

1

Do you remember that painting, that Renoir, that beautiful woman of a certain age, that Madame Charpentier, sitting in a black velvet dress upon a sofa? With two little girls in lacy blue and white beside her. That bourgeois French woman in black, dress trailing all over her sofa and her two little girls and a dog somewhere, perhaps in Madame's lap. Lots of clothes, lots of textures, lots of skin tones.

Well, in introducing Rosalind, our Rosalind Oliner Baumbach Twist, who is American and our contemporary, I want to make sure you remember this picture. Perhaps the publisher will put one in. French velvet sofas and the end of the nineteenth century, light falling lovingly on everyone and all those draperies behind them, that languidness that Madame C. assumes like a drapery — then picture our Rosalind:

A woman more beautiful than Madame C., with pale skin, deep blue eyes, snapping black hair, who is languid and decisive simultaneously. Her clothes, for example, are languid — a gray silk shirt to the knees of her gray silk pants — and so is her pose, leaning against the sofa cushions, feet up. On her lap, a little girl with red-gold ringlets and then a leggy almost teenager standing taller beside her. Say the girls are wearing dresses. I mean, does anybody celebrate quotidian bourgeois beauty anymore, except the ads? But wait, this woman is rising, rushing off, she's got a job to go to, patients to see, a class to teach, the languidness gone as soon as the picture gets snapped. The girls go back to their sweatsuits and activities. It's the eighties, early on. Rosalind is fat, I forgot to mention; it shows now that she is standing up.

The husband is around the edges of this picture, probably out. He's tall, very tall, abstracted. This is a second marriage, for in the center of this family there was a crack, say in 1968, and the first child belongs to husband number one, the second to the second, which you can't trace in the features, because people in families mostly look different from each other anyway. But now I've lost her. Rosalind. She's gone off somewhere. Born or brought up to be languid, she has turned out, like her contemporaries, to live a life that is rushed. It's the eighties. The Reagan administration has stepped into its own golden picture frame as life in these United States flows through a different set of opportunities and molds. Let's step back. It's May. To take another look at this story. That spring. These lives.

$\sim$

For the first thirty-seven years of her life, Rosalind Oliner Baumbach Twist had been lucky. She'd been lucky in work, backing her way from a Ph.D. in sociology into a lucrative and rewarding practice as a psychotherapist. She'd been lucky in love except for Baumbach, her first husband, and even he had left her something: a huge house in Brookline, Massachusetts, and a daughter whom she loved. She'd been lucky in small things, secondhand Volvos, and in large, neither of her two children nor her second husband, Henry, had problems inaccessible to goodwill, intelligence or money, all of which she had. Moreover, Rosalind's brother and sister adored her; her parents placed her at the center of their family's earth. And if Rosalind considered her own character 'impossible, a garden of neurosis,' through psychotherapy, education and experience she'd brought that garden into bloom: she was articulate about her failings, attuned to delicate distinctions among her feelings and complex formulations of relation and dismay.

Only her body eluded her. Sometimes merely plump, and sometimes monumental, she hid her monument to what was fleshy like a crime. Beneath black tent dresses with romantic red roses strewn about, her thighs were large and soft, her breasts like Keats's autumn vegetables, her hips were broad. Beneath her tents, she was still and statuelike. She walked slowly as if in pain and left dishes where she'd dirtied them on armchairs or the rug, as if, her children thought, they had offended her somehow. In fact she had, according to her brother Lev, found the perfect profession in the practice of psychotherapy. For she could sit listening for long hours, her mind as active as her body was inert, participating for good in other people's lives. Or as Lev said, wrapping his knowledge and affection for his older sister in folk talk, like chewing gum in silver foil, "It's what you like to do anyway, Rosie. Sit and smoke cancer sticks and shoot the shit with folks."

Two weeks before her operation, she'd been sitting with her legs spread wide, her ankles thick above her rubber flip-flops on the front porch of a New Hampshire farmhouse, reading to her husband Henry from an article she'd been writing. "A jewish woman tells the following story." She'd paused beside 'jewish.' Something wrong with it. It needed caps. "A Jewish woman tells the following story. She was living near her mother in a city in Poland during Hitler's invasion." She felt a pain split her right shoulder, but went on reading. "With the German army coming closer, a Polish neighbor offered his attic for the mother and daughter to hide in, but the daughter refused." The pain was in her chest by now. "She couldn't stand the thought of living alone in an attic with her mouther for months or years perhaps." Ros stared at 'mouther.' "Mother," she said aloud. Then with her head bent over her legs, she murmured, "heartburn," when Henry asked what was wrong. Then she straightened up. "Three months later, my patient got a chance to leave Poland alone. This time she refused because she couldn't leave her mother behind."

"Hold on," she told Henry. "I have to rest for a minute. But the piece gets better as it goes on." For she'd interpreted Henry's silence to mean that he disliked what she had written. She picked up the rimless glasses she'd set down on the porch and put them on for her last sentence. "My patient eventually left for this country where she prospered. Her mother, alone in Poland, perished in the camps."

Returning later that evening to Brookline from the farm she'd staged the summers of her sixties youth in, where life had been communal and a famous fugitive black man had spent a night, the pains had reappeared. And on Monday at Henry's insistence and because such pains were not endurable now that she'd endured them once, she'd gone to her internist in Cambridge.

Tests had been taken, blood had been drawn. Her friendly, intelligent internist had cocked his head to rest his warm red ear against her breast and listen attentively, then held his cold stethoscope to her flesh. More tests had been taken, more blood had been drawn. A few days later, entering Dr. Kriegel's office, she met a friendly intelligent face that was in mourning for her. "I'm really sorry," he said in a voice that made her think he really was. "Indications, operation, main stem clogged . . ." She'd heard. She hadn't heard. She'd driven home. She'd had Henry call his cardiologist uncle and she'd called her old friend Danny Kesselman, the holistic Berkeley internist, to find out what the West Coast thought.

"I mean, you could change your lifestyle, get away from all that competitive insanity back east, but shit Ros, a left main stem, some disaster could take place before you got anywhere with the organic interventions."

"Yes or no," she'd said quietly, feeling once more that she'd been dragged into this crisis by whomever she happened to be talking to at the moment. Meanwhile in her real life patients and children and an article were awaiting her.

"You're pushing me," said Danny sadly, whose favorite part of holistic medicine was lying in darkness beside his patients listening to the healing dissonances of the late Beethoven quartets. "But given those numbers you've got, I'd have to say go for it."

Hanging up, she'd gone on, called her brother Lev in Oakland, who'd called her sister Lila in New York, who'd volunteered to call their parents, then come for Ros's children's sake to Boston. Then covering her most fragile patients with the empty hours of a psychiatrist friend, she'd informed them all that she was going to the hospital, packed her bags and driven herself to Massachusetts General with her husband Henry beside her.

All of the above had been done briskly as if she were administering the affairs of someone else. A daughter, perhaps, in her early twenties, who had business in a country that was dusty, dry and far from home. Or a patient, who needed clear, unemotional, practical direction.

At the hospital, Henry had listened again to her instructions about the children. "Check on Sophie to make sure she knows I haven't been buried in the basement of the hospital or some such story. Nana will be a help if you let her." He'd nodded, then held her, then left her, which was a relief for a moment, a chance to be alone. And it was only after pubic hair and arm hair and the tiny hairs on her nipples had been shaved that she began, lying by the window in the hospital, to feel alone for real, to feel afraid. Still as a statue, gazing at the afternoon sky, fear like darkness descended on her shoulders. Oh God, let me out of here, she thought. But by then the little white cup of pills the nurse had brought had made her feel drowsy and her evening softened and slid away as more pills got brought to her and she was still sleeping the next morning when her body was rolled from her bed to a stretcher and from the stretcher to a table in the operating room and then her heart was frozen until it stopped and a machine in the corner took over and began to breathe for her while she was gone.

〜

A pause to point out that this is a particular moment in history, a few short years after middle-class women, the former serving maids and handmaidens of middle-class men, have moved with strength, anxiety, intelligence, into the professions and gained what independence there is in pleasing a boss instead of a husband.

Middle-class men, on the other hand, well, consider it yourself, the world defined as your apple or oyster, along with its women, whom you feel lustful towards and also tenderly protective, then suddenly half your population becomes a buddy or competitor — men, well men, for a while, feel bewildered, angry, put-upon.

∾

Henry Twist, Rosalind's husband, stood up from the red Naugahyde couch in the hospital's solarium. He needed news about his wife and so he stood, walking to the window and looking out as if the news might fly in. Besides, sitting between these worried bodies had been uncongenial, and for a second he'd felt, as the elbow of the man beside him had grazed his chest accidentally, that the whereabouts of his wife were unknown and she had slipped away from him.

Everyone on the couch had looked up at Henry as he'd stood, wondering if he'd heard something and how he'd heard it, for no solemn-faced doctor had come striding into the sunny solarium with a hand outstretched to shake his. They'd stared, for Henry was huge, six or seven inches above six feet, and as thin as he was tall, with pale skin, pale brown hair, pale blue eyes and a timid, but desperate air.

Outside the window Henry stood by were warehouses that had been transformed into apartments by Harriman, Ellis, Architects and Engineers. Henry, an architect, knew this bit of professional news. Inside those apartments lived doctors and lawyers and computer engineers who'd bought the places at prices so high they'd astonished buyers, sellers, everyone else.

Those buildings should have roof gardens, thought Henry, filled with sudden tenderness for the warehouses and the men who'd bought them, as the terror about his wife's whereabouts that had shut his mind down floated off. Roof gardens on that building for oxygen as well as pleasure, an idea that seemed especially important and original to him right now.

He blinked and ceased to see the sunshine and tried, feeling braver as a result of his oxygen idea, to picture the machine in the operating room which breathed for his wife, while the vein from her calf and the artery from her groin were used to patch her heart. But no machine appeared to Henry, because no one had explained, in the hurried days before the operation, exactly how the machine was put together. Henry, whose imagination needed real details to run along, folded one huge set of fingers into the other and, with his gold wedding ring shining in the May sunshine, thought about Rosalind.

In his place, Rosalind would have been thinking not about the machine, but about the social and psychic costs of a medical system that performed this operation. It wasn't simply, the Rosalind in Henry's mind went on, that there was no reasonable way in this richest country in the world to deal with the cost of ordinary ailments, but that our psyches were all paying for a culture that could invent this kind of thing. Consider, she said, as Henry peered through the window at the warehouse, the rationality it took to create this machine, the detachment to use it, the obedience to experts to submit to its care.

How happy Henry now felt, as if his possession of Rosalind's thoughts was keeping her alive and in control of the operation, while his eyes were on the warehouse transformed into expensive but uncomfortable luxury apartments.

Finished with Rosalind's thoughts because he had no idea where she might go from there, Henry, who'd never tried to duplicate the being of a being he'd depended on before, returned to his own mind and saw a knife cutting open his wife's chest and a nutcracker breaking her ribs so that her frozen heart could be restrung, while a machine he couldn't visualize breathed for her from the corner.

He looked down, saddened suddenly, weary, undone, and found Thursday, May 5, eleven seventeen and thirty seconds, on the flat expressionless face of the watch on his bony wrist. What good would it do him to know the time it was, if he didn't know if the operation were on or over? What good would it do Rosalind for him to think her thoughts, while she was off that machine or still on it, living, waking or somewhere else he didn't want to name in thought. As if to dare something, Henry looked down at his watch again. Eleven nineteen and seven seconds. Thursday, May 5, 1983. I really would have thought that the damned thing would have been over by now, he thought, without knowing exactly what damned thing he was referring to. Only that it was upstairs. Taking place without him.

~

Pain free, because the woman who would have felt the pain had floated off somewhere, Rosalind lay in the recovery room, beneath a blanket of drugs with a tube up her nose, a tube down her throat, a tube stuck into her chest to drain the fluids from her lungs after the operation. Beside her bed, a machine that was different from the machine in the operating room pushed air into her lungs, gasping and wheezing, like an old man with emphysema.

A nurse in white nylon, ugly and angelic, watched a television screen at the foot of Rosalind's bed. Lines from Rosalind's arms and legs sent messages to the screen: blood pressure, temperature, output of urine, while Rosalind's heart, electrified, drew zigzags. The nurse bent, unhooked a full bag of urine, replaced it with an empty one and looked at her watch.

In the other three beds in this recovery room, each with its lines, its bags, its television screens, its zigzag drawings of the rhythms of a heart, lay three men: a pharmacist, a lawyer, an industrial designer. Nurses, residents and an anesthesiologist moved between beds, bending, lifting, caring for them.

A few minutes later, in the recovery room, a series of irregular blips began to skitter across the television screen at the head of Rosalind's bed. The blips skittered more rapidly. Stopped. An alarm went off as the nurse, who'd once been convented, and the resident, who'd considered cabinetmaking instead of cardiology, grabbed the paddles from a machine nearby and bending over Rosalind's body made shock marks all over her chest until her heart, which had stopped, started up again.

Why her heart had stopped, whether a heart attack or lowered blood pressure or something else had stopped it, was clear to no one, then or later. As it skittered, then stopped, Rosalind, in her drugged unconsciousness, dreamed she stood on a sandy beach before a lake, toes in the freezing blue-black water. Her freezing toes drawn back. A sentence inside her: 'I can't leave the children.'

~

Children, I might add, during the period preceding this one, when there were wars, riots and changes in the lives and expectations of people everywhere, from the very edge of former empires to people at this country's heart who came in skin tones other than pale pink or yellowy white, children landed on communes, in single rooms, with mothers who'd left one father and were going to school at night. With fathers on weekends or summers or alternate nights. With new fathers no fathers female fathers or different men for different nights.

~

Five miles southwest of the hospital, Rosalind's two children sat in the yellow brick Garwood School in pleasant tree-lined suburban Brookline. A school that had been named in the 1950s after a man whose accomplishments no one in the 1980s could remember, it was situated on a street of enormous houses built to represent prosperity to the residents of the 1920s. Since then, trees had grown to the height of the school's second story and divorce had entered this liberal mostly Jewish neighborhood along with a black dermatologist and a physicist from Taiwan. With divorce, a list of single mothers on the bottom of a pile of problems on the principal's desk. For they were unable to pay their after-school tuition bills, but shamelessly insisted on sending their children anyway to soccer or ceramics.

On the second floor in a room near the principal's office, Rosalind's younger daughter Sophie sat by a window with a slender silver birch to look out on. She was building a papier-mâché relief map of the earth's surface. Furious when she understood that the lowest point on earth was the ocean floor and not the land (why hadn't she realized? Why hadn't the teacher explained? The teacher had explained and she'd been dreaming), Sophie had balled up wet pasty pieces of papier-mâché and started over, building mountains and plains and peninsulas up from the ocean. She'd stopped to let the world dry before she colored it with poster paint.

The science specialist, a pretty, broad-shouldered woman, started down the aisle, to see what Sophie, a notorious ripper up of projects, had done.

Sophie, looking up to see the teacher approaching, felt that pounding in her heart again. That pounding when she couldn't stand something. Someone looking at what she'd done when it hadn't come out right yet.

A few weeks before, she'd spent a whole afternoon making and ripping up birthday cards for her mother's birthday, trying to get the card to come out right.

Here was this enormous woman looking down at what she'd done. Saying, "How wonderful, Sophie. You're the only one to get the Italian boot to look like that."

Liar, thought Sophie, pressing her lips together. Just like my Mom. She forced herself not to cover the boot with her pale freckled hand.

Sophie's heart was pounding with this enormous woman looking down at what she'd done. Taking seriously, just like her mother, what Sophie, a little girl who insisted on her littleness for fear of harming anyone, had made. Which might be wrong or dangerous.

As the teacher's narrow waist and squishy behind went up the aisle, Sophie went back to the Italian boot to jiggle the heel, to test it. The boot broke. Now with something that was still wrong with what she'd made, she could bend happily over her world and fix it.

Outside the window she sat by, a yellow bird hopped on a branch of the silver birch, then took off into the sweet spring suburban sky.

~

On the top floor of the Garwood School, Rosalind's older daughter Nana, who was tall and could see over the heads of the shorter students, sat at the back of a room of sixth graders taking a spelling test. A long blonde braid lay on her heart, while beside her long thin fingers lay a pile of felt-tipped pens.

The words on Nana's spelling list were *element, equality, equivalent, excess* and *entirely,* not a difficult list for a grade-six class in a neighborhood where students who didn't do better than children in other neighborhoods were sent to tutors or psychotherapists. For these children were valued not for looks or loving-kindness but for accomplishments. And since their parents, accomplished too, had no factories to leave them or farms for them to cultivate, their only legacy was a childhood in this neighborhood's schools, which would prepare them for the colleges, which would help them to accomplish what would pay enough for them to live in a similar neighborhood when they grew up.

Nana looked down at her words to make sure they were correct. To make sure, moreover, that they looked nice. She liked spelling. She also liked the way her words looked, written carefully in a purple felt-tipped pen. Spelling is like gymnastics, thought Nana. Something you got told how to do, then practiced and got better at. Endlessly consulted by her mother: should I wear my coat or my cape? And endlessly ignored: I'll wear my sweater, Nana loved having rules for situations. So she'd felt a bond with Henry, as the other sensible member of a family headed by a mother who had principles too subtle to understand, laced through with whim and indecisiveness. Henry, who'd come to live with them when she was three years old, had obliged her for a while. With rules about bedtimes and limitations on her allowance and Ping-Pong lessons and trips to the science museum where things had explanations for them. But Rosalind disapproved of rules, because they substituted fiat for reason, passion, need, and the lessons and trips went with them when Henry returned, a few years ago, to life inside his head, where he reigned as Nana saw him, like the gigantic spider king of a dim and distant planet.

Nana changed from the purple felt-tipped pen to a green one and wrote down *Excess.* Tears came to her eyes, because her mother, who was a psychotherapist, which Nana knew meant people came to her for help with problems, was having an operation today and might be lying at this moment, with her pretty face, but fat as a piglet body, on some table being opened.

"She's incredibly lovely for someone so eccentrically misshapen," someone behind them at the school play had said last week, because Ros was normal sized on top and enormously fat on the bottom. Sometimes even her normal half looked weird because she didn't wear a bra and bagged like old balloons under her Pakistani smocks.

This morning at home, Nana could tell from Henry's especially spacy look how serious this operation was and also from Aunt Lila's coming. Aunt Lila was as thin as her mother was fat and had red frizzy hair and an expression on her freckled face like she was on the hunt for something, only that something was unreal and somewhere else. She wore loose cotton pants of black, and purple polo shirts, which were cute in a way with all that frizzy red hair, only Nana wished she wouldn't in Brookline where the other kids could see her. "She's a painter from Greenwich Village in New York City," Sophie had whispered to their neighbors.

Unlike her mother who took a year to come to a decision, then changed her mind, Lila stared at things, like that green willow across the highway from the supermarket yesterday, then started towards them. Without considering, as Nana had pointed out, that the ice cream in the station wagon would melt while they were gone.

Nana, looking up at the clean green board where "May 5" and been written in yellow chalk, wrote *extremely* in her best red pen, then thought, Lila's a little like Sophie, I guess. Sophie had had a horrible stomachache this morning, then been unable to decide what to wear. She'd thrown dungarees and running shoes and dolls all over her room until Henry came up to see what the thuds were about. Then she'd cried in his arms until Henry had said, "Sophie, I've got to go to the hospital now."

Entirely, wrote Nana, on her yellow legal-sized spelling list, which was done.

~

Beyond the edges of this family landscape there were boats leaving Brooklyn carrying Japanese radios to Oslo. Wars everywhere as well as dishes to wash. People living in cardboard boxes and picking in garbage cans for what was left of other people's dinners or furnishings. From this perspective, a question about the operation Rosalind Oliner had just undergone arises. Floating, like smoke, in the air above Boston. For did her death, her resurrection, her chance to live longer than her heartbroken ancestors in Poland, hold out a standard that would apply to all these others one day? Did it say *there,* we have it now, the worth of a life, the value of an individual, the preciousness of the human soul remaining here on earth inside the body for its term, where it belongs? Or were this operation and that machine only the temporary form that a conviction of our preciousness took? A conviction that something like history or the wealth and know-how of the West had made manifest as a heart-lung machine and that had nothing to do with other people's hearts in other times or places.

~

"I'm awfully sorry, sir, but I can't call up there. Someone will come down to get you when she's ready." The friendly woman with the blotchy face behind the counter had her eyes on Henry's breastbone as she spoke.

"I have been waiting for over" — Henry looked at his watch — "four hours now. Surely the operation should be, I would have thought. Four hours is, as I remember, the outside figure for the procedure's length that got mentioned." Henry's syntax got clotted when he got tense. His long fingers spread out upon the counter.

One fifty-two, said Henry's watch. Thursday, May 5.

"Could be four, could be five even." The woman smiled gently. "I promise I'll notify you as soon as I have news to offer." She dialed a number, frowned, hung up and said, "She's in the recovery room now. That's the only information I can get hold of."

"But surely," said Henry, "if they know where she is, someone should be able to — "

"The doctors will come to talk to you, as soon as they are free to." Her voice was sharper now. "I'll page them in a few minutes if you like."

Nodding to show he had no hard feelings, although he felt this woman behind the counter should be taking better care of him, Henry returned to the solarium and the red Naugahyde couch which squeaked as he sat down, squeaked again as he got up and walked to the window and looked out. He had no thoughts in his head now as he stared at the warehouse, only the feeling that he'd had an operation too and all his faculties had been cut out. Leaving a tall, thin, useless body waiting for something, for news.

"I wish to register a complaint. Where the hell are all those doctors? You paged them fifteen minutes ago," Henry returned to tell the blotchy-faced woman, who mollified him by saying that she could understand his feelings and would call up once more if he'd return to the couch in the solarium and wait a few more minutes.

Roof gardens, thought Henry, returning, like an obedient schoolchild, to his seat and making plastic groans and noises as he sat his great length down. They should have roof gardens on those warehouses, for oxygen and also pleasure. His stomach felt strange and his heart speeded up.

~

A few minutes later two men in dark suits arrived in the solarium. One was bald and slightly overweight, like Henry, in his forties. The other was older, colder, a scar on his cheek. The bald man, the cardiologist, stuck his plump hand out to reach Henry's. His careful voice took Henry beneath his wing. "Let's go to my office and talk." Meanwhile the gray-bearded surgeon walked like a crutch on Henry's other side should he be needed. And Henry's rage collapsed into fearfulness.

"The stoppage was brief, of unexplained origin," said the red-faced cardiologist from behind his desk.

"Are you telling me — "

"She's alive." The surgeon, standing stoop-shouldered beside the desk, fingered the scar on his cheek.

Henry followed the words and the surgeon's finger moving up a jagged red line, but felt too stupid to register anything except that something extremely serious had happened while he'd been waiting in the solarium. "Thank you." He was standing and striding to the doorway, then turning round. "Are you telling me her heart stopped, after the operation?"

Both men nodded. "In the recovery room," said the cardiologist softly.

"The operation was successful." The surgeon frowned and laced his fingers together.

"But I thought someone was supposed to watch over her up

there." Henry looked at the ceiling. "She's alive?" he repeated, catching the pale blue eyes of the cardiologist and remembering his decision, before the operation, to trust these men, on the advice of friends and colleagues.

The cardiologist slid a Polaroid snapshot across the scarred wooden desk. "It's a good thing we got in there," he said. "Even with surgery, we can't predict — come look at this." Beckoning with his thick fingers towards Henry to return to them.

The snapshot was of a bloody acorn. No, saw Henry, the snapshot was of a heart. He should examine it, he felt, for information, the way he might a blueprint or set of specifications, but his fingers were pushing the snapshot back across the desk, and he was nodding as if he'd seen as much as he needed or wanted to, then starting for the door again. He turned, filling the doorway, his head grazing the top. "But I thought someone was watching her, that someone would take care of all that," he said softly as a grief-stricken child before he turned and went down the hallway. Feeling, as he sat down again in the solarium, that something enormously important had happened in that office, but he had no idea what it was. He searched his pockets for something he might have left in that office, behind him, and found dimes. Which reminded him. Call home. Talk to Lila. The children. Rosalind's parents and brother.

❧

One reason, as you can guess, that Henry is feeling so shaky is that he is, within this family, the technician. Whose purpose, authority and confidence are based on his relation to and mastery of objects.

Yet these men, who have mastered the heart of his wife, speak to him as if he were a patient. That is, if not under anesthesia, dumb in some fundamental sense.

❧

Henry called the following: Rosalind's parents in Manhattan, her brother, still asleep in California, and his sister-in-law Lila, at home with his kids. He skipped the friends on the list and he forgot in his intense suppressed excitement to speak to his kids, relying on Lila instead to convey his information, which was that Ros was okay, apparently. As far as he could tell, from what little information the hospital had seen fit to give him.

~

Hours after Henry's phone call, which he'd been half asleep for, Rosalind's brother Lev awoke in Oakland. For a second time. Slipped his feet into his battered leather slippers and slip-shodded (was the feel in words for these self-propelled feet) to his rainy window and stared out at a man in a windbreaker who was lifting the battery from his pickup truck to carry it for safekeeping to his home.

It would be stolen otherwise, in this slightly dangerous slum.

Okay, apparently, Lev thought. Okay, apparently, which was the phrase that Henry had used about Rosalind's — was it health they were talking about? Illness? Postoperative condition. He stood, for a long moment, at the dotted rainy window watching the man cradling his battery, like some small and wounded dog. Then tore himself from the melancholy sight, and dressed for San Francisco and his job.

"This is KMRC. We talk about the world." Lev had an all-night radio talk show that he hosted and got paid nuthatch wages for, like the advertisers paid, because nobody but nuts, said the station manager, listened at midnight and beyond. Or worked at night either, was the implication.

He'd married someone who didn't talk that much, so all these words built up during the daytimes. He could chat chat chat while everybody else was sleeping, so that the voices inside his head could lie down later and take a rest. Meanwhile, this question fluttered above his family's funky household: was Lev's choice to live in voluntary poverty a movement of the soul, a necessary psychic tropism, religious in origin? Or connected, say, with his older sister's lavishness. Or was it habit merely, signed on in youth, — this is a question whose answer, Lev decided, at this moment, moving his beat-up Datsun as swiftly as possible onto the great gray Bay Bridge, that he doesn't know or even need to know. Driving to this foolish job. Now he's off the exit ramp, leaving a great swoop of cars, darkness, water, behind him. He's parking over by Polk Street, near that restaurant that's listed this evening's offering as a rack of lamb, on a blackboard beneath a library lamp, for twenty-five dollars a portion. Lev loves food. Especially fancy stuff. He stares for a while, thinks rack, lambs, torture, garlic and olive oil. Rosemary, peppercorns. He takes a Sony from his pocket and plugs it in his ear.

"God doesn't heal you because you're good." It was his favorite radio preacher. "He heals you because you believe. Show some faith and you'll move him in your direction. What kind of faith? Now faith. Everyone's looking for an excuse to stay sick, but God never healed anyone lying down. He made them rise. Take up your beds and walk."

He'd done something right tonight. By simply walking up this block to work. He'd shown faith. In the power of the daily to bring recovery. He'd kept on truckin'.

～

Rosalind's eyes opened then closed. Feeling weariness, pain, the nothingness of the hours she'd missed and the weight of something she couldn't remember, she heard the industrial designer beside her moaning and thought she'd heard her own voice.

～

Was it only loneliness, this renaissance of public discourse his show was part of, people calling up strangers to talk? Lev climbed the stairs of the former warehouse that housed the radio station. Loneliness arriving with divorce, the breakup of families, neigh-

borhoods, nations and empires? He'd reached the second floor.
Shut up, he told himself, as he passed the janitor who was dragging an enormous plastic garbage bag full of wire service copy
and cardboard coffee cups behind him. He waved through the
office door at Andrew, the producer, calling Hong Kong from his
office with his feet up on the desk. Pressure in his chest, for what
he would be doing tonight was weird, even for someone on the
funky midnight to six shift.

"Trade will be a key topic in the talks with the Chinese."
Chuck, the engineer, had the network news turned up when he
came into the studio. "Hundreds of thousands of West Germans
are expected to take part in the traditional spring antinuclear
march. 'We found that those who won, won. Those who did not
win, did not win.' That's how the director of elections described
the recount."

"When the news was done, "Hello, this is Lev Oliner. I'll be
around from midnight to six. What I'd really like to talk about
this evening is my sister. My sister has just had a bypass operation
and she's now recovering from this incredible operation, or
rather, I assume she is recovering. I got a phone call from my
brother-in-law to say she was okay, which was bizarre, because
why shouldn't she be? She's thirty-seven, which isn't very old for
a person to be allowed to live to. It was only after they said she
was okay, that I thought she might not be."

The board lit up with people calling in.

"What I'd really like to talk about is whether or not you've
faced something like this in your life. Someone you love being
sick and you waiting to see how it works out." Lev paused again.

The pauses were part of what got Lev hired. "They sound authentic," one producer had said.

"I'd especially like to hear from people with family who've had
heart operations or who've had one themselves."

Chuck raised his eyebrows through the window and made a V
sign that turned into a friendly version of the finger.

"Hello," said someone who identified himself as Dan. "I'm so glad you brought this topic up. This was years ago and I'm remarried now. Totally different lifestyle, so to say." Dan's ex-wife had had a kidney operation. "I was waiting and waiting for her to come down. And when she didn't, by the time she came back down, I, she, I was furious, everything she'd ever done that bothered me, I'd gone back over."

"Was she all right?" Lev had leaned forward as he listened.

"That time, but not the next. I got to like her again between times."

"I'm terribly sorry," Lev said softly.

"Yes, well, of course, my whole life is different now, as I said."

The Hershey's commercial promised nothing but pure chocolate in your chocolate. No women's underwear, no bicycles, no carp swimming through.

Someone from Berkeley named Miriam came on. "I've never called one of these shows before. I mean, talking to strangers about your private life. I teach. But you can see your audience and grade them." She laughed. "I teach Russian literature at a private school here, whose name I won't mention. Last term we were reading *Anna Karenina*. And I got all caught up with the significance Tolstoy gives our births and deaths and sicknesses. As if people knew what their lives were about as they lived them. A few weeks later, my mother had a serious operation, and after she came down from the operating room, my father took one look at her beginning to vomit, I mean she was vomiting, can I say that on the air? And ran out of the hospital room. I ran after him and started yelling. You know, that he'd always run out on us, and so on. I stopped yelling and thought that this was more of the same in our lives. That nobody had gotten nicer or more serious because my mother was facing death. As if I were disappointed. The funny thing is that later, after I'd apologized to him for yelling, my father said, "Ach, life, it's nothing like Tolstoy, is it?"

"Tolstoy's life was nothing like Tolstoy either," said Lev. He paused. "Thank you for telling me that story."

Another red switchboard light.

"Hello, this is Clark from El Cerrito. I'm glad I got through to you, because I never talked about this really, to anyone. I had a heart operation like your sister. Before they decide to do it, they give you these tests. It's like dying, I mean it. They shoot you full of dye and this dye goes from your leg through the vein to where your heart is. To your heart, I mean, which you can see on the screen on the ceiling beating. And you think you're dying or burning up as the dye hits your heart.

"It's spectacular in a way. Like you're dying and seeing what's been keeping you alive all this time. Life is very different for me now, I guess. If more people had that happen to them, they wouldn't fuck around so much."

Fuck, of course, had been bleeped out.

"Thanks," said Lev, "a lot."

~

At the hospital in Boston, where it was ten thirty, Henry took another look at Ros in her net of tubes and tiptoed away.

2

Rosalind

Ten days later she's going home. She's trying to stitch her life together. She's sitting . . .

Still as a statue, gazing at the noontime sky, Rosalind sat by the window in her hospital room and waited for Henry to come and take her home. Her respirator gone, her tubes pulled out, her legs exercised by walking the corridor each morning on Henry's arm. Her body healed enough to leave this place. Her mind ranging, along with her eyes, out through the windowpane over to the other side, where thought was. (Thought, for Rosalind, was something like Italy is for other people. That is, a picturesque place to wander around.) Some nameless childhood feeling of suffocation, cold came over her. Hand to her mouth. Oh God, let me out of here. No thought had come to her in other words, but only present space and time. The picture in her mind, not of Henry coming or the kids at home, but of herself as a child alone at night in bed. Waiting for her mother. Who came, who didn't come, who touched her lips to her daughter's cheek or forehead. Who picked up clothes strewn like autumn leaves around the green wall-to-wall bedroom carpet. Who came, who didn't come, as arbitrary and important as a heart that worked or not. Oh God, let me out of here, she thought. But Henry, as usual, was late.

She waited, building up (with an impossible false patience) a grudge. Then he came. Looked at her oddly, slantwise, as if expecting something, some news or communication. He wheeled her (orders of the hospital that wheelchair, despite their walks every morning down these corridors) into the elevator (where she inhaled the smell of claustrophobia). Then the cardiologist's office. She sniffed. Found something other than the cleaning fluid, medication, body fluid, smell of the hospital and thought, Professional, has his office around him, felt naked and shivery, alone. Felt ashamed, being unprotected, forgetting Henry was behind her. No feel of the man behind her, she caught a whiff of something else as she sat in the humiliating wheelchair, in that awful office of that bald cardiologist. Henry by her side, at last. His wooden chair with arms. Her wheelchair. As the cardiologist, behind his desk said, "No known cause for these illnesses. No single cause, let us say more precisely." Laying his fingers out like playing cards across the glass-topped desk. Grinning as if his ignorance were a form of boyish charm, the thick fingers on his two hands played with each other. Intolerable. My life in this man's hands, his obnoxious wedding ring, Ros thought. His fingers becoming fists, opening like clamshells, and his voice got louder and he plunged, as of course he must, into what was Her Fault about this. Of course ancestors, those miserable frightened Jews from Poland and Lithuania, some gassed, some shot, some scraping out an angry living in Bensonhurst, or rising to professional and suburban anxiety, but also risk factors. "Smoking, overweight, inactivity." All those years, the doctor didn't say, of trying to diet. Her eyes now focused on the cardiologist's bald forehead as if to dare him to go on. Communard, sex dope politics single motherhood Ph.D. to family therapist and then thank god this chance for money. Stress. A certain — excessiveness. Abortion freshman year. Left Radcliffe for Brandeis because she couldn't fold sweaters like her roommate had. Messy! Ignorant! Masquerading as an intellectual, knew less than she appeared to, knew more than she could get at now, there in there. Pain and itching on the scar on her chest as he went on — ' . . . episode in the recovery room . . . ' — nodding gravely at Henry as if they had been soldiers together in some war while she'd been gone. 'But now she's fine, all systems copesetic.' Nodding, once more, at Henry, as if she were a piece of stereo equipment he had left in the hospital for the surgeon to repair. A World War II vocabulary and Henry his ally, she his enemy, with her smoking, her over-weight, her sedentary life.

Now the cardiologist gestured with his bald head towards Henry, who had something that might interest her, he said.

Henry looked bewildered. Lower lip began to pout, brows knitted. Paler when perplexed.

"Snap," the cardiologist said, winking. "I gave it to you." The colder tones in his throaty scale and agate blue eyes remembered his mistake. "Oh yes" — rummaging in his desk. "You gave it back to me." The man pushed a photo across the desk at her.

But what was this man pushing at her? This was a photo, this was a blur, this was a red, badly exposed, all-over design, this was a photo, as it came closer, of a heart. Her heart, presumably. The heart this man had patched while she'd been gone. Her heart, ap-parently. Picking up her speaking voice inside her head, her tone. (As her real heart beneath her clothing began to pound.) Tiny stitches in the corner of the photograph that would tear open if in real life she went on pounding.

Her index finger on the photo's edge, as pain hit her right arm for she'd moved slightly in her chair to reach for it, she muttered, "Is this a present or a joke?" Pleased enough by the power of her sarcastic tongue to chill these men and stop the pounding. Now she could tuck this abominable snapshot coolly and calmly in her purse as Henry gathered prescriptions. This for blood pres-sure, that for pain, infections, so forth.

"I was never so aware of medical school as a training ground for mystification and cowardice," she burst out as Henry pushed her down the hall. Meaning why hadn't that cardiologist explained what had gone wrong with her and what her chances were instead of pushing pills and hearts across the desk. With her outburst and the ride down the elevator again, to the revolving front door, she found the trail she'd been seeking in that office. For that man, she felt certain, as Henry pushed the chair to the revolving center door, that man had known exactly how bad her chances were, but wasn't telling.

Instead a snapshot had been handed to her. And here she sat in a wheelchair with her heart in her pocketbook and Henry with the prescriptions he'd just filled in the pharmacy in a paper bag. "Henry," she said. "The chair. The door." Because he'd stood behind her before the revolving hospital door, as if to push the chair through.

"Oh Lord," he said. "Unbelievable. How could I could . . ."

She knew it was this, his being an architect that made him ashamed. Trying to push her chair through the wrong aperture. Not her discomfort. Or rather, in fairness, his shame at her discomfort as the result of his incompetence. Failing. A thought complete. Instead of this awful musing, these feelings washing over her. Even a thought that was not entirely accurate, as this was. His patched tweedy elbows rising to push her through the electronic door into the sunny day outside where the breezes she met were an intrusion, an offense against her violated life. (She caught at this moment of air/sunshine/light from the earth that she was furious, but at whom?) More air, sunlight, grit or something in her eye that made her blink. A tear for something, that dog she'd had, whose leg some boy shot off when she was twenty — I'm in despair, she thought. But no, refusing this state, as if it were being offered to her, then, making it voluntary, I can always despair. Having finally got it right. As if the thought were a comfort, a pillow to fall back on, a rest. Escape from rage or sadness. Her own fingers began to knit each other. Giggling. Only inside herself, for in her real life she was a large, slow-moving professional person, full of dignity and (often) dirty feet. Shoes off now, she rested her feet on the dirty rubber underneath the dashboard. Cheerful and content, she looked out the window and saw, as the car began to move, the Charles Street Jail. A high brick wall before a Victorian granite building, tiers of cells around an empty center, where the guards could watch the men. Some shadow over the whole trip home, like that dream she'd had Thanksgiving evening (everyone clanking silverware against their plates and stuffing their faces, while to the left, a young man, black probably, was in some jailhouse agony, locked in his strip cell. This was her best friend's stepson, who'd been put away for stealing a car after abusing his father's new wife).

But that, that stuff about prisons and Victorian architecture was the content of Henry's lecture ten days before, on her way to the hospital, with ho-hum hesitant spaces left in it for her to theorize about societies as she drove. Henry was frowning as he worked his way from the left lane to the center to get on Storrow Drive.

She'd loved that. What brio. Their duet, intellectual in nature, on the way to the hospital. Where she might have perhaps maybe did die.

Stop, she thought, approaching Kenmore Square and the neon Citgo sign and a future shaped out of her past, her home, her children. Some beat again. Some trepidation. "Stop," she said loudly, at Coolidge Corner. Meaning, go back, before all this happened. Then she murmured, "Henry, dear, could you run out and get me some lives?"

Lives were what she fed on, Henry had once said. Not those of the living merely — her patients, her children, her family, her friends — but books on celebrated intellectuals, Victorian marriages, alcoholic movie stars, murderers, and the rich, if they were addicted to something or self-destructively dead.

"And pick up a *People*." They were by the curb.

"What exactly do you" — snapping the ignition off, he turned to look at her — "want?"

"Use your judgment, would you?"

Alone, she felt sweat on her forehead, her cheek, the useless-ness of trying to raise those arms (whose muscles had been cut). Alone, she thought, in a calm, clear, rational inner voice. I can always despair. (If this all comes to naught). Feeling satisfied, as if she'd gotten the sentence and the sentiment right at last and thereby paid somebody back. Nodding at Henry who'd returned with a brown paper Busy Bee Bookshop bag to place between them on the seat.

"I got what the woman told me to," he muttered, then drove towards Dewey Street.

~

And these are the signs of the times on that road. BMW's on Stor-row Drive, Hondas, Toyotas, not so many Plymouths, Chryslers, Fords. There's been, if you recall, a gas crisis. Big American cars have been passed on to poor people, who stand on Rosalind's brother's Oakland street fixing them up. As far as other visible signs of the times, not much. That is, how would you know that the houses they pass cost three, four or six times what they cost a decade before. They look the same, these clapboards, bricks and stucco, stones, for not much new has been built. As for what we've come to associate with the years of Reagan and company, those men lying on subway grates and women and children in hotel shelters, that feeding frenzy on the part of the rich, gob-bling up industries, neighborhoods, national parks, while Marie Antoinette picks at sugarless cake in the White House, these are invisible on this day, this noon, this highway.

"Henry. How are the kids doing?"

"Good, I think, considering."

"I want details."

"Nana's in her room a lot or on the phone or out, she's become a jock. More of a jock, excuse me. As for Sophie — " Henry sighed, as he drove round the corner that would land them on Dewey Street.

"I thought so," said Rosalind sharply.

"I read to her a lot. You'll have to talk to her, I'm not."

"What did you read her?"

"Grimm. Fairy tales. My old, some treasury of poetry. Donne? Browning? Is that possible?"

"Henry? When I'm in the hospital?" Silence. Then she said, "I was sitting on that porch in New Hampshire, reading you my article."

"You were mad. I mean irritated," said Henry. "I'd interrupted you to ask if 'a patient tells the following story' was some psychiatric tag line, like 'rosy-fingered dawn,' and you wanted me to shut up and listen." But his tone was rosy, meditative as they reached their corner and drove into the mild May breeze that blew on their house on Dewey Street that noon. Pretty, he thought, with some scorn. For leaves were rustling before its small-paned windows and so, on earth, were daffodils, irises, paper white narcissus. Scent of lilacs filled the air. Still, their house remained unmoved. Rain might wash it, fog might blur its edges, but their gigantic Tudor cottage looked the same in all weather. Designed to be a sentimental version of what English peasants lived in once, it had been blown up to American size and set safely inside the American present.

I hate that house, thought Henry.

I can always despair, thought Rosalind cheerfully, for luck, as the car stopped and she sat locked in by the belt she couldn't remove, the handle she couldn't, with her muscles cut, push down. Thinking about Sophie, whose fate they seemed to have settled by dropping her in a conversational sense, in favor of that gentle country porch they'd sat on before disaster.

The car door was opened by Henry and she was standing on the gravel driveway, to find a yellow stucco house. Trees, a landscape distant and familiar. Figures began to move, small ones, then large ones, as she began to move herself. Sophie running with her arms held out. "Mommmmmmeee." She flinched as a small body came towards her painful own, held her arms for protection to her chest. Said, "Hello, darling," over Sophie's head, and found Nana waving casually beneath the maple with the sunlight shining on her golden head. Sophie beneath her chest said, "Mommy," and Henry by her side said, "Careful," and her sister Lila appeared with tears in her eyes to say, "Ros," and an orchestra of voices were around her now.

Growing things pulled at her like seaweed at the door and she was desperate, exhausted, reaching the dining room, where flowers and some dish that Nana'd cooked for her cried out for her attention!

"Look, Ma, what we made for you. The food. Your wedding china. Flowers."

Nana ushered her over to the oak table, pulling the chair out, seating her. Pasta on the plate already, must be cold. The wedding china set around. Love flooding her, for that handy bossy careful overseeing housekeeping little girl. Now twelve. Glittering high-handed Nana who had everyone ranged around that table, looking at her and saying, Welcome Home, Mom. She felt the hard wood chair beneath her seat as her fork picked pasta up. Mouthed, it was a replica of that saltless, starchy hospital food.

"It's from this." Nana waved the odorless recipe book she'd left by Ros's plate. "These recipes saved my life," said the author on the back cover when Nana turned it over.

"Good," she said. "I certainly hope so." Cheerful, for irony was her meat and drink (when she wasn't eating cookies).

"It doesn't have to taste good," said Nana. "It's good for you." Her shining hair. Her health. Nana picked a rolled-up pasta piece from Rosalind's plate, tasted and started to laugh. "Awful," she said.

"And look, Ma." Sophie pointed to the roses on the vase, adding, her precious darling, "don't tell," to Nana.

"She stole them from the Rosenstock side of the fence," said Nana, matter-of-factly.

"But — no," said Sophie. In this awed and awful voice. That her sister was actually telling.

"Nobody knew," said Nana. Munching and making a face. Laying her fork down, like a sword into plowshare.

"They came over, really, the fence. Really. Hanging, sort of. They *grew* over the fence, Ma," said Sophie. With a worried faintly nauseated look, oh the dramatic possibilities this child found!

"Sort of," said Nana. Loving her understatement.

But now these children's faces upturned like flowers, waiting for Rosalind's interest and amusement to droppeth like the gentle rain upon them, then, perhaps because they were calling on her, exhaustion overtook her and she murmured, protesting, "I love this all, girls, I really, but I must lie down, I must, to bed, I think, right now." She rose. (The girls, behind her, thought, But she always does that. Wait for the moment of happiness to arrive then flee.) Henry took a year to get off his chair and come to her. Meanwhile the girls had risen, plus quiet shining-faced younger sister Lila. Everyone threatened to follow. But Henry, taller than a stork or a crane, head brushing the chandelier, well, Henry took her arm. "Come, Rosalind." She rose. At the fullness of her name, the kids looked impressed and scared. Hung back.

"Well, maybe you shouldn't be eating now," said Nana. Preparing to clear and have the last word at the same time. As the grown-ups marched over to the stairway, Rosalind saw rug, saw stairs, a mountain of them, and they climbed that stair mountain, and at the top by their bedroom, she looked down again and saw two figures who were small again, seen from upstairs. "I've missed you," she said softly to two small heads below, one blonde, one pale red. "I really love" — as she turned away towards her bedroom. Feeling her voice had laid hands on them. Love had been a mystery until she'd found these children. She turned to Henry who would help undress her.

∽

Picture it. You're lying in bed. The cessation of those ordinary sounds you and your body make while you are standing up, the squish of thighs, thump of feet, babble of your voice to someone else. It's afternoon. You've been driven through the town you drive through ordinarily.

You're — but listen now, to Rosalind, who is lying, listening to her heart while lying down. Thunk. Thunk. Thinking: Imperfect: like a phonograph record with dust on a groove whose needle will skitter away at any moment. Then life came back. After a moment of panic. Small sounds, a fly at the window screen, somebody's mower. Children's voices, nothing particular, high, faint, louder, fainter again. Nana's radio.

But with the return of all those noises, she had relaxed, she had fallen down a rabbit hole, she had heard, as from a distant country, some presence at the door, and then she'd slept and slept and slept. Only babies and the ill are equally comfortable with all the hours of the days and nights for being slept in or for being up. The rest of us sleep at night or feel we should. During the daytimes, we nap.

~

That presence, that shadow, while she slept, was all of them: first Henry, looking down upon her face (how rich, how various, how new, she seemed to him, no longer the diminished and disappointing version of herself he'd picked up at the hospital). Still how displaced he felt, how far from her thoughts, as if some silent process by which she kept watch over them had stopped.

Nana, beside him, shouted, "Shhh, Ma's sleeping," to Sophie, who'd moved to the corner by the door. Sophie was hissing, "Nana, come on, we'll go to the — "

"Shhhhhh," Nana shouted once more with her finger to her lips. Shouting *shhh* was the kind of thing that annoyed Henry beyond all reason, that Nana should wake her mother by loudly calling for quiet. He said, "Nana," loud and cold. Nana said, "Henry," even louder. Sophie said, "I didn't." Everyone looked to see who had woken Rosalind, because that was what everyone wanted. That she should wake. But she slept. And slept. And slept.

The first day. It's Monday. The morning.

He should have touched me when he left today, Rosalind thought as she sat up in bed that next morning. Should have told me where he was going. She meant Henry, of course. Touch meant talk. (Sex, in Rosalind's view, was an event, full of *sturm*, a fight beforehand, despair or hopelessness recycled as desire, while touch, the ordinary arm around the shoulder, never occurred to her.) As for he, that was Henry, the he in her mental life as she had been she in her mother's. Whole mornings spent musing on his frailties, disabilities and, once in a while, his strengths. (Although she believed that thinking well of people was a form of denial, unintelligent and foolish.) As for touch, in their ten years together, except for the year he'd stopped smoking (then they'd made love every morning until she'd said, "Look, with my sleep disturbance, I find this unerotic, let us say, this compulsive, unchosen matinee, let's go back to the evenings, where some spontaneity is possible."), with the exception of that year, let us return to the thought, Henry had jumped from the bed they'd shared as from a fragile raft, pulled his pants on and run downstairs to eat his breakfast. "The breakfast of champions," he joked about the white yogurt mound with the raisin in the center.

"But I'm it," she'd joked too. Protesting. *"La vrai chose.* Woman. Why run for the symbolic?" Meaning a chat, perhaps, on the pillows, about respective dream states. Now wincing as she tried straightening the pillow behind her, thinking, He should have touched me when he left today, told me he was going.

It had been different in the hospital. Buzzers bringing nurses with breathing tubes and trays in the morning, people fed her from a tray. In the middle of the night, a hovering presence, a night-light, a bell to ring, instead of awakening as she had last night to find a wall of bone and muscle that was Henry's back turned towards her. She'd started, startled, wondered, Can I keep going, beating, boom through the darkness, began, in that same darkness, chasing sleep, before her, now, like a lover or a two-year-old. Ahead, catching up, aahh. She'd found it. (She'd learned to do this during years of sleeplessness. Don't get up, don't read, eat something if you must, but don't let yourself wake, entirely.)

She looked up and found the rice paper moon that hid the fixture on the ceiling, left to where her grandparents lived mute within their plastic photo box. They'd been mute when living around the country they had run from. Poland, which accounted for the red hair (her father Sidney, Lila, Lev) in the family. "I don't remember. There's nothing to say. Who wants to talk about such things? It stank, it smelled, of things, of blood." That heavy European contempt, that stolidity. Endurance.

"Where are they now?" Sophie had asked that winter. About her great-grandparents.

"They're dead now," she'd answered. As if dead were a condition, a continuing tense.

Her white linen arm hit the drawer of the bed table.

"Oh shit." She pulled it open. Her life in little: a pack of cough drops, a pack of Merits, a pencil and notebook for dreams or ideas, a diaphragm, some jelly. And in the back, stuffed in by Henry yesterday, that awful photo.

She'd been gone for some episode, dead for a moment in the recovery room. But she was fine now, apparently, according to the doctors, all systems copesetic. A lot they knew. She knew them (from teaching family therapy to idiot M.D.'s practicing psychiatry). She thought of Henry jumping from their bed this morning. That table downstairs with roses yesterday as hands plucked at her to listen! Pay Attention! Help! she thought, the way she used to, at the moment of pleasure, underneath the shower, with its warmth. A yawn. The biography of that movie star on the top of the bed table. She reached for it. She hurt and stopped. She looked at her lap. She plucked the least bent cigarette from the four she had emptied at some unremembered moment onto her lap like grains of sand, drew the matches from their place beneath the cellophane skin of the package and puffed. Dizzy, nauseated, feeling, temporarily, like Nana yesterday, or

was that Sophie's face about those roses, but prepared for anything now, she rubbed the cigarette out against the cover of the
cardboard pack, dropped the pack in the drawer and left it open.
Then she leaned back against the pillows and fell asleep.

She was awakening from a dream, a breathing tube that nour-
ished her even as it consumed itself, when someone bent over to
kiss her forehead.

The lips, as she awakened, became a voice. "Can I kiss you,
Ma?" A face construed by her returning vision to be eyes, mouth,
Sophie. "I had to come home from school, Mommy. I wasn't feel-
ing too well."

"What's wrong with you?"

Sophie shrugging, indicated with her hand that Ros should
make room on the bed for her to tell a story. "I met Birta
Oglethorpe this morning, Mommy. But in Language Arts they
said, 'Write what you did on this weekend in your notebook.' I
didn't feel like it. I couldn't. So I did nothing. Then itching came
out all over." Scratching at her arms and chest. "The nurse said,
'There's nothing wrong with you, Sophie, no temperature, but if
you're feeling bad, go home. There's all kinds of chicken pox and
everything around.' Lila came and brought me home."

This wasn't a story made to be believable. Only pitiable. Be-
lievably false. Says help! thought Rosalind, like, waving her hand,
forgetting how much it hurt, to say, go on or stop, it's all the same,
you can stop and stay with me. All this is fine with me, with you.
She barely bothered to follow Sophie's version of her sister Lila
saying, "You know how fond of you I am," and Sophie answering,
"I know you are, Lila," in a confident voice, "you bought me bubble gum shaped like a frankfurter in the minimart."

But a child's voice ran like a river beside her, and a tiny heart
beat like a bird's beside her. Adjunct to her body. Alternative. See.
A tiny self. "Well, if you're home, we might as well turn on the
television and see what they've got for us."

She breathed better as more voices and more people joined
them on the screen, then a shadow passed across her eyes and

settled on her shoulders. "Sophie, would you peek in that open drawer, and get me a cigarette, like a darling?"

Puffing she could stand returning life. The fullness inside and outside her now. The pleasure she felt with her daughter beside her. The bone of my bone and the blood of my bone. But those couldn't be the words she wanted, flicking ashes into the top of the box.

～

"For unto us a child is born. For unto us a son is given." Since Ros had heard those words from the *Messiah* she'd wanted not a daughter, but some child of unspecified gender, a son, perhaps. Or even, she thought sometimes afterwards, a littler brother than Lev, a bird, a fish, a puppy (which she got later on). At thirteen she'd gone to church on Christmas Eve and heard a red-robed chorus promise in unison that the rough places would be smoothed and the mountains made plain. The rough places smoothed. And the mountains made plain. She'd murmured going home, round the corner, in the falling picturesquely falling Christmas Eve snow. (It was the *idea*, at that time — This is me, Rosalind Oliner, walking home from church on Christmas Eve in the gentle snowfall — that had pleased her most of all. Not the damp tickling her nose, her cold hands (refusing gloves), her wet feet (refusing boots). Something high, clean, purified, as well. That chorus and that snow had signified to her. And those words — made plain, made smooth — had made her certain that whatever had been broken with her mother too long ago to name or date would be mended with the daughter she would have. As she entered their lobby, looked blank as the doorman greeted her ('Merry Christmas, Ros,' one of a large cast of characters in her life she barely bothered to notice) and then turned and gushed, 'Oh yes,' remembering some inherited liberalism that went with her black stockings, then up the elevator six flights to glare at her mother, who hadn't wanted her to go to church. ('You're Jewish,' the reminder. As if she didn't know.)

Still later, after college, she saw her child to be as someone to hold, cherish, educate. Someone at the heart of her life, which would be rich with love and work at its edges. Someone confident, stable, slender, bright. Not fat or stormy as she'd been, battling a mother she'd considered stupid, weak and cold. (Brilliant, her mother called her, which felt like an insult, a slight, when all she had was insights, a flash in the pan of her essential ignorance.) She and her child would be intimate. She'd be empathic. Loving, forgiving, intelligent, mom. Murmuring with this marvelous little girl around the edges of some dinner that someone else had made. Together they'd what? "We two form a multitude," it had said in *The Family of Man*. At twenty-five, she'd had Nana. She'd waited at the hospital for Baumbach to come pick her up. Nothing. No one. No answer when she'd called. She'd come home in a cab with the baby with her heart pounding (talk about operations!) to find a note on the butcher block island in the middle of the kitchen: "I couldn't tell you this before. I'll be living with someone I met last year. We'll be in Burlington. I'll be in touch. P.S. I know you'll try to lay some trip on me about this, so I'm prepared."

Prepared by a lifetime of men she couldn't count on and by Baumbach in particular for this defection, she hadn't been prepared for Nana, the tears, the colic, the certainty, for the first time in her nonprofessional life, that what she was doing was necessary, but not necessarily up to snuff. She wasn't prepared for the time she'd spent searching for sitters, money and companionship, while Nana grew to be herself: practical, self-reliant, unintellectual and mildly contemptuous of her harassed, intellectual mother. Don't you realize there's no soap to wash the dishes with?" Nana would stare at her. Or, "Don't wear that thing again. It looks funny." "Come on, Mom. We'll be late. Can't you get organized?"

"Nana has the values of her peers," said Ros. "She'll be a real estate agent," said Henry. Respecting Nana and her right to be herself, Ros yearned at times for other women's daughters. For the rough places had become rougher instead of smoother with Nana, and she'd catch her daughter looking scornfully at her, as she'd looked at her own mother.

Sophie had been different. Ros had had a practice, a full-time housekeeper, a sense of herself, Henry's love and Henry's help. If breast feeding still made her feel cowish and the shit work, as she called it, went to Henry or the girl who cleaned for them, the reality of growing Sophie — her fears, her storms, her vivid imagination — was so engrossing that Ros's fearless, stormless, imaginary daughter died. With her died the mother Ros had imagined for her child. For as she watched her daughter grow, she watched herself. Comforting Sophie, as she hadn't been comforted, tender with Sophie's friends and feelings, engaged by Sophie's conversation, she loved doing with Sophie what she loved doing with everyone: talking, listening, making suggestions. Preferring at times her thoughts about Sophie to Sophie's actual presence, she avoided picnics, birthday parties and the mothers of her daughter's friends. Ordinary life wasn't sufficiently something, she didn't know what exactly, she told Henry, to interest her. She'd chastise Henry, who didn't mind filling in, for taking Sophie roller skating: "She'll be bored. It's not stimulating enough. She needs something more related to people." She'd been grateful to the friend who'd pointed out that it was Ros who wouldn't like roller skating, not Sophie. To Henry for not listening to her. For there were gaps, she knew, in her consciousness that kept her own behavior as a mother from her. Still she counted on something, was it tone, touch, feeling? Was it a fact that Ros could count on Sophie? To keep things close, to keep things humming between them. We two form a multitude. We too form a body.

～

A pause. As the story settles into nowhere land, the land of the drunk, the anorexic, the eternal land that poetry speaks of, dope land, lying in bed land, being carried back to babyhood, that merge, unspeakable, repulsive, blissful place, where we barely exist. Barely exist and only exist, soak in the essence of being there, some pleasant unpleasant sensational lump.

People rush into dope dens to get these feelings, push guns in people's faces to get money for them or stop other people from having them, by shoving guns in different faces. Whole counties and countries are ruled by gangsters as a result. But the impulse, pure and corrupt as a baby's bottle, is simple, universal. I mean that Rosalind ate and smoked her way into oblivion, for fear of losing pleasure, the grasp of life that is dwindling from her like sand. But also she found pleasure in this land of nod, by sitting, munching, smoking dope and cigarettes, sleeping, dreaming, being there with Sophie for the next ten days or so.

~

"I could be bounded in a nutshell and count myself queen of infinite space except that I have bad dreams." Ros giggled as she laid her joint temporarily in the ashtray. Giggling at this fact: that she'd wanted in high school to be an actress and play not Ophelia but Hamlet. Now here she was. With his beast, she meant best, speech. Olivier. However. It was not dreams but awakening visions that made her reach for a Merit, a slice of peanut-buttered toast. Joints laterally. Not too much. Of that cardiologist's fist closing, opening on his desk. And from his mouth. You will die too soon. You will die too, was it swoon? Her vision founded, like Plymouth, Mass., upon the rock of the man's ambiguity. His sentence interrupted by something stuffed into her mouth.

She'd had a hippie paratrooper as a patient years ago, who'd learned to jump from airplanes without conquering his fear of heights. Jumping from an airplane has nothing to do with climbing a tree or walking across a bridge, he'd told her. 'I jumped and jumped. But I'm still afraid of elevators.'

Counterphobic was the word for what he had been. Going beyond where the fear is — to avoid the emotion and feel, simultaneously, that you'd conquered what you'd avoided. A form of hysteria, common to males. But she had better things to worry

about than her, her thoughts perpetually interrupted by something, Lila with her terrier's brown dog expression in her eyes,
her white hand in the thick of her red hair. Twisting strands and
glancing at the ashtray, had Ros checked with the doctor about
the dope and the cigarettes? I mean, if this, these things, are okay
for you? The last time, was that this afternoon? This morning? A
couple of weeks ago? Lila had been glancing in a worried way at
the bed table, so Ros had opened the drawer and handed that
photograph to her. Here, you take it.

"Why should I check?" she said now. "I mean, they don't know
ant thing, anyway, anything." Remembering 'mouther' from that
article she'd read Henry that day at the farm that this mess began
and searching this messy room — was that a Mallomar? a pizza
slice? — for that article, but nothing. These motherhood mani-
acs, she thought. Because it's only one job among many. Her
speech was slurry, she could tell that from before. Giggling because her sister so earnest and anxious, should take something
into account. Besides doctors never recommend what could con-
ceivably give anybody pleasure. Now do they? Batting her eyelashes. Like some forties movie star. And nobody said it was
forbidden. As Lila's eyes searched the hall for somebody.

Ros understood that Lila was looking for Sophie. And the
function of Sophie was to be a watchdog, to keep the other family dogs away. By the time she reopened her eyes Lila had gone.
Sophie returned with taco chips and cheese dip. Only Sophie (lying down beside her) didn't accuse her, asking questions as she
dipped, licking salt, reliving flavors, comforting herself, good-
night.

3

Sophie

The night of the day that her mother came home from the hospital Sophie had . . .

Sophie had lain in her white bed that night thinking about those pirates who put this woman and her baby in a zoo cage on an island. Real pirates and real people on real islands, near some war and Uncle Lev in rowboats. They had been rowing a boat across the ocean and then Henry met them in the Architecture Department after they got off the island. And real anything can happen in the world, thought Sophie, wiggling her toes beneath her quilt, which was too hot. But maybe the father will come to rescue them.

Sophie turned over and pressed her front parts to the mattress, which was hard beneath her body. And all that hardness made her brave, so she could open her eyes and turn over and throw her quilt on the floor — Take that — and get out of bed, then tiptoe through the darkness to the closet.

Pam, pam, pam were her feet on the cold floor. The door — wide open. Some squidgy dust. On her hands and feet in the closet, where her shoes were squirmy things, she touched a cardboard shoe box with a broken doll inside. This was the scariest thing in the world, worse than pirates. Inside the box the dolly's head and arms and legs had fallen off and lost its body in the middle, because the rubber band that held it all together had snapped coming home from that farm on her mother's birthday. She had wanted the doll to see everything going backwards from that farm, so she'd twisted her dolly's head so hard that her head, legs and arms had fallen off. And she'd screamed from her big mouth before Henry could stop the car. And Henry had said he'd leave her if she screamed like that again. She'd cause an accident They'd all be broken.

Now in the smelly closet darkness, she lifted up the lid and bent to where that dolly's legs and head and arms were in a jumble, and kissed what she prayed was the forehead of that doll. Then she crawled out of darkness and raced with her heart pounding back to bed.

Now it was morning and she was dressed in jeans. And Henry, taller in the kitchen, where all the pans were hanging after a flight of stairs, where she skipped every other one, pam, pam, spooned the yogurt from his bowl. As she watched, the same yogurt every morning went on disappearing down his throat. The bowl got empty and Henry was writing something with a pen. Pinning what he'd written to the white refrigerator door with a magnet.

> Dr. Kriegel. In case of *anything*.
> 491-2986.

She came up behind him. She let him leave.

She traced the numbers with her fingers. And anything, she thought, can happen in the world. Real pirates who cut off breasts. Real dolls with all their arms and legs cut off. And there was *anything* underlined on their refrigerator door full of Nana's soccer meets and "Henry remember!" in her mother's handwriting. "Pick up Sophie from school." He forgot sometimes.

"Is Ma going to die?" she asked suddenly.

She'd kept him there.

He stood.

Now he recognized and saw her. He saw her, heard her, kept his eyes on her. For she had learned at school: raise your hand and ask a question and you could stop things, like why wasn't America called by a Viking name if they discovered it? Why not? She'd asked and asked.

"No, I don't think so," he said, whispering from his tallness.

But then everything got confused and the air felt bad and stuffy because he left through the back door slam. Even though he'd already checked her pack for lunch money, glasses and got your pencil box and all, he left before she left for school. And she left too, because on the sidewalk Birta Oglethorpe was waiting for a real little girl with all her arms and legs attached. Her mommy. Then remembering spidery long-legged Henry, she pretended at the moment that she stepped outside that all his arms and legs were hers. And greeting Birta, with a waving hand, felt sure of everything for a moment.

"Hi, Soph. We're late. Let's run."

So she went to school, then home again to see her mommy. Like that. I have to go home to the nurse and the teacher. And Lila picked her up. And that Mommy's bed, for all the days that came, it was a raft, an island, with *Peoples* and television noise and food she brought up for them and hazy smoke — "It's dope," said Nana, sniffing. "You dope." "Which is impossible," said Sophie, "because it's Mommy! Besides, she's sick."

Here she was like a Guardian Angel going upstairs and down. "Be an angel, Soph, and get me some." This was the thing she could never explain to anyone. How these little winds blew from Mommy, be an angel, be an angel, Soph, and on her mommy's face, this sadness that meant Sophie *had* to do these things. Get me something, little mommy like a doll in that bed, with her blue eyes and hair staring out, little mommy wants. And later, in the hot part of a day, her mommy brought this photo out and said to Auntie Lila, "Chat with me, I miss conversation," her fishbowl eyes, all over the room, ordering up some chat.

"Oh me, I'm dying to," said Auntie Lila.

"Lila, do me a favor, get this horror out of here. But not now. Stay. You can take it later," said her mom about some photo. Then she made a face and swallowed the pills that Lila was holding out to her. A handful of ugly-colored pills with water. "Now take those down too. I already told Henry . . ." But her mom was purring, wanting something. "Now tell me. What was it like for you being here, darling, while I was gone?"

Lila said, "Oh, what a relief to be doing this. Chatting instead of hovering. What was it like? I felt even your ghost had departed and *it* was hovering over by the hospital. While I was hovering here. Over here, I'd think. Summoning *it* back. Nuts. The kids were great. We had a picnic the day you were . . . operated on."

"On the living room floor," said Sophie. "And Nana made taco pizza for us."

Mommy raised her eyebrows. "One of Nana's dad's inventions, God help us." Looked down at her smooth place between those breasts.

"Seeing that hospital place, like a middle-income project for the ill." That was Lila. "To the left of that bridge. As if I should keep my eye on that place, so you could come . . . to . . . come home to us. Here I felt so helpless. Sophie wanted stories every night, and Henry read her — Grimm, I think — turning to Sophie.

She made a maybe face. She liked being read to. She didn't care what.

"I kind of like that scariness," said Lila.

"No," said Rosalind firmly, from the cover, her eyes sparkling. "I dislike those stories intensely. They're not folk stories, but the stuff of those bizarre nineteenth-century psychopathic Germans. Besides, it seems sadistic to me. Or thoughtless." Picking at the fringes on her covers. "Of Henry."

"But you like it when he does things with the kids you disapprove of." Lila stuck her tongue out for a second.

"So I can correct him," Ros said. "Do you remember that conversation in *The Golden Notebook?*"

"I — never — read it."

"About these two women, who have been friends forever. Like me and Valerie. And one of them says, 'Do you remember so-and-so? He said something insensitive in nineteen forty-three.'" Mommy laughed. "The book takes place in the midfifties. It's why I don't mind Henry doing Grimm to Sophie." Mommy laughed again, then lost her laugh, and closed her eyes. "Come on, honey, lie down beside me." Sophie lay down and her mom spoke like a mummy to the ceiling. "So take, Lila, in the drawer, there's a photo. Downstairs . . . And those bloody pills."

Sophie lay listening to breathing, hating it, then sat up and hopped off the bed, downstairs, tiptoeing not to wake her mommy up, stopping in the kitchen. "What is it?" Sophie hissed. At that *it* on the kitchen island.

"This photo? From the hospital, I think."

"Mommy's," said Sophie, who ran right up and grabbed it, sticking this picture under the magnet on the refrigerator before either of them could think what she had done.

It looked, that bloody thing, lost in all that refrigerator whiteness. She took it off. Watched Lila make a mouth. "What do you think?" Because Lila always asked kids (like Sophie) what she should do. Sophie shrugged. Lila shrugged and put it "for now" on top of the refrigerator, which Sophie nodded at, wisely, because they agreed with looks, that this was an okay "for now" place for this mommy's heart to rest. Beat, beat.

∽

"Mom isn't coming down to supper. She said to be certain to tell you guys." Sophie had told everyone that first night. She said it and she said it. Then she didn't have to say it anymore, because nobody expected her mom to come to supper. Nobody noticed that Sophie was home from school that whole week except for Lila who didn't care and the next she had some stomach flu that made her feel so bad she had to stay in bed beside her mommy, watching the soaps and all the other grown-up programs.

Sophie watched her mom. While Mommy watched the television people.

"Tell me, Melissa, you must remember who you saw, the night of Susanna's murder."

"Sophie sweetie, run down to the freezer, we'll have ice cream or whatever you find for us."

So she went down. First for peanut butter sandwiches then for Nana's frozen Milky Ways, which were dark and hard and mysterious. And she never climbed on top of the refrigerator even though she knew that photo was there. Beat beat.

"Love is people needing people," Mr. Rogers was singing when she came up. "Love's a man daring to liberate his brother."

Her mom had put a match whoosh to a cigarette between her lips. Smoke came out.

"Wait a minute, Mommy." She went down again for brown moony Mallomars to tuck into her mommy's mouth. When they got eaten, her mommy went whoosh and lit the cigarette she'd put out.

"Cigarettes are shit." Nana was coming into the bathroom when Sophie was brushing her teeth. "Especially for Mom. Don't bring her any, Sophie."

"I didn't," Sophie told her. "She already has them."

Then this day was over too, and she could go down for supper and make her announcement about their mom staying upstairs again, though what she wanted to do was bring her down by the hand and shout surprise like a birthday party.

Mommy started to pile up books, she asked for trash. There, in my office, behind *The Merck Manual.* All those biographies of movie stars. Special mental books, and notebooks, so she could read and write about her work. All these were piled, with the cookies and the magazines and the television, on around the bed. Sophie was on the edge now, with her own notebook. She went on writing on that composition (*what did you do this weekend,* which was the first weekend Mommy was home), then tore it up. Jumping off the bed. Because she thought: I have to get back to school before it's over.

"Sophie. Could you go get me a pack of cigarettes," said her mom, looking up. "At the minimart. I've got an account."

"Aw, Ma. I'm — "

"This is my last" — laughing — "carton."

Sophie saw it. That if she got this now, she could be free, go back to school.

Everyone was saying things: "If Mom asks you to go to the minimart, say no," Nana had said. Sophie had nodded. Lila had said, "Sophie, please. I'm here to run errands."

Caught between her mommy and the rest of these people who were *saying things,* she prayed this afternoon on her way to the minimart for this to be the end. "Let Ma stop being like that." She changed her prayer to keep her mother, who read minds, from feeling bad. "I'll be better." Not knowing, as Birta Oglethorpe came up the block, whether better meant going or not going to the minimart. Pretending to be a little girl on the television set, she tilted her head and smiled a tooth-out smile at Birta.

"Hello bello. Sophie dophie. Go bot your pin din?"

This was Birta's language. Sophie didn't like it. It made her cold. But Birta's beaded safety pin, the sign of friendship, was still on Sophie's sneaker when she looked down. "I can't talk now. I have to go to the store for my mother."

"I'll come too."

"But you can't go into the minimart." Birta might tell Nana, who'd tell Henry, who'd tell Ros that Sophie told. "Beat you to the fish store." But there were no pretty silver fish today in Mr. Ehrenreich's window, only a letter printed on cardboard.

Dear Mr. Ehrenreich,

Thank you for letting us visit your fish store. We liked holding the lobster. It was moving and cold and heavy. It was alive. The pink ocean perch had a million eggs in two sacs. The wolffish had sharp teeth, for eating the clams you showed us.

Love,

Mrs. Sabin's kindergarten

Devotion School

"Little kids," said Birta happily, who was also in grade two.

Wolffish with sharp teeth ate a million eggs in two sacs in Mr. Ehrenreich's fish store window as Sophie said, 'Stay here,' to Birta, walked brave and straight to the minimart, down the skinny aisle to the big counter. "A box of Merits. The big box, please." To the man.

"That's an awful lot of cigarettes for an awfully little girl." The big man smiled with his big teeth. "Okey dokey, Sophie. I'll put them on your mom's account."

A long brown paper bag with the Merit carton sticking out came back at her.

"What you got, Sophie?" Birta was waiting outside.

"Let's go swinging, okay?"

Running so fast down Browne Street, pell-mell across the street (against the light, oh no), past the school where no one was in the playground in the park that — oh no, Nana was there, swinging with her long legs up before Sophie could stop.

"Sophie, Birta." Nana dragged her feet on the ground to stop the swing. "Where you been? Where you going to?"

"Nowhere."

"From the minimart." Birta looked down at her sneakers. "To swing."

Nana's eyes fell on the bag. She put her phony voice back on. "Are those for Ma, Soph?"

"Sort of." Sophie's hand tried covering where the carton stuck out from the bag.

"Why don't I bring them to her?" Nana jumped off the swing.

Sophie shrugged her shoulders forward. To say, Please don't, because I'm miserable.

"Okay. Hand them over." Nana's hand reached out. "On the double, idiot."

"I can't." Sophie tossed the bag up in the air, ran to pick it up. Looked down at the carton in her hands, then ran and ran with tears and snot in her mouth to their house. No one was behind her when she looked.

4

Nana

Nana takes charge of her destiny (with a little borrowed capital).

Nana, swinging in the park, spotted Sophie. Long before Sophie spotted her. Way out on the edge of the park. Meanwhile, she, Nana, had been banished from that bedroom, no thanks, honey, coolly from her mom, but take care of things downstairs, make supper. Of course her mom was never down to eat it. And — well. There was that other thing, that certain sum of money that she'd asked for from her mom and now she was swinging and swinging in the baby park (she'd vowed to keep swinging!) until she came up with some other way to get it, pointing her toes towards that sum of money she had to get, to buy some sweats and running shoes. Because once her mother had banished her from that bedroom — why not? — she'd run and run right around the high school track into that miracle, those high school girls, who'd asked her could she join their relay team this summer and now she couldn't be on the relay team without the special shoes and sweats. And that card Mom had given her for the money machine at Coolidge Corner had had

INSUFFICIENT FUNDS on it. Not that Mom hadn't been, "Sure, take the card, go get your sweats and shoes and stuff." That head sticking out of the covers. No haircut. Smelly arms. Those magazines and candy wrappers. Dope smells.

Sophie now with something brown and baggy in her arms was coming closer. Running right towards her without seeing her. Blind.

"Stop." She jumped off the swing to where Sophie with that bag ran right in front of her. That Birta was there too. Crybaby. Curl twister.

"Help! Nana!" Sophie shrieked. Looked down. Deciding to cry as Nana looked down too. Up again at the package. In her paws. The package was long. Narrow. Brown baggy. Cancer sticks obviously. Heart attack. Crash.

"Are those for Mom?" Nice big sister voice on. A little scary and a little wise.

The package tossed — wildly — like a football to the left side, then quick, before Nana could swoop to pick it up, Sophie grabbed these Merits — good recovery! — and ran, with Nana close behind. Nana stopped. Let Sophie go ahead. A big lead for a little kid. Then she caught her down the block near the house. Ripped the back of her jacket. Which was amazing. This little kid could run so fast. "I'm going to torture you." Hands on Sophie's neck above the rip. "I told you not to do it."

She held on to Sophie and pushed her back to the house, then down to the basement, where it smelled like a cave, and she ripped the carton and took a Merit out and scratched the little bendy match against the bottom of the little book, and whoosh, the match flared up.

"Okay, Soph. You take a puff." She puffed first, coughed, handed the cigarette over. Sophie's eyes grew wide. A tiny gasp. She puffed, coughed, sputtered, gave the cigarette back. "Come," said Nana gruffly. Sophie followed her to the downstairs little toilet where Nana dropped the cigarette they'd puffed on into the bowl. Watched it together — drown. That brown stuff spilling out of its white cover.

"Pee on it, Soph."

"You first." But little Sophie was crying.

So Nana did it first. Cold toilet seat. Then Soph.

"Like dogs," said Soph, giggling. She'd had the seat warmed.

A whole box of cigarettes took a long time and a lot of pee so they let them drown finally.

"Now you tell her. No more, Mom. Go on."

"I can't. You're older."

So Nana dragged her up from the basement and together they came to the bedroom. "Mom," said Nana. "The cigarettes are gone. There's no money. We don't want to get you any more."

Their mother opened her mouth and things fell out. Resent this, your business, ridiculous, appreciate concern, go away. "Good-bye," they both said, feeling terrible. Then Nana got her real idea, staring at the closet as she went out, of how to get her running suit and shoes, out of revenge in a way, because Mom had sent them away again, and here they'd taken care of her.

"Mom's not coming down to supper," she let Sophie tell Henry, when they met him on the stoop. "But we can make it. From stuff in the freezer. How's that, pa."

We go back again.

No one had seen Nana the day her mother came home from the hospital standing by the open bedroom door as Henry had searched the closet for a nightgown. Nana had seen and heard her naked mother. "I want something that buttons up the front, so I don't have to raise my arms to put it on." Her mother naked with her arms at her sides and a red scarry line that ran from her neck to underneath her creamy breast.

But on the bottom, her mother was still herself, with her smallish waist, her biggish hips, her cave that had no hair now above the biggest thighs of anyone. Her strong feet with thick toes.

Nana's nipple, hiding under Henry's blue shirt, had felt funny when she touched it. Looking at those mother's feet.

"That one's too heavy," her mother murmured to a bathrobe Henry held. "And that's a dress, not a nightgown. Yes, I do need something or do you think I should wake up and be greeted by this thing?" Pointing to that scar, as Nana looked up at her mother's nipple like a handle, in the middle of the door they'd cut to open her. Down at her mother's feet.

But on the bottom, her mother was still herself. Saying, "That's okay, Henry. The wedding shirt will do it." As Henry lifted her left arm and pushed her hand through a white sleeve, then the other arm and hand. He buttoned the embroidered shirt from her mother's neck to her knees, and the scar was out of sight. "Now would you take those pills down to the kitchen? I'll remember them better if they're out of here," her mother said. (It made no sense.)

Ten carpeted stairs under Nana's racing feet before Henry could catch her as he brought those brown bottles down. At the bottom of the stairs stood Sophie with two hands tight around the middle of her vase.

She didn't try to scare her. (But she did.) She said that it was pirates that cut her mom, then laughed, ha ha ha, felt bad for her little sister, led her upstairs, towards her mom, away from those pills, down the hall, to Nana's room, where they did bounces, admiring their sweet clean feet with admiration, curiosity.

A few days later, Nana had come home from school to find Lila, not an exactly real or authentic aunt (that was on the spelling list this week) sitting on the back step with her shoulders folded down like broken wings, sucking on a pen. As she came into the gravelly yard.

"Hey Lila, what you doing?" she asked. This was the day after Henry, who'd started telling her things, like all about his life, had had this awful day at work, which she did and didn't want to know about. And there was Auntie Lila sitting with her shoulders folded down like broken wings.

"Nothing. Sitting. Looking around. Trying to draw that thing." Lila took the pen from her mouth and pointed towards a bamboo rake leaning up against the fence where the roses Sophie had picked for Ros had grown. Now there were roses drooping because it had gotten hot. And on her aunt's skinny thighs a black book was open to a blank. "Your mother brought that rake back when she and that Jonathan went around the world, in 'sixty something, they were always mailing back some object. Prayer cloth. Hammock. Rake. They fascinated me, the things, and also the idea of Ros and Jonathan, hitchhiking all over . . . like royalty in backpacks. I thought they were harbingers of something, some wild and adventurous life."

She had had no idea what to say. To Lila, who talked sometimes as if she were thinking out loud. And sometimes said nothing. "So come run with me, Lila." Nana didn't feel like hearing. Or rather she felt so much like hearing, she couldn't stand it, being in somebody's head, like listening in front of their parents' door for things she didn't want to hear. "I'm going to where that marsh is, across from the park with the little kids' swings. To run."

"Sure. If you don't mind. I could be company for you."

"You could be what? You got your sneakers on?" As they started down the block. Lila nodded yes. Faster, faster, speeding up, breathing hard, back to jogging. Down the street, beneath the trees they ran past the marsh and to the park.

"Company for you." Lila grinning, had turned towards her, funny leaping for a second, with her feet cutting past each other. "Entrechat. From dancing class. We had to know everything, you know, when we were kids in New York. Music, art, dancing, skating, science. Except for Ros, who refused to do anything much except dramatics after she was about your age, I guess." Breathing hard. Leading with her elbows. Which Nana knew was not the way to run.

"Not me now," said Nana. "Only Sophie. Has to know things in our house." Streaking past her aunt. Turning back to laugh. "I don't have to know anything, if I don't want to. Ha ha ha."

As she'd laughed she'd heard these grown-ups (Henry and Lila, *par exemple*) trying to *tell her things* (about their whatever, sadnesses, or lives). Then in the center of this park there was a pond with smelly water and yellow goslings and a heron. And slip, slip, pound went Nana's feet around the pond with the cool after-school air on her shoulders. Knees high, she ran on her toes, brought her heels down — heel, toe, brought her arms low. Let them hang. Round the pond four five six times for luck. Seven faster to be real. Her heart pounding. Stitch in her side. But she'd run round and round the pond.

When she'd looked over at Lila, who had dropped out, her aunt was sitting cross-legged buried in the tall marsh grasses all over her shoulders. Dark blue sky above her red hair with only a streak of pink sky, which would not come crashing down on them, Nana knew, if she'd only kept running and running. This was her secret game: I keep the sky up by running. Daring, she'd dared to stop. On point. With her arms wide. Like from that ballet class that Lila took. "Come on. We're going home." Her arms high and wide including everything. "Come run with me now, Lila." She'd given an order, started the sun going down, ha ha. The trees. The cool marsh grass. Lila standing up.

She'd gotten so silly, running in this silly way on tiptoes with her silly aunt that she deserved what happened next, after they'd sprinted together like sisters by light leafy trees with heavy trunks and houses on either side as the sun was going down. Lila, whose legs were so much longer, went faster. Nana went faster as they got close to their house. Their gravel driveway. Their garage.

Lila, surprising her, took a springing leap at the end and beat her inside the kitchen door.

"We made it." Inside the kitchen Lila's white face and red hair got stuck out the open-top Dutch door, while Nana kicked gravel against the bottom.

"But you won, Lila." How obnoxious Lila was. Winning then saying, 'We made it.'

"That didn't count." Lila flushed like a red-headed sunset. "There was no race. I just took a leap at the end because I felt like it."

"Yeah. For sure. You felt like it." As if that were any reason to change everything, all the rules, at the last minute. Her mom did that too. All the Oliners, aunts and uncles.

She should have kept to her training rules. Run like in a race. Or gone alone altogether.

Sophie's red-gold head appeared by flushing Lila in the doorway. "Mom won't be down to dinner tonight. She said I should be certain to tell you guys."

Big-eyed Sophie worried about being *responsible*. Saying 'certain' in that grown-up voice about their mom.

So Nana had stepped through the door but everything wasn't right inside, including the stuffy air and this aunt who'd beaten her into the kitchen and this mom upstairs. Sophie talking stupid like that. The clock on the wall which said eight, which was pretty late for Henry not to be home. There had been two redheads in this kitchen while her own blonde hair was glued by sweat to her neck. She'd felt a chill, a lonely chill. She'd reached back to smack her sweaty neck, like the beads of sweat were flies.

She'd hated this place. Where she was so lonely. Maybe she should cut her hair off. Change everything once and for all.

"Forget Mom," she said loudly. "Let's see if there's anything for dinner around here. In the freezer?" The phone rang. It was Henry.

"I'll be late," he said. "Do you want me to pick anything up on my way home?"

"Pick everything up," said Nana. "We need it." She'd hung up and said to Lila, "I've been thinking of getting a haircut. What kind do you think?" Although it had just occurred to her. As if changing her hair would fill this empty mirror she felt in the pit of her stomach. Change everything. For everyone. (Now she felt wilder.) Lighten things up. (She felt frenzied and wild for a second. Thinking these things.) Besides, coming out for a moment, into the easy air of kitchen stuff, it was nice of her to ask Sophie, whose hair was cut like Mommy liked it, and frizzy Lila, whose hair just grew wild, how her own hair should be cut.

They'd debated Nana's hair for a while. Lila said, "What a great idea. I'll, if you want, come too. I adore expeditions where somebody else has the business to do and I hang out and watch them. Although I can't stand my own expeditions. Also Ros and I used, when we were kids, to *accompany,* was how she put it, each other for haircuts. To make sure they didn't do anything too drastic or too cute. But mostly I accompanied Ros." Lila was peering, her brown eyes a little desperate at the top of the refrigerator. "But then I hardly had my hair cut after I got out of my mother's clutches."

"What do you mean 'clutches'?" Nana had watched Lila's sad eyes find something up there. Return to her.

"I have no idea," said Lila, her white palms turned up, then raised, to throw her hair back over her shoulders.

Lila was always playing at being someone, thought Nana. Making little pictures of her attitudes and feelings with her hands, eyes and shoulders.

"You can come if you feel like it to my haircut," she'd said nicely, feeling weird being so nice, when Lila had been obnoxious a few minutes ago on the home stretch. Really, if she wanted someone to *accompany* her, like her mother said, it should be Jenny or Anitra, who were her age and her friends. But *really,* in some other voice, Lila was sad-eyed and from faraway and had no one but Nana in Brookline to take care of her.

～

Two days later, because if she put it off, she'd never dare to do it, there was a mirror in front of Nana at Supercuts. Nana's narrow face changing shape as a plump dark woman who was, she'd said, from Santa Domingo, took blonde hair off the sides. "Are you sure that's not too short?"

Nana had nodded, brave about the shortness. Looked at the picture stuck in the frame of the mirror. There were three dark children on a beach. She kept her eyes on them as her blonde hair fell in clumps and wisps on the plastic sheet, which, like a cape, she wore around her shoulders. Nana's neck got clear and no sweat, she'd told herself, about this dark, sad-eyed woman with the scissors leaning over and the three little kids stuck in the picture on the edge of the mirror behind the jar of combs in slimy aqua glop.

"Of course I knew it would come out okay," she'd told Lila afterwards. "Maybe I'll get a streak next time. Purple. Or green. What do you think? This cut is for running. Did I tell you about what happened to me?" Giggling, as she and Lila walked through the funny winding Cambridge streets to the river. It was only a little rain really on her new haircut. Like mist or hair spray with no smell but the street's gasoline and the roses in these yards. The lilacs were over. "I run at school, the high school actually. I went over there one day and started practicing with the high school girls and they asked me. For their summer team." This was almost true and Lila liked the story. "Oh yeah? How wonderful, Nana." The only real weirdness was how Lila's pale face looked twisted as they bent over the railing of that bridge to wave at those Harvard boys in rowboats on the river.

Nana tossed the wave over her eyes, like a boy and a runner. Waved at the boys and the boats. Thought about rowing with them, instead of running with the girls at school. But didn't shout "go for it" up the river as they rowed, although that was what she wanted.

With her new haircut on when she got home (after two subways and a bus), she went to her mom's bedroom, where Sophie was, and said, "I need your card. Your other card," when her mom didn't answer. Uncut hair on the pillow, eyes open, some magazine in front of her face.

Sophie took a look and scurried away like a guilty crab.

"I need the money machine card, Mom, where it it?"

"Why are you asking? You know."

"Do you want to know what I want? To get with it?"

"What?"

The magazine lowered.

"Sneakers, sweats."

"What for? Don't you have?"

She gestured for her mom to make room. She sat to tell her story. She told and told and her mom listened and said hmmm, and asked how long her legs were compared to the older girls', estimated chances, congratulated, "You think, if you practice, you'll be — they'll put you in the relay team?"

Accepting her estimate. Nodding at her chances. "Sounds wonderful, I'm thrilled for you" — this was her mother's good point, her listening. Nobody else was enthusiastic like this. Nobody (as her mom told her to get that bank card, there, in the purse) else was as generous. The magazine got raised again before her mother's face.

She'd glowed. She'd left the room. She went out to Coolidge Corner where the BayBank was and found INSUFFICIENT FUNDS on the screen.

"I had this thought" — her mom was sitting up in bed when she got home — "that perhaps on Friday, that restaurant, I'd planned to go after my birthday, Nana? Would you like to?"

"Mom, there's no money in there."

"Really? I can't imagine . . . Henry. I'm surprised at him." Her mother frowned, waving her hand, which came down in her lap, picking up her magazine. Dismissed. "I need some space right now, my dear." But Nana refused to budge and stayed staring at the closet. Where her mother had a thousand things she never wore (and had paid for with some card). At her mother who dropped the magazine and went back to chattering about that restaurant. Fat fat eat everything. Remembering she couldn't eat so much because of running and that her mom shouldn't either (that closet full of uneaten ha ha clothes or thrown up ones, torn, outgrown), she felt crazy and her mom was back in bed. Itch, desire, tearing into her at the closet, like standing in that kitchen when she had decided to cut her hair. "Mom, I think you ought to take a walk with me."

Her mother looked surprised, but only faintly.

She shrugged, said, "Slippers, please," and Nana found them in the closet, among the thousand shoes, and brought them and slipped them on her mother's feet.

Sticking out from the bed, so naked-like.

They linked arms. Walked, with grimaces on her mother's part, down the stairs. Her mother got ahead, and when she said, "Mom, don't you think I should stand by you?" she turned and said, "For God's sake, Nana, I did this every day in the hospital with Henry, this walking, there's no trick to it."

As if she hadn't been lying there like a vegetable all these weeks.

But that leap at the end, that was Oliner.

"Okay" — her mom had slipped into her office — "I'll stay on the couch right here and read a little. Catch up."

Dismissed again. Good-bye.

It was she who got her Mom walking and Sophie to stop bringing her cigarettes (and she'd had to be tough! to do it. That weirdness with the toilet). All that pride made her even more *bitterly* disappointed, in her grown-up's voice, when she went outside to the special telephone booth to make her call to Henry, who answered without even listening, saying No no no to her about the money, just because she had no *real* father. So alone, she had to get what she wanted, in the jungle.

Maybe she should have said how wonderful *he* was before she asked, but between the two of them there was hardly any wonder left in the universe. Professor Twist, she'd shyly asked, to the operator who was at Harvard. Professor Twist had gotten found by a secretary and then she'd told him: what an honor and what a good thing for her permanent record card at school, this race, and if he didn't care about her record, because her mother pretended not to, what a good thing for her body. Sixty-five dollars is all for the running shoes and thirty for the outfit.

No, he'd said. We haven't got the money for your running shoes and outfit. I'm not a professor, actually. Only a part-time, temporary, adjunct.

Sixty-five dollars is all. I could wear shorts.

No, as if this question were insulting. She knew this wasn't real money they were talking about, but Henry getting stubborn, like she did sometimes. Starting down Harvard Street, kicking mica glints with her rotty sneaks, she said shut up to her mind.

"People are people," she sang, "children are people," scuffing with her old sneaks on the mica on the sidewalk outside the telephone booth, taking off.

Nana in the jungle

It had been easy for Nana once she'd gotten her idea to carry it out. Easier having been so brave, standing up to that nut in the bed upstairs (her mom). Easy for her to stand inside her mother's bedroom closet, while her mother was asleep (my God!) collecting clothes. (Her mother lay snoring and moaning.) Nobody had bothered her as she'd stood inside her mother's closet picking out jackets and caftans and Mexican peasant blouses. Sweat smells, pocketbooks, dirty nightgowns. Dresses from Pakistan, Afghanistan or whatever other country had a stan in it and poor babies with staring eyes on the hunger posters. She folded the stuff in the cardboard boxes she'd found in the basement in her closet. (Who'll get custody of Nana if Ros dies? in Henry's handwriting on his workbench in the basement. Which she refused to even think about. It was so dopey.) Folding clothes instead of stuffing them in boxes, so they'd be nice instead of wrinkled when she took them out. On Saturday morning. Baaam at six thirty. The clock radio. The first box carried to the kitchen. Yes. But in the yard, she'd spotted Lila and slipped back into the kitchen, climbing the stepladder to temporarily store her clothing box on top of the refrigerator while she made up quick what she'd tell Lila if she came in. This was stuff for school, she'd say. The rummage sale for the single-mother kids to play soccer in the after-school program. She had to be at the playground early to help set up. Or was it weird to put the box up there? So she got back on the stepladder to bring the box down and knocked some photo down.

Okay, okay, as she climbed down. Setting the box on the floor. Scooping the flash of a photo up into her hand, her jean jacket pocket. Braver and bolder, now that she had her story straight, she went out into the yard behind Lila, with her clothing box.

This was the surprising part. Her heart beating, getting clothes from that closet, carrying them out behind Lila, but no panic, no speeding up, no grabbing at things the way she might have. Say she was still a kid. She carried her box down the block to Coolidge Corner, where she left it at the Bagels And. "Please, I'll be back in a minute. Would you keep this for me, please?" The bald man behind the counter nodded at her. The golden smelly whitefish stared at her. She ran back home and got two other boxes. This time Lila noticed her, blinked, went back to drawing and Nana went back to the Bagels And. Another box, sir.

Four boxes got dropped at the Bagels And before the deli man said, "Girl, we need the room, the customers will trip."

She bought a pickle to make him happier. She went outside and knelt on the sidewalk to spread the clothes on a blanket so that people could see them.

There were three customers before her now, reaching down as she reached up.

"Can I? Are you? How much?" And thank heaven for none of these kids or grown-ups being from the Garwood School or Browne Street or knew her mom. "Take as many dresses as you want," to a grown-up woman. "They're a dollar each if you take a lot."

The woman had a glint in her eye: "This, maybe, at a dollar, why not?" Orange, pink and red-brown shawls got draped over people's shoulders and arms and sometimes Nana charged four dollars for everything, this sweatshirt and these old boots, and sometimes, in her excitement, fifty cents.

"How come you never find such good things for men, second-hand. I mean, have you observed this phenomenon? That only women sell their clothes before they're wrecked." A handsome man like Uncle Lev with all his different kinds of language and golden hairs on his thick arms, squatted beside her with his thick legs apart.

"Gee, I never," she said. So pleased to have him talking to her. "Maybe they don't wear out."

More people came and some dresses were too big for anyone except the pregnant girl with the skinny braid down her back who said she was from Chelsea. The sun and Nana's stomach said Noon, so she paid a boy a dime to watch her things while she went to the Bagels And to buy a bagel and cream cheese with chives with a cool pocketful of money she could touch when she reached in for it. Shadows on the street and leafy trees and glints of mica on the sidewalk made her feel proud. For she belonged, with her pocketful of money, to the street and the world now. Felt her shadow stretching tall and skinny, wavering before her on the sidewalk as if it had substance.

5

Henry

But what's been going on with Henry? And who is paying for all this lavishness, this lifestyle?

No, Henry had said to Nana, no no no no no. We can't buy those running shoes and sweats. Our lives out of control. His dependence. Their expenses. That illness. Dark dense awkward twisted difficult. No way out except to start saying no to things. But back now to that first Monday after Rosalind came home from the hospital, and everyone went off to work. We are with Henry.

⁓

"No, I don't think so," Henry had said, spooning up yogurt at the butcher block island in the kitchen. The morning Sophie had tripped down to the kitchen and asked this going to die business: this questioning of everything, this kicking at foundations. Like Kierkegaard, who if Henry remembered correctly had said, "The dreadful has already happened," according to Professor Whatshisname in Hum Six where he'd met Ros.

That was freshman year at Harvard. He'd just met Ros. That

plump and beautiful New York girl, that Rebecca (from *Ivanhoe*). He'd come east for this, what Harvard had promised him! Dark, exotic, passionate, smart. Here in this marriedtoher kitchen light this question came from Sophie, standing in their ordinary kitchen's Monday morning light. So he'd thought of nothing, tripped over nothing, backed into his regular kitchen sink, heard bumping his buttocks that his daughter had asked an ordinary question: is she going to die, Dad. "No, I don't think so," he'd answered in an ordinary voice.

Blah blah blah on that telephone as Valerie, Ros's friend, went on and on, and he answered: 'seems to be,' kicking himself for picking up, changed tones to be that other Henry, cold when he was flustered and good at getting off the phone. With a sense that justice had been served, by his getting finally off the phone, he went down down down the path and out into the gravel driveway. Jealousy (at all those people calling Rosalind). Although at first he had been grateful, took their inquiries as kindnesses to him; now with her return, they were friends for her alone. Kicking gravel, stones, and trying, fleeing from that kitchen, to regain that ordinariness, that equanimity, that me Daddy, you child thing. But kicking stones was wrong. Even in the car, that Volvo station wagon, orange ethical grown-up's car, voices intervened. "Like a house on fire," as he drove over the Mass. Ave. Bridge, into Cambridge fast. Past a Salvation Army, and a liquor store, a post office. But nothing in this red-brick neighborhood would stay proportioned as he drove by. Was that the Necco factory? as he drove by. Speeding up and slowing down. So he practiced: "No, I think your mother will stay alive for us." Feeling certain, as he parked, that his father in Minneapolis would have drawled: "She won't die." That was mastery. Or was that someone in the movies? He was wimpy. Or merely human . . . lacking certainty. The clarity of his . . . dad. Long dead. As he walked down the path towards the architecture building, whose leaking glass tent was a disgrace to the profession practiced beneath it, as his attempt to push his wife's wheelchair through the revolving door of the hospital had been disgraceful. This 'think she won't' business handed to a child. Like some rationalistic overintellectual caricature of a Cambridge intellectual parent.

Think she won't business, handed to a child.

But how, to a child, did you convey this other thing? This slip-slidy, slip-slidyness of life, as it turned out to be, not gray, as alleged at Harvard, when he was a student and Kissinger was still a presence there — that brilliant and murderous career that took off from this place like a rocket — aha! — exploding like a bomb in Cambodia and beyond, but slippy, sloppy, mixed, unmatched, elusive — *This* was life. (His wife was dark, plump, exotic, brilliantly successful, the Kissinger of family therapy.) And his father, a thin, fair Milwaukee moralist, the author of certainty, had been wrong. This was unusually philosophical for Henry who had a public policy kind of musing inner voice or a technical tune he was turning over, like earth, much of the time, and feelings, like aquifers, that ran below.

And very strange, his wife, crisp as mental bacon, her sagging flesh, now hidden in her bedroom like a naughty child. Put away to learn a lesson. Waving his enormous ringed hand, as he walked up the pathway past Memorial Church where services had been held after the Civil War had eaten its young. This was the oddest sensation, that he had in his brain the capacity for the first time right this minute, the brain cells trained and ready, for the first time right this minute, to capture, encapsulate, the complexity of this woman who was his wife. Then something exploded and he had failed to do so. Lost it. Despair struck him. He sagged. As if capturing her would bring her back, not to this life, but to that other. The one before.

A faint breeze stirred the tree before him.

But Life was still buoyant. Hands waved at him. He put this nonsense behind him, in that bedroom, where it belonged. There. The project manager standing with his clipboard by the leaking glass tent of the architecture building. Waving as if birds still whistled and the sun were shining. "Henry, how's it going?" "Fine, fine," daring to wave back. Students carrying books into the building. He thought, as if he'd stumbled on something, maybe, in middle age the consolations of philosophy will come back, that reading to Sophie from the poetry, he once . . . could he have read Browning to her? Playing the piano. He'd been a Beethoven . . . Schubert . . . Mahler. As a Frisbee sailed from behind Memorial Church. Now he turned his back on the church and on his previous thoughts, by straightening his shoulders and deciding that he could master all this illness, stillness, fascinating scariness that had sailed into his life if he only had some facts.

A Note About Facts

Facts came in with the nineteenth century and are about to leave us, leave Henry, even, for whom they once served as an organizing principle instead of punctuation. Meaning this, that while it's a fact that his wife has had an illness, everything else — the mode of treatment, the whispers people speak about it in, the prognosis, how Rosalind feels and what she thinks about it — is not just a matter of opinion (which was what Henry learned in college was the opposite of fact) but something constructed, learned, artifactual. Subject to change depending on the questions you ask, the frame you've put around it. The prognosis, here, in Ros's case, is vague, statistics slither in either direction. (Life or death.) In other words, there are hardly any facts here. Or even answers to the question Sophie's asked. Is Ma going to die? (Leaving wars, floods, fires, and ax murderers out of the picture, as a cause of Rosalind's death, which might be silly in general, but is sensible, for the members of this class in the time and place we are discussing.) Does it help Henry or will it help him when he sees that? The absence of fact? Not in the slightest. For Henry like other members of his class can barely distinguish between his knowing something and his ability to change what is or act. Meanwhile, he's turned left at the door to his office and cut back across the campus in the opposite direction. Following a girl with an orange braid down her back, a crowd of hats and asses, briefcases, book bags, legs across the Square into the Harvard Coop, where he now stands staring at breasts, asses, well-exercised thighs, in a book he's found in the Health and Beauty section of the Harvard Cooperative bookstore. He'd come, you see, looking for facts about her illness. But here, certainly, there are no facts, only breasts, asses, well-exercised thighs offered to their readers by breathless authors as a means to triumph, in your person, over time and mortality. (If you eat right and exercise correctly.) A fact, at this moment, is in order. It had been six weeks, at least, since Henry and Rosalind had fucked or made love, depending on your orientation and their mood. Henry was, despite his conscientious attempt to be considerate, and solicitous, hungry. Especially hungry for her body, in the face of all this death. Still, Henry couldn't even ask the doctors how long before they could again. It seemed too selfish.

He'd lain so stiff in bed the night before, trying not to touch and maybe hurt his wife that he'd been sore when he woke up. Had touched her accidentally once. Had heard her moan. This bed had once been sex and comfort. Calf over calf. Sole to Ros's anklebone. Touch the flesh of someone known to him. This bed had once seemed — a dangerous raft at bad times, and at good, jumping up in the morning, so that he didn't feel tempted, which he knew, from experience, bothered her (in the exhausted mornings).

Fixing hearts must be like fixing pipes, he'd thought sitting up that morning. A fog of fright and longing about him. Bad temper or rather distemper, out-of-sortsness hanging round him. Lust and that expensive spirit. Fixing hearts must be like fixing pipes, he'd thought, attempting to capture will and cheerfulness. Once the new length of pipe gets fitted in and soldered, no sweat. But he'd been sweating. Placing his long legs, long feet on the floor beside the bed and looking down at his long toes that morning. Body heat and body weight. The flesh on her buttocks, the creases on her thighs. The breathing he'd taken for granted.

Losses lay behind him in childhood. Although he barely remembered what they were. Losses lay before him. Although he didn't wish to dwell on them. Instead, swimming in his consciousness as he'd looked down, was that dark October day in class when he'd met Ros and he was still a virgin and a physics major. A chill in the October air. Late afternoon. Even the weather in those days had been intellectual. 'The dreadful has already happened,' said some dark depressive Dane the professor had been discussing.

Your Heart and How to Live with It was an oversized book on the top shelf that he spotted now with an undersized gray-haired faculty wife standing below it. So he closed whosever's exercise regime he'd opened. Got rid of bodies. Reached above the braid on top of this Quakerish woman's head and brought it down. That your heart and how to — "Excuse me." Smiling as she blinked. Opening up the book he found leafing through drawings of all-over-branching fan-shaped arteries, veins, a representative blockage, and turning pages, a blurry photo of an operating room and that machine he couldn't visualize on the day of Rosalind's operation. While he leafs through the other offerings of this section, I'll offer you a few facts about their early life and courtship.

They'd met in a freshman humanities course at Harvard. He'd been destined for physics or some other combination of abstract thought and carpentry, and she was considering transferring to Brandeis, although she'd just arrived at Radcliffe the week before. Because she couldn't do something he didn't get straight until she told him years later what had made her wave her hand, over her coffee cup, towards the college ten miles west of them in Waltham. "I got through high school on a talent for making up answers that sounded better than the right ones. Even if everyone at Radcliffe seemed equally glib, most of them had gone to private schools and actually seemed to know something. Besides, my roommates' drawers were full of neatly folded sweaters, which indicated something darkly significant, I felt, about my unfitness for the place."

At Christmas, she'd announced to an astonished and virginal Henry that she was leaving school altogether for a semester. "I'm, it was this person I used to go out with senior year at the Bronx High School of Science. We went to see *Breathless* together over Christmas. I thought I owed him something. Because we used to be together, I guess. But I didn't actually expect I could — I know this sounds nonsensical — get pregnant. I had to go around to all these doctors telling them how crazy I was and how I'd kill myself if I had to have a baby. Now, I don't, can't get myself to concentrate, I'm so depressed and sad. But maybe I'm only trying to make the lies I told the doctors seem true." He'd been depressed by his naïveté about this large dark woman whose hands he'd held at Swedish movies he'd never heard of in Minneapolis. For he'd assumed some decent wait before he broached the subject of their sleeping together and expected, meanwhile, that they were pledged to each other in some way.

Later he couldn't remember whether he actually felt betrayed or felt that she should feel that way. But he avoided her in any case. Meanwhile, something about this abortion business stayed with him. Her courage and competence. Her forthrightness. (Who were these doctors she'd lied to? How had she found them? Why had she not leaned on someone, that guy she went to the movies with, or him even.) Ten years later when he'd heard from a mutual friend that her husband had left her with a baby, that same something propelled his car into roaming her neighborhood until he found the house. He went around the back and stuck his head through the open Dutch door of her kitchen. Inside he found a living replica of a Vermeer: a plump woman in a blue smock with fair skin, dark hair and shining blue eyes, holding a baby in the crook of her large white right arm. In her left, a ladle she stirred some soup with in a large red pot.

He'd never seen her like that again. Even now he had no idea why she hadn't been at school or at work at Cambridge Hospital that morning. Leading groups of delinquents, anorexics, schizophrenics and their families or the merely difficult, obnoxious or friendless. Or opening take-out cartons, unwrapping sandwiches (she rarely cooked), working at her typewriter on her thesis. Still, he'd never forgotten that woman with the baby and the pot of soup for him to eat. Standing there like something he'd longed for, unnamed until that moment. Something to stir in the depths of himself for years after, for if he'd lost the real-life painting by marrying its subject, the longing behind his vision had been fed by his act. For Vermeers were in museums and Rosalind and Nana and the baby Sophie who came later were his mortal fleshy ballast that kept him so detachable and detached, on earth where he belonged.

Outside now. He stopped. He saw. With that *Heart and How to* book under his arm. A disappearing sari across the street. Which might have been but wasn't the sari of his colleague Veena, now back in Delhi, the only woman in the architecture department and Henry's mate and confidante.

But no. She'd turned around. A broad face instead of a narrow one, and flash, over there, Hello! But no again. He dropped his eyes to his feet (those shoes! how scuffed and dirty), then followed them (his feet) back to the architecture department, past Memorial Church, and something something passing thought about Longfellow, the Civil War, these tiny New England boys so brave and cheerful, going off from here, then up the stairs to his office.

He'd had an older brother in Minneapolis. Now in Hawaii. Not dead, but doing well. Only silent. Hardly in touch.

The sight of his cinder-block office walls stopped him. As if someone else had been walking through the streets of Cambridge with these thoughts, and he, Henry, had only entered the day at the moment he'd entered his office. Shaking himself like a terrier, to bring himself to his senses.

"Your — is the word program manager? — from Washington called." William Howell, Henry's round-cheeked, gray-headed office mate looked up as Henry entered their windowless concrete-block office. "Setham? Sextant? Somebody at the Department of Energy." Howell adjusted his wire-rimmed glasses. "I found his speech somewhat difficult to understand. The southern touch. Or do they all sound like southerners in Washington since the late lamented President Carter?"

"I doubt it. Especially now. The prevailing accent, if I'm not mistaken, is Californian." Henry looked up at his office mate whom he'd lived with and avoided for ten years. Hopelessly mismatched, they were rarely together, being part-timers in this office.

I need a friend, thought Henry glancing at Howell, who was leafing through a manuscript, sucking on a pipe. Someone to tell my story to. (It had been Ros.)

Now Howell was staring at the white wall before his desk. "Thanks for taking the message," said Henry, feeling warmth in his heart for the man, and the sense, looking down at the steel-gray desk, that they'd been through a war together, been buddies if not friends.

Tears would come to Howell's eyes when he spoke about Thomas Jefferson, the last real architect, he believed, in a world that was hopelessly corrupt. Conviction ruled his clipped tones when mentioning Harvard, which should, he thought, teach only certain perfect classic forms to its students. People like Henry, Howell thought, had ruined education, standards, order. Still it was this side of Howell that Henry was secretly fond of, the romantic conservative bent on moving backwards (as Henry was moving forwards) to find some nonexistent perfect moment.

Henry slipped the book out of its brown paper wrapper, looked at the sales slip and thought, It's now or never. As if he were a teenager, about to assert himself with his father (a dry, depressed pharmacist). Henry has had friends, people he's worked with, played with, joked with, but now nearing forty he's feeling stranded, these were acquaintances, he saw, it was Rosalind who had friends (look at all those people calling). Meanwhile, he was desperate for a friendly word from this snide and prissy conservative who disliked him. In fact, the more disliked he felt, the more he wished to make a friend of Howell. While, to his left, at home, where half his psyche still resided, he felt some deadly dissatisfaction with himself for not knowing how to handle what he'd glimpsed. How to bring it all over to that desk beside him. How say, My wife came home, long awaited, and nothing is the same, things are a parody of the normal, a negative, a not. Also, do you like me now? I'm yours because I'm lost.

"So this is how it works." Henry leaned over Howell's desk and spread the pages of the book he'd bought in the Coop out. "It's simple, in principle. I thought you might be interested."

"Well, what do you know?" Howell traced with his finger the flow of oxygen from the machine to the body lying on the operating table in the photograph. "It's a million-dollar bellows that breathes for you while your heart takes a rest, so to speak." Pausing to grin, pleased by his mouthful. "My favorite kind of machine. A manmade extension, shall we say, of the body. Like those — what do they call them? — police locks in New York City. You must have seen them." Howell rarely left Boston except for Houston or Milan. But his look at Henry said, 'You, surely, must have some connection to that wicked city.' "Cast-iron arms that get held up against the door while the owner is away from home." But now Howell seemed to be remembering as his bright blue eyes behind his steel-rimmed glasses got narrow, and he sucked on his pipe until his red-cheeked pugnacious grown-up schoolboy's cheeks got hollow, that he and Henry were antagonists. "Or perhaps you don't believe in locks, since as I recall you don't believe in second-story men or muggers."

"I'm almost forty years old," said Henry. "I believe in everything. I was twenty-four when you first got to know me." Picking up his book and carrying it back to his desk. Feeling vulnerable, naked, silly, like laughing or crying. As if he were a kid and he'd just exposed something private unnecessarily. The scab on his elbow or his knee. Why had he brought that book over? He'd forgotten already.

"Nana, could you, I'm just calling." He tried her next.

"I'm fine. She's sleeping. As usual," said Nana.

"Looks okay?"

"Well, pale. Why isn't she thinner from this operation, Dad?"

"Don't know. Probably is." (He hadn't looked.)

"Well, got to go now."

"Hey wait. Your day?"

"Running. It's fun. Hanging out, otherwise. Judy is coming over. Maybe."

"Great." A yawning silence. He'd never noticed. How uncommunicative she was. "Are you running? How far?"

"Three miles. A mile and a half in the morning, and the same around suppertime."

"I never heard of anyone doing it in two, aren't you supposed to work up to something?" He thought of those books lined up at the Coop, maybe he'd buy her a running one. He heard her silence. He read her silence: why do you have to *tell* me about things I already know, all the time? He said, "Great. When did you start, I mean, running?"

"A few weeks ago. It's okay, Dad. When she went into the hospital. I'm good. Long legs and, I guess, wind, I guess."

"Of course. And Sophie?"

"Upstairs with Mom. Asleep on the bed. I didn't know, I left them alone. Together."

"What about school?"

"She says she's sick."

"I doubt, have we got anything . . . ?"

"I sent Lila out. She'll probably bring . . ."

They both laughed. Lila had in the last few weeks bought cottage cheese, Japanese soup, red peppers, carrots, fresh tuna fish for supper, Lila had brought everything but ordinary dinner food, and when somebody, maybe Nana, had pointed it out, Lila had spent the afternoon making meat loaf and mashed potatoes (with cheese stuffed in the meat loaf and red pepper flowers on the mashed potatoes, as if there were no frozens, no takeout, no ordinary).

"It's okay, Dad. If you tell me where the money is, I'll . . . pizza or something."

"Thanks, Nana. Just get the card from your mother's pocketbook. For the money machine. BayBank."

He'd hung up. Better for some reason. Whole.

⮜

Three weeks later, Henry was sitting, but we all sit and sit and sit at our office desks, with the phones glued to our ears and a comfortable feeling of timelessness, as if office or institutional calendars and routines cut change from the pattern of our lives and make the same things happen and happen and happen the same way, no matter what. Students coming in and out. The same as when the weather was this way last year. For the same grades, old papers, end of the semester apologies and thank yous. Meanwhile, the over three weeks since Ros had come home amounted in that office to only this: some notes in Henry's top drawer for an article on windmills, Xeroxes in the drawer below from the med school library on fat intake and beta blockers, along with medical bills, Sophie's shrink bills from last year and the gas and electric for last month. The argument with Nana about the sneakers shelved. (He'd put his foot down and that was that, only some scribble scrabble done during the argument and stuffed in the drawer to remind him.) In keeping with these burdensome drawers of his, Henry had stayed late in that office, it was six when we've looked in.

"But Henry, what we're facing is a multifaceted problem." Geoffrey Seccombe, Henry's project manager at the Department of Energy, was on the phone from Washington. "So when the situation arises, someone should have the sense to do a decision tree analysis. Not with the exception of developing a cut-and-dried answer. But as a means of getting, so to speak, a methodological foot in the door ha ha ha." Seccombe's vocabulary had been acquired in Washington, but the accent that shaped his sentences was southern, for as Howell said, he'd come in with that Georgian peanut farmer.

What Seccombe had just said was nonsense. But what he has said was always nonsense. Even earlier in the day. Before he'd sent out for bourbon and barbecue. Only once it had been soothing nonsense, whose accent was charming and whose tone was warm: I like being in touch with someone as kooky and creative as you, Henry. Or Hinry, as Seccombe called him. Whose underlying soothing sense was that Henry would get the grant after this one. After all, how many physics majors had become architects and how many architects could be practical and innovative simultaneously on energy questions. Now some sterner note — like medicine — had slipped into the orchestration. For research into architecture that cut fuel bills wasn't of interest to an administration gazing heavenward toward billion-dollar weapons for the stars. Or to this government's gas and oil backers. This would be Henry's last grant, he felt certain, for the duration. (The grants from other agencies had already dried up.)

"Most of the numbers are in," Henry murmured in response. "But they'll be a trade-off between roof-tilt angle and upper-story living space if anyone ever uses what we've got. For public housing, say."

Both of them knew when the ritual had been performed. A question to chew over, a chance for both to speak, a murmur, open-ended until the next time. Now Henry felt better, something doable had been done, despite the fact that on this Wednesday, June 8, 1983, both he and Geoffrey Seccombe knew that no public housing was being built and that no one but the two of them would see this study.

That sterner note bounced back like an echo to his ears. With that echo, his certainty, that this would be his last grant from this department for the duration.

Henry's eyes closed, as he rang off, while the woman he'd been lying by each night groaned in her sleep. He opened his eyes. Restrained himself even in memory from turning over, touching her, comforting her, comforting himself. With his eyes open, as if the office rite had set it off, he heard from nowhere or rather from inside himself the joke that he'd been handed along with his B.A. in architecture: 'What should an architect do when he gets his license?' Heard the answer to the joke as if the man on the phone had just handed it to him instead of a grant. 'Marry money,' said somebody with Geoffrey Seccombe's sweet southern voice and the Department of Energy behind it.

Henry's vanishing professional life

Henry's first few years in his profession had been exciting. For his thesis project, a solar-heated community center in Roxbury had been built by a coalition of community organizations, then reviewed by *The Boston Globe* as a tribute to what Harvard and real life could accomplish when and if they got together. His thesis had gotten Henry his lectureship at Harvard and his lectureship had gotten him a place in an adventurous new firm, where he'd built air-supported public tennis courts, prefabricated libraries and a disastrous project that had been his baby: a housing complex where people from rich to poor would pay whatever they could afford for the same well-designed duplex apartments.

This project had appeared in *Progressive Architecture*. Praise and blame had rained down on Henry's head. For what would happen to the real estate market, or even ordinary values, if the apartment you got to live in for having money was the same as what your neighbors had been given for their lacking it?

In 'seventy-seven the firm had lost its friends at the bank and gone into receivership. With public money drying up, Henry had lived on grants from the Department of Energy and part-time teaching jobs, writing articles and remodeling summer houses for Rosalind's friends. Little by little beneath the barely paid pleasures of his temporarily unsettled working life unrolled a carpet of wealth from Rosalind's. A carpet so thick it embarrassed him to think about it. So he didn't think about it. For he'd have thought of his discomfort with the cash that passed into their household, then flowed out again to shopkeepers holding out French children's dresses for Sophie and Italian virgin olive oil bottles for their salads. Ski trips for them all to Colorado.

How this happened, this revaluing of everything, houses, corporations, airlines. The flow of money like blood through those old arteries of this world, carrying away more money as the arteries themselves, unfixed and uncared for, thinned and twisted, or clogged. There's despair behind this. Loss of power, loss of face, loss of a war, but you don't need this lecture. Our heroine is meanwhile making good, because newly rich kids get confused and even anorexic worrying about what, if anything, to put inside them. Meanwhile some teenage girls handed Rosalind ninety dollars for a fifty-minute hour, while other girls sponged her kitchen counters with pine oil for three fifty. Ros stopped seeing those families of schizophrenics at the hospital, who were so much less lucrative and gratifying.

It was irrational, said Rosalind, who'd begun by trading therapy hours for carpentry or paintings, not to charge the families of bankers and lawyers and stockbrokers rates at least comparable to what they were commanding for their own services. Equally irrational for either Henry or her to do the work that someone young or unskilled could be hired for. Finally, definitively closing the discussion, which treaded, Henry felt, on territory that was her business, not his, she had therapeutic discounts for interesting members of the middle-class poor. "You know, like whosis, the documentary filmmaker and his second wife, the women's commission member."

She was right. She was right again about those jobs he had considered taking when his firm had collapsed four years before; they were morally questionable, aesthetically thin, and the pay he'd get was negligible. No one, these days, was asking him to Roxbury to build community centers or housing projects, however tame and conventional.

Nine years before, as a thrifty, orderly man, marrying a spendthrift, messy woman, Henry had made budgets and lists of chores on index cards for them to do. (Henry had always believed you should, in all senses possible, clean up after yourself.) Ros had hired a boy to rake the front lawn, her chore, and left his, the back, alone. "I don't share your morality of manual labor," she'd drawled when he'd complained. As for the budgets: "I don't want my consciousness cluttered up by the price of what's on sale at the supermarket. I'd rather make more money." He'd been outraged (by the values), but they were hers, and therefore (according to his) to be respected, as an individual's right. Still when she'd dropped dirty underpants on *Progressive Architecture,* then spilled red wine on his precious architectural drawings, he'd written her notes that were enraged, and dropped them on the items. "Had I known you were this censorious, this is my home and you've created an atmosphere I find unbearable," she came back at him one Sunday breakfast morning.

Coming from a household whose censoriousness was so pervasive no one had named it, he found her disappointment in his character more unbearable than the mess she'd made. Besides, this was her house, left by Baumbach when he'd fled. (He had put solar panels on the roof, the year he'd moved in with her, then given up when the first real snow had knocked them off.) Pushing aside the *Globe* sports section and looking down at his plate of greasy eggs and Sunday sausages, he'd vowed at that moment to give up even noticing those things she did which would elicit this crippling impotent anger, and had given up, simultaneously, without intending to or making bows, his interest in discussing her no-smoking plans, her diets. They were her business. And dull as greasy sausages to talk about, as it turned out. Besides, he rather liked the bounty of her body, as if her excess repaid him for a childhood in a lean and self-denying house.

He went on giving things up, his plan to work on this house he hated, which she'd want "input" into and would, besides, mess up. His place in Nana's upbringing, which Ros pointed out was overly stern and restrictive. When the firm he'd been a partner in went under, he gave up noticing things: the closetful of clothes she didn't wear, the jobs he might have taken that she'd have questioned, the money she handed the children without asking them what they wanted it for.

Still, he remained uneasy with something undefined. Was it the kids their lives were bad for? What to do with this sense of himself as an angry onlooker as the money in architecture moved into expensive renovations, ugly luxury apartments and installations for the military, or Department of Defense. He comforted himself by wearing old tweed jackets, consulting with suburban neighborhood groups about playgrounds and neigh-bors about solar devices and coming home early to look for *Henry Remember Sophie's Swimming Lesson* on the refrigerator door with a magnet. Which paid somehow for the money he wasn't earning, as the pickup jobs or articles he wrote stretched out to fill the hours he had to kill.

Henry Remember (on the refrigerator door with a magnet). He forgot sometimes.

You've noticed something. This man is a personification of something about this country, slipping into marginality as his wife rises up, but let him, for the moment slip further.

~

"Be patient," Henry had told Nana a few weeks before when she'd complained that Ros was out to lunch. Besides, he'd joked at the end of week three, 'Out to Lunch' was not the same as 'Closed.'

"Oh Daddy, you're so dopey," said Nana, groaning.

But Henry knew how pleased she was: she loved his dopey jokes. He'd been patient himself at first with Ros's spaciness and then preoccupied. His last student projects in and his grant for the DOE to get written up and out of here. An article on windmills he'd promised *The Nation* last February. The research on Rosalind's illness he'd decided to do himself to calm those anxious flutters he felt each morning, awakening to look at the woman asleep by him to make sure she was alive. What exactly were those pills she was taking, what kind of diet might she follow? A *New England Journal of Medicine* symposium whose participants debated the value of her operation: it might be useless, several said, or have actually harmed her. (Depressed by his findings, he'd finished his research with that article.)

There at the edges of his consciousness, he began spotting ice cream containers or Frito bags around the house. They were Nana's, he decided. Those cigarette smells were from the teenager with the eye makeup, who cleaned for them but never cleaned herself. He ought to speak to her or Nana about the smells of dope as well. But that was the sort of thing Ros was so good at. Tactful, straightforward, firm, compassionate, polite.

There were holes on the campus lawn the noon that Henry left his office, in a suit, on his way to the Faculty Club to meet his chairman. Holes he stepped around. Now dope is nothing to the confusion of false certainty. That high that came upon Henry who'd gathered those dope smells, that stasis, his ambiguous future, his drowning wife, the bills in his drawer and decided he could resolve everything by moving briskly towards the man who'd been his mentor to see (stepping around those holes decisively) if he'd find him a full-time job.

The chairman's genial face shining, his handshake firm and cold, he'd been gentle in his inquiries about the family, then serious about lunch, choosing first chicken, then the tuna plate, then he closed the menu and brought up Henry's work for the Feds. But as Henry fed his research to this man, he found his heart pounding, sweat on his palms, and all he could do was bow his head and hope this fit would pass.

There'd been holes on the college lawn when he'd walked over here. And the same lack of attention, he saw, that had him falling from his state of grace as a young architect had brought his dear wife's body to this pass.

The chairman, obliging, leaned forward, his large pockmarked face half-covered by his black-framed glasses. What could he do for Henry (to pay him back for the research findings), hmmmm?

"I, well, as you know, my wife's illness."

"Certainly, we were just talking — "

"Well, as you know" — then Henry went on — "projects, nothing very lucrative, two kids, dyslexic" — that had been Nana the year before — "a full-time job."

"Henry." The salt spilled on the table, poked at with a toothpick, as the chairman himself went on to the times, the contracts, the university, the real world. "Henry, the work you do, marvelous, but if you were willing . . ."

"Oh, I'm willing."

"Still . . . would be embarrassed that a man of your talent and distinguished, we use young people to do drawings, which is all we have in the firm right now. Absolutely unsuitable." The chairman, elected for his skills in dealing with unpleasantness, looked around the room. Another coffee? "You must keep in touch" — tracing the salt spill with his finger. Looking around the dining room again as if he might be missing another appointment.

There was a hole filled with shame inside Henry as he walked back to his office, for he'd taken the wrong tack. Not your need, he heard Rosalind murmur, but his. Not need, in any case, but entitlement. First you say how well you're doing, then you ask for a job. He'd become a case, even to himself, instead of a colleague. But surely he didn't need to rehearse these conversations with Ros before he could, how did they say it, go for it?

How long, exactly, had he been wandering? (What had possessed him to try the chairman, who'd never been reliable?) A gasping for air, up against glass, still searching, as he neared forty in a desultory way for a lost channel.

6

Lila

We are inching forward. How Lila sees these things.

But how many times, Lila had thought the day that Henry had lunched with his chairman, but how many times, Lila had thought the day that Henry had said 'No no' to Nana, but how many times, Lila had thought, the day her mother phoned, could she climb the stairs to ask the same things over: "Are you sure? Did the doctors say? And will you talk to Ma today? She's calling." And face the same stoned answers. And go on lying to her mother who kept on calling. And watch Sophie's face shut down when she said, 'Please dear, let me run the errands for your mother,' to keep Sophie from buying junk at the minimart. And be afraid to talk to intimidating Henry who was out of it when he was home, or was out of the house. And must, besides, have known what was going on.

Meanwhile, she went on fixing food for Rosalind, saltless vegetables and oilless salads that she ate herself, giving up coffee to encourage Ros in the mornings and in the evenings giving up sweets.

"I have become my sister's garbage can. I have become my

sister's body." Feeling so heavy and so different from herself this morning when she'd looked in the mirror that she'd been surprised to find herself. Red hair, white face, strain on her cheeks. Instead of someone large and dark and sullen.

That evening Sophie arrived in the guest room downstairs with colored paper, felt-tipped pens, ideas. She had a — hesitation, frown — card for her mother to make. Could Lila help?

Get better. Growing like a rose, from the center of the drawing. This was the first time Lila had felt useful here in Brookline, lying on the floor on Friday evening with Sophie, saying, "Sure, do that. You know how to do it. Great." Instead of drowning in her imagination or worrying about having said desperate things the other night to Henry, who thought she was hysterical. Or murmuring from the doorway to her sister: "Are you sure? Should you? Don't." Or brooding about how she'd be back at the Alcott School in September, without having done a drawing even, teaching arts and crafts to eighth graders.

"Oh Lila, I've made a mistake." Sophie's gray eyes found her own. Over and over.

"No you haven't. Turn it into something. See, now you can do it." Pointing with her finger.

As Sophie's pencil went back over the faint line she had drawn and the line got thicker, blacker, extended.

So this morning she tried to work out in the yard by the no longer rose-covered fence. A few remaining roses drooped. Standing with her sketchbook in the early morning light, Lila saw her sister stretched out on top of the fence. Where the roses had been. A dark overweight angel reclining on the fence instead of her sofa. Looking, as she reclined, like one of those fleshy bourgeois women in Renoir, but with dirty white wings sticking out of her back and a filthy Mexican wedding shirt instead of a velvet dressing gown.

Stretching herself, back bowed as if for love, this angel made some move too sudden and too violent for the narrow fence to hold her, then dropped to the ground, where she picked herself up. No reclining bourgeois angel now, but some impoverished rural fat lady with sweat stains beneath her arms squinting suspiciously into the sun. While the tall skinny man, whom the rake propped up against the fence had become, stared straight and solemn beside her into some camera's unblinking eye. They looked like the people in *Famous Men* something, that expensive book full of poor people that Ros used to have on her waiting room coffee table outside her office.

The sun coming bright, to Lila's squinting. Warmth on her shoulders. Now from the corner of her vision, she caught sight of a real Nana dragging a cardboard carton down the block in the suburban early morning's light. She blinked.

Now the bamboo rake leaned against the fence alone.

The woman and the man were gone.

She carried the rake back into the garage. She carried her sketchbook into the house.

"I've got to go home on Sunday," she'd tell Henry, who'd barely seemed to hear her talking to him on Thursday evening. When she had tried: "Do you see what's going on with her? Do you notice?" But now she'd say it simply. Without reasons, without worrying about Ros, without anything to back her up for going home other than necessity, her need, her right.

Still it was one thing for Lila to decide to leave Boston via visionary means: glimpsing filthy angels tumbling off fences in the misty light of early morning. It was another to tell her brother-in-law or sister in ordinary language that she was going home on the train. For Henry and Ros had this in common: they were distant, intimidating, needy, requiring not her services exactly, but her servitude. What she'd heard in both their silences was that she should stand by and witness what went on in this house. Until somebody asked her to testify for them or released her from her bond.

Instead, she'd grasped something this morning in that backyard, staring at that angel and that rake with her pencil in her hand. Something large and undefined about the world: who people were when they didn't have their houses, hairdos, health or graduate degrees around them. Something more particular to her sister and herself. That it was time, she'd understood, to release herself at twenty-eight from Rosalind's power. For she'd felt slight beside her sister's massiveness, solitary beside her sister's family life, marginal beside her sister's professionalism, poor beside her sister's riches. Naked beside her sister's closet full of clothes. Even Ros's troubles seemed substantial, while her own, like her paintings, were imagined, imaginary, or nothing she had heard about.

Go home, talk to him, she told herself. But not like the first time.

Henry had been raking the grass when she'd gone to talk to him on Thursday. Henry had been raking. What's wrong with this picture. His raking. That rake brought back from Thailand. Those things that never got used. How they littered this house, rejected, dejected, brought from everywhere to lie untouched. Depressing her.

"Henry, can I, talk to you?"

He'd nodded. She'd said, "Ros?"

Asked with that one word: Henry, do you know about what's going on with her? I'm sure you do (all this is left unsaid). Is that why he's out of it, because he's out of sight, up there, so tall? "Henry, I'm sure you . . . can see what she is doing."

"Yes," he said.

But to what? The dope, the cigarettes, the cartons she found all over. The rotten food. The will for will-less death. The arrogance. The *arrogance* of self-destruction.

She could have questioned, been concrete, but here is the *loyalty* question. Ros as a big little girl. Grilling them. Did you tell? To her and Lev. About their mother.

"Good," she said. "Fine. I'm glad."

As he'd gone back to raking, the grass, the long tall grass, the guilt she'd felt about Ros, for some reason, become the grass, his raking her, caring for her, high above the earth, with his cropped head looking down. And she'd felt, 'Good, I'm glad,' that her miserable sister was being cared for. Now she should be able to go home.

Fine, she'd thought. It's all taken care of.

Still by the time she'd reached the sidewalk, she'd seen that nothing had been done, not even her talking to . . . Henry . . . how strange, and that she should glimpse, almost simultaneously, in that late dimming light this knowledge of something else: that the problem with her painting all these years had been, the objects leading the figures, instead of the other way around. Once more, she thought, with feeling. Tell him.

"Oh, it's you." So this morning, which was a Saturday, she'd peeked through the railings of the stairs to the basement where it was cool and musty away from the sun. Henry had bent over his workbench in the corner.

Henry hadn't looked up at her. There was a doll on the workbench. His long fingers had brushed the doll's dark head. He'd looked up at the steps and at her. The doll's head had begun to roll. His fingers had grabbed. His head had gotten bent again. The head, torso, legs, arms, had gotten repositioned as Lila had come down the steps to arrive in the basement beside him.

"This is Sophie's. You didn't hear her wailing this morning?" His fingers had stretched a huge rubber band as if he'd snap it at her. He'd reached into the doll's neck feeling for something. "There's a hook in here somewhere. Where were you?"

"Trying to draw outside. I didn't succeed."

Now Henry had hooked the rubber band. Now the head was on. When the arms and legs and torso were all together, she'd say to him: "I'm going home."

"Daddy. Did you do it yet?" Sophie's head had appeared in the space between the railings.

"I'm doing it," he'd said as Sophie crept down the stairs. Slowly, pointing her toes, and counting something.

With this little girl standing beside her breathing so carefully as the doll got lifted and set on her tiny feet, Lila couldn't say what she'd intended to. But had waited until the doll had Sophie's hand around her waist, following the little girl up the stairs behind her father, the miracle worker and surgeon. Everyone happily climbing the stairs from musty basement to the sunfilled Saturday morning house.

∾

Rounding the corner from where the trolley stopped at Coolidge Corner on her way to buy good-bye gifts for the children, although she hadn't announced her departure yet, Lila spotted something that reminded her of home and New York City: a blanket on the sidewalk spread with clothes. With Nana kneeling to pick a flannel nightgown up and hand it to a girl. Only it took a second's second sight to see that this was Nana. For Lila looked first at the clothes, thinking maybe she'd find something (a good-bye gift) for Sophie or Nana, then at Nana seated on the blanket with her many shades of blondeness folding bills into her wallet. Which she placed in the pocket of her blue jean jacket. Serious, financial, twelve-year-old Nana, whose blue-green eyes squinted when she saw Lila.

Lila moved closer. Now she recognized Rosalind's clothes all over the blanket. "But what do you want to sell these for?"

"I need to." Nana's face lifted. Her legs were folded under her. "For running stuff, so I can participate in a race, which I can't do now, because of the money and the uniform." Inclining her head towards her right shoulder. "There's nothing in the money machine and Henry is being strict. My mom says that Henry is strict sometimes because of being from Minnesota, where they're waspy and it's cold."

Nana's hands now on her slender ankles, as Lila, touched by any aspiration, running, jumping, playing the pennywhistle, asked, "But did you ask your mom, sweetheart?" Moving to block the blanket, so nothing could get sold until the answer unfolded.

"Sort of. Wait a second." Nana lifted a paisley skirt to reach the hands of someone bending down. Lila stepped aside, sniffed the air and imagined she smelled bourbon, because once she'd had a boyfriend who'd lied about drinking, and afterwards, when she heard lies she would smell liquor.

Nana didn't want to tell her, she could tell. Breaking into other people's secrets was worse than breaking into their closets or stealing their clothes, she felt. So she stood still for a moment to let the sale get finished.

"You better tell your mother or your father, Nana." Unless she marched her home right now, Nana wouldn't tell anyone. "I mean it, Nana." In a strong voice. She started down the block, so Nana wouldn't feel pressured, stumbling a little and worrying as Nana stayed cross-legged on the blanket, that Nana's soul would be scarred if she did wrong without confession or punishment.

Maybe there weren't souls anymore to scar. Reaching the corner. Maybe souls, like angels on fences, only existed if you believed in them. Maybe Nana, like the boys Lila'd gone to high school with, now dealing coke and kicking old people out of their apartments to deal real estate, didn't believe in souls and therefore wasn't bothered by her theft or even harmed.

Envious of all these guiltless young people for a second, she saw that filthy reclining angel fall from that fence again and began running home towards her sister in her office to tell her, not about Nana, but about her own going home. Instead of all this crazy secrecy, they'd giggle together, like they used to, about how overconscientious Lila was. Unlike Ros, who needed other people to keep what she described as her 'mild psychopathy' in check.

Breathless from her running, she reached the house, the kitchen, the hall where her sister's patients waited for her. She stood before the office door and knocked.

"Can you come back later? I've just gotten started looking at my article." Ros had her tortoiseshell glasses on, and was stretched out in her soft leather Norwegian shrink's recliner. Her dirty bare feet propped up. A manuscript held up before her.

"Another time," said Lila. Who got beckoned in and treated to a rambling discussion of the article Ros was, had been, was trying again, to write. Which was a treat, she guessed, for Ros rarely talked to anybody about these things and was *brilliant* in their family reputedly, even if Lila sometimes didn't see why it was important to say the things she said. How they related to life as people led it. Or even felt in their hearts about things.

"Tonight," said Ros. "Meanwhile. I've got to. Work" she said with great gusto. A false gusto. Or a true one, but from some other time.

Waving Lila back toward the door, which she escaped through, going step by step backwards, crabwise, into her own life. She could feel that. These false starts leading towards a real one. That painting life hidden behind the door of her apartment in New York.

7

Rosalind

Three visits. Ros returns to civilization. It's Sunday morning after Nana's criminality. That evening they all go to a trendy restaurant in Cambridge. You know the kind.

Rage had sent Ros downstairs. That cigarette outrage! Then Nana bossing her. Walking her around. Still, the cigarette thing had been *the both of them.* Her kids. But it had been organized by Nana, that little prig, thought Ros, trying to remember, as she raged and simultaneously stepped down the stairs, one step at a time, admonishing her mind — as if she hadn't climbed stairs before — to be careful! Outraged at her own timidity, her preaching to herself. Because it was all these moralisms that she had tried to avoid in the raising of her kids that were rearing their serpent heads now at her (vipers!).

Now she was enraged no longer. Excess (those vipers!) did it to her. How hilarious, her own inflamed imagination, rhetoric.

Trying to remember (as she stepped down the stairs, that last step which was sure to trip her up unless she clung to the banister). Now step, she told herself, trying to remember the smooth of Nana's neck, love entrapped in silky hair, her hands. That being she'd loved, not her prissy daughter's qualities. Something wrong with Nana's neckline now. Some redness or was it bare.

A calm descended. A happy state. Desire for something. Nana's neck. Still, forbidding her own mother cigarettes! As she sat, with the seat squeaking beneath her on the giant leather couch and Henry's remark passed beneath her too.: 'You like things big, husbands and houses and couches,' passed under her thighs along with the leather in the spot where her robe had been twisted. Twisting, then giving up. Something caught about this flesh in the space between where the cushions sat.

She saw, without looking, redness there between her thighs, like she'd seen looking down, when she was a child on the beach, welts or bites or flesh rubbed chafed from warm weather walking.

She slipped her hand beneath the pillow as if looking for something, dust mites in childhood, old unvacuumed toys or crackers or tags (percent of stuffing materials), and then her fingers found the smooth greasy feel of cellophane, the cigarettes she'd hidden some months before lifted out, the smell of nicotine in her nose before she lit up.

A hit. A dizziness. And while she passes into a slightly different state of mind, I owe you this piece of information. That our heroine who feels so bad (smelly and sweaty and aching with her feet up on the coffee table) rarely smoked in her life before this operation and as for dope, she'd left the stuff in her twenties except for lovemaking when it relaxed her. But now she drew this smoke into herself, then out, cuddled against the pillow, squashed the damn thing! Take that! It's made her nauseous, and when she can't stand it, the nausea and discomfort any longer, she stands, walks to her file cabinet and slides the drawer on rollers open to find her patient files, which comfort her. The finding of them. The chance to lose her body when she uses her mind. The thought: I was loved once. Competent. Needed. Within boundaries that were tolerable, not choking or burning up or buried and used for ashes. Little girls running me everywhere. Husbands gone. This despite the laugh she'd had earlier, at her own excess (those vipers!). As if a moment later, a veil had been placed on her capacity for detachment or humor.

Each morning, after they all had left the house, 'Go on,' she'd said to Sophie, who was still hanging around looking uncertain, to school, but Sophie insisted on hanging around) she came to this office, as to an assignation, smoked a Merit, snuffed it out, reentering that rage. Who were these kids to order her around? Reentering her rage as if it were a room until the files on her lap had caught her passion, like wind looping up a kite, and she was pulled along to an interest in something. Away from exhaustion, hopelessness. "You're like that xylophone on a string," Henry said once, "that Nana had. Remember? She'd clap her hands and grab for the thing when the bells went off as it got drawn along the floor, but somebody else had to pull to get it started." She'd exclaimed at the metaphor, how apt it was, but had forgotten the toy. It had been Henry, most likely, who'd pulled the thing. But to return, she felt a lot like herself in those mornings (although she did nothing, saw no one, sat with her feet up on the couch reading these files, as if to acquaint herself with what she'd lost, then leafed through her notebooks or her books). Reading a paragraph here, a chapter there. What had she noted, what had she underlined?

Cheerful, which was why this comedy tumbling around her in the next few days seemed so, waving her mental hand — unnecessary. Made her feel like the little piggy whoever he was, the sole surviving member of a house built of brick that had tumbled down anyway. (They'd forgotten the mortar.)

Nana — why was it always Nana — had started things. "Hey Mom. I'm here," cheerfully on Sunday morning. "I mean. It's not." She'd stood in the doorway. "Important, I only, Lila said I had to tell you. So here I am."

Her stance was tentative and bold simultaneously. I'm clean, said the eyebrows, shoulders, I have a right to be here. Let me not disturb you. I can return, said one foot on top of the other.

"Hmmm," Ros's own motor humming. Ros's eyes dropped to this girl's long legs in cutoffs, fuzz where they'd been hairless, then the beautiful large hands bunched up, some explosion, like *what the hell* with Nana's body, as she shot herself straight through the door, paused, to flunch and flounce and hunch and hounce over to the couch as if she resented her own actions, then sat carefully down on the other side, legs up on the hassock, carefully casual, at ease, two people on a log, Ros's equal.

"Well," — she bit off a nail — "I *took a few things from your closet and sold them.*"

"Hmmm," said Ros, so startled that she moved in tone and inner life from Mommy to shrink as she backpedaled (never be surprised, that is, never show surprise, was rule one in her shrinking arsenal, although of late she'd gotten so experienced she knew how to show surprise in a way that wasn't judgmental). "Hmmm," she said waiting to see what she felt, which was oddly cheerful after the shock wore off, as if at last she had a problem to solve that wasn't her own, or merely her own, or impossible, or her body.

"Hmmm," she said. "Which clothes? Which ones?"

"Old and ugly stuff," said Nana. "Nothing you'd want. I mean, you don't throw anything out. Some of it was nice. This was stuff that doesn't fit, old stuff. Things like that."

Ros laughed. "Of course, I never . . . a thousand purses from nowhere, I mean, god knows when I stuffed them in the closet." But her tone changed, her feeling followed. "And may I ask, when? And where I was?" Stuck somewhere. In bed, of course, as Nana answered, giggling a little and swinging her feet onto the rug, as if she were both enjoying herself and trying to flee.

"You were asleep. You were always asleep. You were doped. Smoking or eating junk." The last two words Nana said primly. "I guess this made you sleep more."

She wanted to cry out. She did. "You little prig. What do you know about life?" Feeling better immediately, real, whole, a lot older than Nana, but losing her whole agenda which had been to proceed calmly with questions. "Where did you sell them, Nana?" Righting herself, for apart from parental dignity at stake, there was a good and interesting story. "At Coolidge Corner," said Nana plainly, who had chosen a firmer stance, back straightened, when she'd been yelled at and who chose in any case to pretend, when she remembered to, that she was the factual side of the household. "Where the, you know, African T-shirts get sold, you know that stuff. With the pictures and sayings. Slogans? They did well. The clothes, I mean. I mean, people wanted them. People who were signing those petitions for the, abortion rights and stuff. Mom. Things you would like. Be for."

"That's nice. I imagine some of that *stuff* you sold is pretty good. I mean pretty expensive. Some of it is probably rather nice. That is, I liked it. Well, in fact, there's no telling what you sold. Was it fun?"

"Yes."

"Did you take anything you've seen me *wear* recently?"

"I don't think so."

They understood each other. A weak attempt at a smile on Nana's part like lukewarm sun in early spring. "Now," Ros yelled and twinkled simultaneously, for now she *really* was enjoying herself, "you owe me this. You know that I don't care about the clothes or money, really, but I must know why you decided to pick on me, all of a sudden, when there were other ways you might get cash."

Nana stepped back. For Ros could see her eyes acknowledging that her mom had pulled her trump. Which was the power of truth, said plainly. Nana shrugged. "You remember those sneakers and sweat clothes and stuff I wanted, asked for the money for? You gave me the card. You *wanted* me to get them. For my — running career — do you remember? Those are your words. There were insufficient funds on the screen."

"Of course I remember. But we have other accounts. You could have asked Daddy." Ros started in a normal speaking voice, but then the chance for a scene overcame her genuine interest in what had happened to this child. "I despise stealing," she heard herself say (although Nana was still talking: 'I know you wanted me to get those sneakers and I didn't want to bother you again'), then she saw herself stealing everything when she was young. Candy, books, Bob Dylan records, dresses that were too small or too expensive. But stores were different from mothers. It was only shoes she'd taken (without permission) from her mother's closet and ruined. She groaned at herself. "You're rich, I'm poor," Nana was saying, by way of explanation. As Ros leaned towards her daughter's feet, to see what she had on, Nana rose, shouted, "I despise shrinks, they think they know everything." There was something about her running out with that remark in cutoffs, old and faded, ripped, she had chosen to wear for this drama, that infuriated Ros, who reached out and caught a rip in Nana's shorts which ripped further and Nana ran from the room, yelling, "Don't touch me, you're violent," shrieking, "I'm scared of you," pounding from the room.

Shhhhh, Ros told herself. Heart pounding. Scared of Nana and her accusation for a minute. Then calmed herself. Where did this little girl get these accusatory, hysterical tendencies all of a sudden. Who could be scared of her, Ros? Battered, betrayed, full of plastic piping where her heart had been, no, it was veins from her legs sewn into her chest, heart like a patched pair of cutoffs, shirt pocket over the ass.

She thought for a second of that photograph, wondered idly who had it, then answered the ringing office phone. Breathing heavily.

"Doctor," the man exhaled his words, said the man's voice. "How are you? Thank God. I know . . . how . . . ghastly it must be, these illnesses, so sorry to trouble you, do you think . . . possibly . . . whenever and however it's convenient, of course . . . and only if you're well enough to see us."

She had a pencil by the phone, a notepad, and wrote, listening to the rich, well-socialized, spoiled Jewish Prince's voice: *Dr., cri-*

sis, male, ten-year-old, twin. Tuesday on a prescription pad for Thorazine, then sat with *People,* leafing through somebody's life crisis. The phone rang a second time and she wrote *Carla, eating, pregnancy, what? Wednesday seven thirty.* That evening, she left the stale office and joined this staring, accusatory, ill-at-ease family for dinner, then did what the cardiologist had recommended, afterwards, which was washing dishes to get the muscles working in her arms. Behind her, like Cézanne's cardplayers, the family sat, stiff and white and staring. 'What an irony,' she turned to say, 'me washing, when we have a dishwasher.' Nobody laughed. Or shrugged. Or looked impressed. She thought, Oh Lord, everybody is either mad at me, or mad at each other, or miserable. Sniffing the air to see what brand of autumn leaves was burning.

The last call the next morning was from a colleague, a nutritionist with a son who'd self-destructed and landed in McLean, the hospital where Rosalind had been an intern. The therapist wanted to talk, she said, about his options. Assuming her son was somewhere between furious at her and her ex-husband, and schizophrenic.

She would enjoy that, the delicacy and mutual recognition of dealing with a colleague.

She had three appointments, she told Lila, who poked her head in that morning, three appointments. "I simply," said gaily, "have to get back to work." Believed it for the moment. Underneath that false tone, that la-di-da belief, she *really* believed it, that she *had* to get back to her work (but no one, including her, could hear this *really* as anything but bravado for the moment). Lila just stood there. Head in the door. Stating her mantra. "I have to go home." Standing like a four-year-old.

"What? As if — since?"

"Going home" — Lila waved — "This thing with Nana."

"I know. Tell me your version." Instantly sympathetic. Ready to work. Waving towards a chair. She sat. Lila sat. Lila began with the two of them running. Way back when Ros had just got home. Your daughter, she's like some deer, and oh the sky was violet, evening-colored violet, amazing."

Ros nodded.

". . . ducks on the pond, how lovely, not realizing — we were at home again, having run back and, without thinking, I landed in the kitchen before she did. It made her furious. 'Well, you won,' she yelled at me, slamming the door and standing against it. I was shocked. Because she was right. I never knew I was competitive. She calmed down and ordered me around for a while, fixing supper. My meals were impossible, she said, they all hate those raw vegetables and that grainy stuff and meanwhile Sophie kept giggling. She hangs back, but she joins in. Lila giggled.

"Then like some princess, Nana graciously included me in an expedition, to get her hair done, and began confiding about the money machine and these sweats on the way; she's like you, she seems rational, but she swings this way and that, while Sophie seems tempestuous, but actually she's quite steady."

"I don't know which story I'm in." Ros leaned towards Lila who could go for months wrapped in quietness then, suddenly, open the drawer where her conversation had been kept, and a whole winter's wash came out. Whoosh.

"I drowned," said Lila. "In the Charles. That is, I felt I was drowning, saw my body under the bridge instead of on me, as if it had dropped away; it's been a nightmare," she added, "watching you suffer like this."

"Suffer?" said Rosalind.

"You're — " Lila stopped. "I think you are killing yourself," she said quickly. "Or — I'm no doctor, but it can't be good all that junk and smoking and aren't you supposed to be exercising, getting up? It depresses me so much that when I looked into the water and saw my own body floating, I thought, If I died I could go home. Get out of here. Besides, I need to get my painting done. One way or another. So maybe this is an excuse. If so, I'm sorry. But here I'm just standing around watching."

"What watching?"

"You, the kids, Henry."

She stumbled on a fact. "You're going?"

A headache across the front of her head.

She said "Well, go on," and waved Lila away, deconstructing first. "You always abandon and flee before you get fled from," leaving Lila, she hoped, as bruised as she was. Then she sat back on the couch and stonily didn't weep.

The colleague called back. Her son seemed better. Could they talk this over on the phone. The pregnant girl canceled.

∼

"What a mistake," began Henry, that evening, in the Louisiana Bayou, a restaurant so trendy they'd reserved eight weeks ago. "What a mistake," repeated Henry, "those Louisiana fishermen are making." For if they imagined they could earn enough selling crayfish up here, to get in on a middle-class lifestyle or even buy their own fish back to eat, well their weakness determined the price they'd sell for, but the price they'd have to pay would be determined by people who had strength. Power, he meant. Which meant money in this country. Fingering the pile of crayfish shells in a bowl by his plate with his long fingers, he went on about how these provincial types would find themselves with white bread and McDonalds after the goddamned Cambridge gentry had robbed them of their culture and their independence. Here he stared at Ros, who was listening openmouthed. Continuing his lecture about how pieces of everyone's culture were being expropriated by this big-mouthed gentrifying monster: working-class housing stock, peasant wine from Tuscany, crayfish from Louisiana. Fingering the pine panels by the table, then glaring at Ros, as if she'd owned or built this place which pretended, he said, to be a shack in the American vernacular but was really a middle-class Disneyland.

Give me a break, Ros wanted to say. Go back where you came from, where it's boring and cold. Instead she said, "I like this food." Then. "I fail to see why people shouldn't eat food from everywhere once they've traveled beyond their culinary origins."

'But what,' she had been writing that afternoon as Lila peeked in, 'would happen to a family that had no mothering person in it? To a society. A world.' Peering at the pile of crayfish shells beside Henry's plate as if they might tell her.

"I bet you don't like this food. I bet you've ordered the one thing on the menu that's not as great as you expected," Nana burst out, tossing her head so that the wave over her forehead dropped over her eye. Ros turned to Henry, who nodded knowingly.

Nana, unfortunately, was right. She should have gotten pan-blackened redfish or crayfish like Henry had. "You could be right. I've never figured out," Ros said, "what was out of whack. My expectations or my choices. Didn't you get a haircut?" Looking sideways at this accusing daughter. Who looked like a teenager suddenly.

"Weeks ago, Ma."

"It looks wonderful." Adding on for Nana, who unlike Sophie didn't do brilliantly at school, as her plate got whisked away and pecan pie came by and her fork broke off the whip-creamed top. "You know what I feel" — taking a bite — "about this place, is that good work of any kind can be important, cooking or hair-cutting say, that gives pleasure to people." Smiling at Nana. But the faces around the table were so scornful that she took her MasterCard out and set it on the table, in anticipation of the end. The end. She'd done what she could with this family for one night.

"Oh no you don't," said Henry about the card and Nana raised her eyebrows as if to say 'What hypocrisy, Ma.'

"I actually. Doesn't she only like people who are intellectual like her friends, Henry? Or lawyers from Yale or something."

"I'm not intellectual." Lila put her fork down as if the thought had stopped her from eating anymore. "Or from Yale." She looked happy or was it smug about something.

Henry ostentatiously reached into his wallet and delivered another lecture. On credit this time. Hidden costs and god knows what to middlemen and banks. Had Ros read the MasterCard bills lately? He practically shouted.

"Of course not. I've been ill if you remember."

Sophie, who'd had a fit earlier because her doll got locked in the Volvo trunk and couldn't breathe, said, "Mommy, I have to go home now, I promised Birta." Pushing her chair back.

"Sophie, dear. Wait a minute while we pay. I'm sure Birta will do fine without you." She let Henry, quixotic, pay cash, mentioning the tax advantages of credit as they stood up. Passing a table near the door, where he stood chatting with the two men who'd greeted him, she stood smiling by.

"Tomorrow then." His hand outstretched to the man closest to him, tall, mustached, and bald, beneath a cap. The other short and muscular, crew-cut, blonde: "In the morning."

Saintly afterwards, in the car going home, she didn't mention that these men renovating their barn in Somerville were the people he'd been complaining about. As she was. But how obvious that he was furious not at some abstract Cambridge gentrifiers but at her for being successful while his own star had fallen. And what a star he'd been when they'd married. How many people had congratulated her on the work Henry did in those days and how lucky she'd been, overweight and with a kid, to marry him. How patient she'd been in the last few years as he'd floundered, making much of what little he did these days, while she went on supporting them all financially and emotionally.

No one spoke in the car. But she sat in a backseat at the bottom of an ocean of feeling, currents passing and repassing, fish, seaweed, unspoken murmurs. Then what she'd sewn together by way of pride in her coming out tonight and dealing with her crabby family came apart. For after she'd opened the Volvo door and stepped out on the backyard gravel, Lila touched her sleeve and murmured, "I'm going home tomorrow, did I mention the actual date? There's a train in the morning. I should have told you before."

She felt cold all of a sudden. As if the warmth of late June had deserted her.

"As you will, Lila," speaking coldly from her throat.

The card, slipped under the rug near her office door, said *Get Better*. She saw that when she bent down, pausing on her way to the bedroom. Why not *well*, she thought, following the line from the first page which read *Get* to the folded inside place where it read *Better*. Why not *well*, she thought, turning it over, to the back where it read *Sophie*. A message like the rest, of farewell and abandonment, although it claimed, turning back to where a sun's rays stretched when she turned it over, to be sunny.

Still she felt better. After that restaurant debacle, wondering idly, as she opened the office door and slipped the card onto her coffee table, how long it had lain beneath the rug.

An apology, she saw. From Sophie. For her joining up with Nana about those cigarettes. Breathing better for understanding something, she took the card and pinned it, like a corsage from an admirer, onto her bulletin board (full of invitations to speak at conferences that were over). Then she left the office for the stairs to climb, not so carefully this time, because up, if more tiring than down, was safe somehow, and opened the door to where Henry sat, ready to blame her for everything, and more.

8

Lev

Everything that had to happen before Lev could pick up the phone and call his older sister. We begin back in time, say around Henry's meeting with his chairman. We end on Monday after that Sunday visit to the restaurant, with a call from Lev to Ros.

"'It was about ten thirty in San Jose, California, and Murial and Tom were at home,'" Lev's stepson Oliver was reading from his autobiography at the kitchen table.

There was a knock at the door.

"It was about five o'clock in Oakland California," said Lev. "And Hanna Bloomcella had knocked on the Oliner door." Lev left the oilcloth-covered table and went to the door to open it.

Just as Lev had predicted, a snub-nosed peasant woman stood before him, with blonde bangs big teeth gold hoop earrings and a thrift shop Persian lamb. For Murial's old friend Hanna, who never knew what she might feel like doing until she felt like doing it, would arrive spontaneously at suppertime Fridays, which was early, so Lev could go to work afterwards.

"You're looking wonderful, Lev, let me hug." Hanna's ancient blue thirty-six-year-old eyes appraised him.

Into her arms. For Hanna was family. And like the members of his family, Lev didn't like her, only loved her and felt a thousand times better because he'd found her at his door. Body love between them as if they had been married or been kids together. Hanna's plump arm around his shoulder, breasts in mounds against his flat.

Those shiny aqua breasts slid past him in the narrow hallway. Like an obedient boy he followed. She was family. Hanna kissed his wife and the baby in the kitchen: "So big, so adorable." Her blue eyes landed on Oliver, who dropped his own eyes to his plate of spaghetti with bolognese sauce. For Hanna, who looked at what was male like meat, could tell that Ollie at eleven had become a little man or little hamburger since last she'd seen him. Settling her butt on their rickety chair, her high heels caught on the rung. "I shouldn't," to the wine she held up to the light. "But I will."

"Josh's waiting for me at Jaks." Oliver's eyes darted, looking desperate. "I have to go soon."

"Jaks is the palace of the video games king." Explaining his eleven-year-old stepson to Hanna, Lev, at thirty-four, became a grown-up again. "But Ollie can't go out until he's finished eating."

"I finished," said Ollie, wolfing food as Hanna nodded — "I shouldn't, but I will" — to the plate Lev slipped before her. She spooned grated pecorino on rich tomato meat. "Mmmm, delicious." Her fork and aqua sleeve gleamed in the fluorescent light as she lifted her plump hand. "Bolognese is my favorite. Dante's mother served us that on Sundays." Hanna, named Helen Rosenbloom then, had married Dante in Naples one summer morning. Returning through divorce and Panama to the East Bay and a spiritual life to become Hanna Bloomcella, Psychic Counselor, M.A.

"Okay, Ollie, you can go." Murial waved at her son, leaned towards Hanna. "That blouse is lovely. Is it rayon, silk?"

For blouses like wines or husband were priced first, prized afterwards by these women. Lev had once exploded at Murial, "You only love me because I can walk and talk and make love nicely and make a living sort of. And you and your friends have this idea that most men are basket cases."

"What else would you like to be loved for?" Murial had asked in a deliberately colorless voice.

"Nothing. I'd like to be loved for nothing. Existence, or my individual self. Not for qualities everyone has or should have."

"What about me? If I were lazy and sexless and a rotten mother, you would love me, right?"

"Bye folks." Ollie's windbreaker got grabbed from its hook before anyone could remember anything they wanted from him.

"Be back by nine."

The door slammed.

"Lev" — Hanna had finished her bolognese and was examining her gray-stockinged ankle. "I want you listening, even if you think that blouses are merely femme stuff." Tugging at a looseness. "Where was I?"

"At Damashek, Bezozo and Lippman," said Murial, who had handed her part-time bookkeeper's job at this law firm over to Hanna when she'd moved on.

"On my way to the bank to cash my check before it bounced. You know they're crazy there. Going broke, I think. Anyway all last week, I'd been on a juice fast, and I felt so centered, walking along and well, you know me and the city, it gets so sexy at dusk — is that the dust in the sky, Lev? — that I die to have a drink or a trip to the Caribbean. Here's where I want your attention, Lev darling." Hanna grasped a slice of sourdough from the bread basket, ripped it in half, buttered, nibbled.

"I'm listening." Butter on her lips. Lev grabbed the other half to make sure she didn't get everything and stuffed it in his mouth.

"Well you know how out of touch with my feelings I get, I had to do a reading to see what I was dying for. You know that churchyard where the pigeons are always shitting on the Jesus

with his arms . . ." Hanna's arms were now outstretched, sourdough between her fingers. "I glimpsed this rose closing up." Her
hand became a fist. "At first I thought, Aha, that's my sensual side
dying. So I walked all the way back to Magnin's for this incredibly
expensive blouse I saw last week at lunchtime. But no, as it
turned out, once I had the blouse on, I had to read a second time.
Guess what, Lev?"

"You did the reading in Magnin's dressing room?" Lev made a
don't-drag-me-into-this-psychic-stuff face. Because Hanna was
Jewish and all Jews were in his family, which meant he knew how
irrational they were and how they had to try extra hard to be extra rational, like Marx or Freud or he did. But no. Here was
Hanna rushing towards false gods, silk blouses.

"That's it, Dee." Murial picked Dee from her high chair. "Lev,
take her cup."

Lev took the milk cup he'd watched Dee playing at spilling to
the sink, feeling vaguely cheated. "Dee, if you don't stop it, I'll
have to . . ."

"It was your sister," said Hanna. "The rose in the vision."

"Spare me, Hanna." Dumping the milk down the drain. It was
the chance to watch Dee spill the milk that he had missed. Disaster in miniature feared, observed, clasped to his heart.

"I can't, I wish I could. You have to call her, Lev. She's in trouble. I can feel it. But if she can get in touch with her feelings now
that she's had that operation, her arteries will stay open."

"Bullshit." Lev had come west with a sack full of dead souls,
family guilt and responsibility, to dump into the ocean. So he
could soar, obligationless, into the realm of freedom over the Pa-
cific, where none of his relations lived. Here was Hanna reminding him of family, flesh, how bad he'd felt about them. How
much he couldn't do for them. "Why assume that the relation between mind and body is so simpleminded?" he asked Hanna.

For in that sack he'd packed an education. Eastern, costly,
rarely useful except in arguments. Now for the sake of this argument with Hanna, he would reach in and ally himself with com-

plexity and with those doctors at Mass General he had so little faith in ordinarily. "I find it unimaginable, this emotion causing that material effect without time or biochemistry intervening."

"Dee would like a song." Murial came back from the bedroom.

"Sorry, Hanna, got to go." Grateful for the interruption. This pleasure to go towards. For among the happiest moments of Lev's life were Dee tucked into bed and his guitar brought out for 'All I want in this creation/ two little girls and a big plantation/ Hey, pretty little black eyed Susan/ Hey.'

"Talk to her, call her," said Hanna. Sliding past the sink Lev said, "Look, if it means that much to you," and some needle pricked his promise through his flannel shirt into his skin. "I obviously always call without reminding," he added huffing. But sickness made him sick and he'd had trouble with his breathing calling Boston.

"I feel bananas." He started for the bedroom, leaking his admission like steam from a valve in the radiators at home in New York City. "I know you do," said Hanna as Dee in the bedroom called 'Daddy.' For now that he'd turned his back to Hanna, he could speak to her and she could read him.

Yes, of course, Lev had promised Hanna. "If it means that much to you, I'll call Ros." But that was Monday night and Tuesday morning he'd had the chance to sail with his old friend Andrew Eliscu across the bay to greenest Tiberon. Magic Island. Like in *The Tempest*. Then back across the windy bay past the brown sea lions on the black rock in time to dock in the city and run up the hill to the studio. Like in some *Dolce Vita* life. Rack of lamb again on the blackboard at that restaurant on Polk Street as he ran past, sniffing the air for garlic, thyme, cilantro.

At the beginning of the next week, as he got ready again to call Ros, Andrew called again. "I promise not to mention what show your name came up in connection with until we've had a bottle of zinfandel and a major lunch," he said. "Does half past sound tolerable? I'll pick you up in Oakland. The Santa Fe Grill. I've been known to drive across the bridge to get my friends."

"Drive away," said Lev. "I can't imagine what show my name came up in connection with. I'm not sure I want to. The weather? *The Shadow? This Is Your Life?*"

On Friday, Andrew had leaned across the table. Oxford blue elbows, red suspenders, on the white cloth. "What's so incredible, Lev, is that everyone at the studio agrees. I mean, who else but you could deal with all those freaks at night and make it radio? So to think about this, talk to Murial. From our point of view, we want you moving up to a daytime slot. With some modifications, of course. And lots more, ahem, green stuff. Goes with pine nuts, ha ha. What we want to do is bring in experts, you comprehend, on blended families, real estate. Parenting problems. Nothing parochial — gay or straight or hip blue collar. Even in San Jose, everyone needs to know what IRA to put his hard-earned money in. All you have to do is stroke the experts, set them up, let the listeners take over."

"IRA is some dopey kid I went to high school with or the Irish Republican Army, right?" Lev loved passing bad jokes like dubious playing cards to faithful, fatal, straight-arrow Andrew, who'd followed him like the Ghost of Christmas past from Amherst in 1969. That was the year he'd fled his own competitive drive and settled in at mellow Santa Cruz and changed his name from Lenny to Lev and written his mother and father:

> Dear Stella and Sidney,
>   I am tired of trying to assimilate myself to this plastic country, and am returning to my real name which is Lev after Tolstoy and Trotsky and my grandfather, Leo, the Russian draft dodger.
>   Yours,
>   In the struggle,
>   Lev Oliner

"You will always be my son whatever you chose to call yourself," his father had written back, strangling him further in the coils of love he'd tried so hard to cut. His mother, whose impossible father he'd named himself after, was too annoyed and incredulous to call or write.

"I love it." Andrew now said about his IRA joke. "Dessert, brandy?" Andrew had rescued Lev from his first marriage and from that listener-supported radio station, when Lev had been too loyal to leave what had made him miserable and bored.

"I can't imagine," said Lev, "reversing everything — I mean for money? — I've spent my life on. What you're talking about sounds slick, no texture, Teflon. Excuse the negativity. Nothing personal. But experts. You know what I think about doctors and psychotherapists? And their cornering the market on the bodies, the souls of this republic?" In fact, he'd never thought about the subject, but could improvise a diatribe to suit some feeling, which could become, if he weren't careful, something he believed in, some conviction.

Andrew's grin offered the answer to why he went on making opportunities for a reluctant Lev. For Lev was Andrew's last college friend, an authentic sixties curmudgeon, who wasn't stoned, wasted, humorless, sold out or impossibly sectarian. "Oh shit." Lev looked down at the wine stain on the tablecloth. Shy in the face of Andrew's love for him.

"Give the money to the farmworkers, some alcoholic blues guitarist you meet in Oakland." Andrew reached to pick the check up, slid his MasterCard over it.

Lev looked up to find a frizzy-haired woman in the corner nodding yes to the corruption the stocky man across from her proposed. The man's big hand reached over the tablecloth to grasp her wrist.

Don't do it, Lev shouted silently with his eyes. Picking up the glass whose wine he'd spilled and finishing the zinfandel, feeling love and gratitude for Andrew and the family Andrew had helped him to support. "Good wine," he said. "I was looking forward to being an authentic old fart," he muttered. Craning his neck to look at the blackboard they'd ordered from. For authentic wasn't people, but ingredients these days: corn bread, sun-dried tomatoes, goat cheese, raspberry vinegars, wines.

"That was a great meal," he said loudly to Andrew, because among his commitments was one to truth and this lunch had been great. Paid for by someone else.

~

"Can you talk, Murie?"

"Barely. Let me take a bite of this sandwich. The Brothers Bagel don't like their bookkeepers bleeding mayonnaise all over Accounts Receivable. Now let me move the phone to the other ear. This one hurts."

"Well, I dropped off Dee at the Rainbow School, then Oliver and I hung out and I got to tell him the story of our courtship. 'I liked your mother so much, I felt shy,' I told him. 'I mean it. I could barely say anything, if you can imagine such a thing.' 'I like my mother,' he said. 'And I never feel shy with her. How come?' Plus some other things, I won't report to you right now. The minute I got back into the house, your mother called because your wicked sister won't let her come over to the house unless she stops drinking, which is ridiculous, she says, because she isn't hardly drinking. Only beer. An occasional whiskey for strength. Then my mother to ask: 'How come I only get Lila at the Brookline house? Doesn't Ros feel capable of answering the phone?' As if I should know. Plus Hanna wants you to call. I've decided to start tonight's program with the peripheral canal, then move into something sporty. The A's maybe. What do you think, Murie? I feel ridiculous about that show about my sister."

"Don't get jittery, Lev. People liked it at the station. You're *supposed* to be a little outrageous. Or they wouldn't let you talk about whatever."

"You make me sound like a spoiled child. I know damn well what I can't talk about. Or more accurately, *how* not to talk about things. Too intelligently. Or too long."

"I'm sorry, Lev. My sandwich is finished. I've got to go."

"Who's stopping you? I'm taking Oliver to pick up groceries. Maybe we'll take a walk, good-bye."

∼

"What's wrong with this block?" asked Lev.

"Nobody speaks the same language," said Oliver. "Where Jason lives in Berkeley mostly everyone speaks English. And plays regular games. Skateboard and things."

"Everybody here speaks Thai, is that the name of the language? You know I don't even know what Cambodians speak, is it Khmer?"

"Dope addict talk." Oliver nodded at the street corner nodders as they entered the Lebanese grocery, where a boy poked his black silk head through a hole in the ceiling and fluttered his lashes at the grocer, his father, below.

The grocer looked up warily as Lev and Oliver opened the door and let the misty Oakland rain in. "We're shutting it," said Lev. "How about the hills after we get some stuff for supper?" Punching his stepson in the shoulder. Roaming narrow aisles looking for red beans, hamburger, taco shells. "This is my idea about these languages, Ollie. Somebody held the world upside down and when it got turned back over, everyone had slid down the globe to somewhere else."

"Silly." Oliver grinned. Picked up a green banana.

"Well actually, I think it *was* something like that. Don't stick your finger in the scale with that banana. There have been so many wars in this century. So many poor places with a couple so rich, that people have been scurrying to find somewhere safe, that has groceries."

"If we take this home" — Oliver lifted his green banana tenderly from the scale — "how long before it gets ripe?"

"I don't think it gets ripe. I think it's *supposed* to be like that."

∼

"Yccch." Murial pointed to the bathroom ceiling. "Mildew." She lifted one broad and beautiful soaking wet foot from the rusting tin of the shower stall below her.

The foot was only beautiful to doting him; Lev groaned inwardly at his fondness.

"Look at the ceiling," she said. "You're not looking, Lev."

"I'm looking at your foot. I wish you'd look at something else. You're not supposed to point that mildew out. You're supposed to pretend this is a hot-shot hotel, like the ones we went to when I lived on the boat and you were, hey, cop to it, living in that basement with Oliver, which was worse than this apartment is."

"But there are more of us here. One, two, three, four."

"Let me wash your face," Lev ran his soap-holding hand gently down her face. The washcloth in his other hand. Her sweet face gleamed from soap and hot water and the flickering fluorescent light above.

More shower rain on them.

"Would you like to have your hair washed?" she asked gravely.

Her hands when he'd noticed, squeezed the aloe bottle and began to rub *a natural treatment for normal scalps* into his head. With the water running down his forehead and his nose, down his neck chest belly off his cock, some knot inside him unloosened, untied. "Go ahead. Complain about this dump. I can take it." Thumping his hairy chest as the water flattened his curls.

First he washed her sandy hair. "Close your eyes or I'll get soap in them. I'm almost done." She opened them. Gray blueness.

"It's Oliver. He's too old to be shut up at night, unless we walk him places. Which you'll never do. I can't. I'd get a full-time job to get us out of this slum" — Murial stepped from the shower stall. "except . . ." She grabbed a towel, wrapped it around her middle.

Her wet footprints, thick toes, narrow heels for him to follow to their bedroom. She got into bed, propped her back against the headboard and looking like an English barmaid said, "I've got to talk to you, Lev."

"Talk." His mouth to her neck.

"I'm pregnant."

A miracle. Not the pregnancy, but the headboard which had become a Grand Rapids halo around her sandy head.

"I don't believe it." He followed her into bed, reached beneath the covers for her hand, missing it, moved to her belly, her cunt. "Dee is just a baby." Rubbing his palm around her mound. "What about that diaphragm? All that waiting for you to put it in."

"Dee is three. It didn't work. Hey, cut it out, Lev." His fingers began to work inside her. His hand pushed away as if he were a child.

But now he was a child beneath the blanket with his face buried and his tongue lapping salt and softness and inside his head before his pleasure at her pleasure, those pigeons cooing on the roof above, became intense enough to lose the words, he knew *you could go home again,* by marrying the right woman and taking a shower together and making love.

But where, his head emerging, would the money for the baby come from? And fuck it, he was being railroaded by everyone right into Andrew's tunnel of a proposition. Now he wanted to be inside her. But fuck it, sitting up. He was supposed to be a grown-up. Besides, inside his head, this thought sat at an angle: she doesn't have her diaphragm in and what if she gets pregnant?

"Let me tell you what happened with Andrew last week. I meant to." Leaning against the headboard himself. Brushing his cock with his fingertip fondly. Letting it go. "But I forgot."

∽

"This is from memory, you understand, but if that hall was a few feet wider, you could make a sleeping loft. But no. I can't imagine you getting another bedroom from your place, no matter how clever you are." Henry was obliging, if cold, when Lev called a while later to ask what would decide things. (Either he had to take that job or not.)

"Still, the place is cheap," said Lev, "and I'm attached to it, like you must be to your house." He was frightened of Henry. Or why be so puny and extra nice.

"I hate our house," said Henry. "It's expensive to run and architecturally monstrous, apart from its essential ugliness. If you must know, I feel like the handyman instead of the owner."

"Well, I guess I'm glad in a way, to know this place is impossible." (Actually he was relieved to know that Henry hated his house.) "Tell Ros I'll call her. Tonight or tomorrow. Actually, don't tell her. I'd rather this call be a little bit private." So you could hate them, according to Henry. Little houses. Big houses. Where you landed and got stuck.

9

Rosalind

A phone call and a chain of consequences. How people help to resurrect each other. As well as let each other drown. It's Sunday. Lila leaves. Ros's clients come on Wednesday.

"I wash dishes as a form of exercise and everyone walks around on tiptoes as if I'm already dying. When I'm not the person whose fault everything is." The phone held a little distance from Ros's ear, because Lev had a tendency to shout.

"Give them a break, Ros. They're probably just nervous," he said softly.

"I'll consider it." She'd forgotten. Lev's oscillation from shouts to whispers depending on who he had decided to be that day and what was being talked about. Lev speaking softly meant that things were so serious that he'd control himself. She could tune herself in to him like a radio. "And you, Lev?" She got up. Moved with the phone from the couch to the chair she'd used to work in.

Used to work in. Her ass felt good.

"Do you remember Andrew? Well, he's got me this insane daytime show to do with child development experts and financial planning types and so on. This is expert city. Blah blah blah."

This got said loud, fast and humorous. A pause. As he waited for her to tell him who he was, or ought to be.

"Sounds great. An opportunity. What do you think?" She swiveled the chair around to face the couch.

"Daytime radio is another ballpark, financially. We'll be rich, or more accurately, upper middle class." His confession. The heart of this golden ambivalence. Said softly. He was sympathetic to his regrets, ironic about his dilemma. (Who but the Levs of America had gotten these choices?)

She stood, put the phone down. The thrill of listening to this music, these undertones, again. Once more. No more key in the bedroom door, the twist of the bagel, the mouth hungering for sounds, that could only come in through the ears. She sat, put the phone where it had been. On her shoulder. The phone hurt her earlobe. Reached to take an earring off that wasn't there.

"It's useful you'll find, money." She heard her own refrigerated tone. This was her least favorite Lev. This man who'd imposed his voluntary poverty on his wife and children. Who celebrated, denigrated, denied his choices, made fun of his comic but serious stance in favor of downward mobility and funk.

"Shit, it's not the money I'm uncomfortable about. It's, well, I kind of love this flaky life."

"But Murial doesn't, does she?" Asked too quickly. Pause, listen for the sounds of his silence.

"Tell me, Ros. If we'd been poorer, would I have been so, what should I call it? Bad? About knowing my limitations or what necessity is? Would I have been handier at fixing my bike instead of taking it to the, where did we take our bikes anyway? I bet we got new ones when they broke. And would I have felt, more in control, if I'd known how to fix my bike. Less bratty? Or is this merely, in this country and quarter century?" But he'd lost his question. He had wound himself up. This was rhetoric time, filling in while he got his breath or his emotion.

"Do you remember that plastic bubble we used to say we lived beneath? We meant our friends, not other people, none of whom, as I recall, were even real to us, can you believe it? Older, poorer, richer, greener. We meant those smart young people at good colleges, that's who we meant, that bubble that *we* lived underneath. Made of security and money. Pretending we wanted out. Not now, I guess. The kids want in, I bet. As for that bubble, we never considered that we'd constructed that bubble ourselves, with all that us and them stuff.

"Or that our own fortunes depended on that American Empire we were all excoriating. Besides, it was easier to get what we wanted then, traveling, old houses, even those Volkswagens. That bus I bought for something like a quarter. Those trips you took. We thought we didn't want anything because what we wanted was inexpensive and different from what our parents had. And another thing."

Rosalind held the phone to her other ear. Considered not listening. (He was seriously wound up now. Manic, but interesting.)

"Another thing. This being rewarded for bullshitting, like making up statistics at the supper table about how many dogs of Republican contributors got lost and Lila believing me. What did that do to me as a kid and why should I go on doing it as an adult, on the radio, no less. For real money."

They had reached the guilt, spread like chicken fat, over everything.

"She only pretended to," Ros said. "Lila only pretended to believe you. Maybe you can help her out, if you're so rich, all of a sudden. She'd die not to have to drag herself into that silly school when she could be painting, Lev." She heard herself, directive, as everyone said, managerial, well good! Assuming her soul, instead of this nightgowny thing that had been draped around her, strangling initiative or a walk to the bathroom.

"Andrew said something like that. But maybe I'll start feeling like all the people I know with money, overextended and overdrawn."

"Like us, you mean, me." But all she heard was herself, for she had a couple of things wrong with her too. Or didn't he remember? When had he called before? She hadn't been answering the phone, but still. Drawn back into those covers, dirt, smells, farts, belch, hiccup, give birth again, now engaged, here in this room, this civilization, her mind, her senses, intuitions useful for something. Tapping her bare foot. Big toe. Dirty soul. Reminding her, as she lifted her feet to the ottoman, how good it had once felt to be working in this office. How cool, necessary, entitled, in charge, no sense of her body, when she was working engaged with someone else. Then bam. Listening to him. Her self reappeared, like a cousin whose name she had forgotten. "I've lost the cliché I was looking for," she said. "Now let me tell you, I really want to go back to, Lev. This bizarreness. I've drifted, been drifting, in some quasi-alcoholic stupor, made of oh sugar, probably, and do people on the coast still do dope?"

As soon as she'd found the words and gotten them into the warm office air — turn on the air conditioner, a note to herself — she'd lost the feeling. That drifty drift. Her tone had been crisp. The air turned crisper around her. The pillow beneath her ass. On top of everything. In charge. Her head lifted. The comfort of that ordinary middle gear gone as soon as it appeared and the woman who ran this family in charge again.

"Do dope? A little. Ros, everyone knows you're a fated, drowning princess summerfallwinterspring," said Lev. "I'm trying to say that you adore drifting, when you're not in charge of everything. Didn't I ever tell you this before?"

"I, you're too needy. To tell me anything. Or too self-absorbed." There. She'd said it. "I'm too — " Yawning, not so managerial, kicking her feet, shower time, she stank. She'd sink. Beneath the waves of a bathtub.

"Well," said Lev. "I guess this is a bad time to talk. I better go. Good-bye."

Click, off, abandoning her, for calling on him. The weight of her self on these men.

"I'm not saying it's all your fault." Henry had said the night before when they'd returned from the restaurant. He'd grasped his ankle boots to pull them off, looked around the bedroom. "But you've done nothing since you've come home except demoralize the population."

That wartime vocabulary again, she'd thought. Like that damn cardiologist. Where had these men picked it up? None of them had been in the army. Musing as if for some paper about the residues of militarism on males, even the best of them, blah blah blah as she watched him, she should write . . .

The boot pulled off, he'd gone on from his perch on the bed's edge about Sophie and some doll he'd had to fix and Nana, never mind, she'll tell you, now Lila, whom he could hardly blame, was going back to New York tomorrow morning. The implication: it was her fault. She'd been thrilled, given her military musings, at the flip-flop. HardonebyHenry in the boot camp of family life, she thought. Suddenly he'd lain down fully clothed on the quilt.

"I'm sick, you're well," she'd told the body beside her. "How can everything be my fault?"

Silence. He drew his knees up. Held them with his hands. "Ros, you're — it's frightening," he'd said before he let his legs go, turned on his stomach. "You're frightening us."

His legs had nothing to do with how she'd felt. As if he'd stuck his finger through her scar into her aching sewn-up heart. Straightforward-enough-when-he-felt-like-it Henry. Now there were two ways to plug the hole he'd made. She could question him casually: 'I'm doing what, Henry? That's got you so frightened.' Or assert something. About him preferably. "This has something to do with your career, doesn't it, Henry? Or lack thereof. This anger." She could tell by the way he sat up to unzip his pants that she'd gotten to him. She'd been thinking for years that he must, despite his silence, be suffering. This failure she had married. Surprised by the snip snap of her jaws, wanting to bite him.

He'd gotten into bed. Silent, breathing hard, it was terrifying suddenly, the anger that came off his flesh like heat or desire.

She felt smug, sleepy. She slept, conscious and afraid of him, like a fire burning beside her, smoke smudging her consciousness mixed with dream, on the left side of the bed. This was good sleep for a while. Not sweating, pain filled, trauma. A dream took place on her left. A house in the suburbs. Leaves falling. 'You're too old to be a waitress,' somebody told her beside a lake or marshy pool. 'Besides, you're sick, forget the lake.' 'Remember it!' This voice. Woke up puzzled. Still seeing trees, back to black again.

This morning she'd awakened with Henry downstairs already and Sophie peering in. "Come on in," she'd said because Sophie in the bedroom was better than that little white face peering in. Dear face. It brought tears to her eyes. Made her irritable. Sleepy. Headache starting. "Why don't you go with Auntie Lila to the station? With Daddy, dear." Sophie's small hand had turned the doorknob. Closed it in her face. She had gotten out of bed and followed her girl downstairs, pleased with her formulation as her nightgown billowed around her: that she didn't want Sophie around because her daughter was clinging to her, disguised as taking care. Clinging disguised as taking care. As she'd caught up to Sophie. Took her hand. On the other side, Sophie's fingers were glued to her billowing nightgown.

Her office, when she'd reached it, had looked peaceful and orderly. Her files were filled with patients who liked her, needed her and paid for her presence and advice. Her calm and her competence. Then a brother who called from California for her attention. That music that came to her underneath his voice. Her own music — catchable — for a second. Still, she'd turned her own need back on him finally. Good-bye, he'd said. While her article (that was how well she was!) had been rolled into the typewriter yesterday. (Lila's peering in just as she'd picked her papers up. To announce, Ros saw this morning, her own departure). "My pa-

tient flourished in this country," she had written before the illness came on, stealing her from life as she knew it. "Her mother
perished in the camps. It seems peculiar to have to ask, as we are
all either mothers or the children of mothers or both, but why
has nobody pointed out that it's the role, not the people in it, that
lights the people up to seem so peculiar, arbitrary, idiosyncratic,
powerful?"

Bam. A hesitant but startling knock on the door turned out to
be Lila. And instead of hissing, 'How ungenerous you are to leave
me,' Ros waited for her to come to the chair, then rose, took a
step towards her, hugged her narrow sister's shoulders. Hugging
her sister's narrow shoulders, nine years between them and not a
single memory of this sister till when? Eight maybe. This life
pushed before her like a shopping cart full of old clothes, furniture, expectations, too heavy in the present to have much past-
ness in the past where it belonged. Full of this stuff (enraged by
life!) Now. Remind me of that sometime, she reminded herself.
She watched her sister leave her. Gave herself instructions. Move
to the desk where the article is. Work if everyone's abandoned
you. There. There. There. Rosalind.

"Ma. It's Grandma on the phone," yelled Nana from the hall.

"Tell her I'm busy. I'll call back another time when I'm
stronger." Feeling decisive.

A note parallel to the one on Henry, on Rosalind's professional life

The year Nana was born and Baumbach left her, Ros became a
family therapist. She'd been an experimental psych major at
Brandeis, studying statistics and running rats through mazes,
until her trip with Baumbach around the world brought human
history and suffering into view. Then she'd switched to sociology. Her dissertation was on the women's consciousness-raising
group as a form (she happened to be in one) and as a political,
psychological and ideological phenomenon.

Baumbach had blamed this thesis and that group for the fail-ure of their marriage. "I was married to a bathrobe, a typewriter, and a fucking female chorus."

Two weeks before Nana was born, Ros had defended her dis-sertation, and two weeks after Baumbach left them, she'd found a temporary job at Cambridge Hospital. The work, assisting some-one treating schizophrenics and their families, became the core of her vocation. 'My whole life, I felt, had prepared me for this work. My place in my family of origin and my love of groups and talk and drama. Plus a commitment I hadn't known about to making sense of the subjective side of life.'

Incisive, articulate, authoritative, and imaginative in a thera-peutic sense, she listened sympathetically to her clients, offering them alternatives to their conduct, if not their goals. She also at-tended a psychoanalytic institute, where she found a 'richer, more complex view of individual character,' an opinion she kept from her mentor, who thought treating individuals separate from the families they came from or inhabited was foolish and even reprehensible. Her own attempt to bring feminism into family therapy, charting the ways in which unequal power be-tween men and women in the world affected everyone's life in-side the house, was only starting to take shape in that article on motherhood she'd read Henry the day her pains began.

～

The first thing Rosalind noticed about the family she ushered in that Wednesday was how prissy and unreal the air they brought into her office was. Brisk, efficient, the father first of all. Everyone scrambling, everyone seated. Ten-year-old twins, and a toddler. Glum looks, then a smile, from the goody-two-shoes mother who began: "We were doing fine until last Monday, when I had to go out and speak at Wellesley. You've been there, recently?"

Ros shrugged to indicate, it doesn't matter, although she'd given a seminar at the health service there some months before.

"These are fancy shoes." The three-year-old girl perched on

the tiny Mexican chair in Rosalind's office stuck her black Mary Janes out to admire them. Smiled at everyone.

"Not recently," Ros said in answer to the woman's question.

"Well, it all started at the breakfast table naturally. Where he" — the woman pointed to her husband — "had *The Globe* spread all over the table, which he didn't deign to move as I was clearing up around him. I didn't have the heart to force the kids to do what their father won't, which is to help get things minimally tidyish so the Chilean woman who cleans won't have to deal with another houseful of spoiled North American slobs."

The stocky bearded man beside the woman recrossed his legs and leaned forward. His face attentive but inexpressive, as if what had been described was interesting but far off. The ten-year-old girl arranged her face to look concerned, dismayed and mournful, her expression changing as her mother talked while her twin brother, who had a Band-Aid on his nose, tried looking scornful, bored or out of it.

"This one" — the woman indicating the boy —"gave me this look. Like, Mom, are you at it again?

"I went upstairs to put a suit on, so I could drive out to Wellesley and sound reasonably intelligent in front of these historians I had contempt for when I was a stringer in Buenos Aires. Instead of a housewife trying to write articles on Latin America from Boston. Should I go on?"

"Why not?"

"It's not individual therapy, I'm sure I'm taking up everyone's time. But to make a long story short, I gave this simpleminded answer to some question about some issue, trade maybe, and came home mortified. On my way downstairs, after changing, I peeked into his room" — pointing to her son — "and there he was. Sitting like a pasha on his bed, lighting matches and dropping them into the trash basket. After all those sessions about why he kept that damned diskette box full of matches under his bed. And why he lit them. And those exercises you gave us with him lighting matches one after another, whatever that was supposed to accomplish." The woman adjusted her glasses, looking apologetically at her husband. "I was the one who insisted we come to see you." Sighing. "I *can* report some progress, however, because this time, he poured water into the trash can after he'd dropped the matches in. Instead of just waiting until the fire went out. I was the crazy one this time. I took the matchbox and slammed it against his face and broke his nose, I mean I bruised it."

The ten-year-old boy's lovely face turned, so Ros could see the Band-Aid below his limpid brown eyes, his thick eyelashes fluttering as he turned some more. See what happened to me, the eyelashes fluttered as he turned back. What do you think of it? Or her, my mom. Or me.

"We think she ought to get some help." The husband bent to pull his sock up, as if he'd forgotten to do so when he sat down. "Which is why we called you."

"What kind of help?" Help! had been her cry this morning in the shower, alone with the dizzying tile surface, the water's heat, the reluctance of her body to move at a speed that would get her down the stairs to work, the fear of falling. Help! had been her thought in that bed these past weeks, ordering Sophie to bring her cookies and Fritos and Coke. Help! was what she'd thought standing twelve years ago before the fridge at two A.M. after Nana was born and Baumbach had disappeared into the wilds of Vermont with his student and she'd spend her nights with a colicky baby and her days at the hospital running groups for schizophrenics. Help, help, help, help. Always the food alone had answered her. And she in her wisdom, her training, her experience, her insight, had answered when others asked. Searched in her depths and come up with something. Tired, suddenly, she saw a sandwich floating in her fantasy — flip, flop, all over the room.

The woman said apologetically, "I've just stopped therapy, perhaps I might . . . again . . . but really, I feel I've had enough."

"Should the cleaning lady come in more often? Or should you

all start clearing the table? Or should he throw the matches away?" She heard herself, she heard her mother's voice. Practical. Crisp. Sarcastic. A disbelief in metaphysics, depths and a belief in clean dishes, straight seams, enough money for help.

"Come now, Doctor, surely that's flip," said the man, a recent convert to depth psychology. "This is serious."

It was flip. It was serious. How sick she was of these depths, this scrutiny, that undertow, those weeks or was it months in the hospital, and upstairs in bed. She turned to the son. "I assume you've been told how sorry she was."

"Ad nauseam. Besides, I wasn't lighting matches. I was lighting the stuff in the wastepaper basket. I'm a human fire engine." Feeling his nose. "So even if I light it, I also put it out." He frowned at the floor, perplexed by himself. Looking up. "You know, it's really not that dangerous. In the wastepaper basket. I know it's wrong. But my friend Luis does it and nobody makes him go to any therapist."

"Fiyah truck," the three-year-old murmured passionately. "I love dis toy. I like to have it."

"Luis is the son of the janitor at the local elementary school," the husband said in a tired way, as an explanation, apparently, of why it might be all right for Luis to light wastepaper basket fires.

"What do you think?" Ros turned to the twin sister.

"Mom's not like that usually. Maybe she had a headache."

"Bam, right into me." The boy's hand dived for his nose.

"Well, I am definitely concerned," said the man.

"I'm not trying to excuse myself, but I felt like a hostage to a destructive child. It drove me nuts," said the woman, dangling one shoe on the tip of her toe.

"Anyway. It's over." The boy stood up. "I threw the diskette box away and put the matches underwater."

"Yea." His twin sister clapped.

"And I'm not," — looking around the room — "gonna get any more matches at the minimart."

"I wish you'd saved the diskette box. Someone keeps eating

them." Growling like a bear, the husband also stood up, adjusted his belt and flashed his teeth, grinned, bowed towards the children.

"Well," said Ros, "before you decide this is over — "

"Thank you," said the mother, nodding to Ros, standing as well. "You've been extremely helping — helpful."

Everyone stood. Ordinarily, in a firm voice, she would have said, 'Please sit down the hour isn't up,' Done some magic, pointing out. That this was the family style, this everything is copesetic after drama (the tone was middle-class tragedy, then something cheerful and brisk), but instead, she took a dive back down into silence, that room upstairs, that younger daughter bringing her help, her husband gone to work that didn't pay their mortgage even, and where had Henry been, since she'd come home? As if she were seeing something new, the presence of his absence in the house. The divine surface of things, she thought, dizzy for a second as everyone left her. She also stood. Now that the session, entirely theatrical, was over. She'd been the audience, and the revelation that the danger was over had come at the end. As she ushered them out, an intuition. That they would never return, no matter what troubles they had, for she'd been flip, according to the husband. Openly on the woman's side. Ignoring the unspoken rule that women in power should bend over backwards to be fair to men and compassionate towards children, despite what men in power do to women.

She closed the office door, straightened a magazine on the hall table, crossed to the kitchen. Felt anticipation, excitement, a thought. How could she not have known? That priests, judges, therapists and even witches were supposed to work unbiased magic. That unbiased magic was magic with a bias so ingrained that nobody noticed it, including the magician.

Meanwhile, the facts of her grown-up life had been: that Nana had wailed at four A.M., while she'd stood before this same fridge drinking sweetened condensed milk for strength and willing her baby to sleep so she could work the next morning without exhaustion. Her husband with some student in Vermont. Most of her money going for child care. Still, compared to most of the women she knew, she'd been blissfully, unspeakably privileged.

Now she opened the fridge door. Peered to see what was on the middle shelf. Lifted this and this and that out, onto the butcher block island.

Sandwich, although it wasn't lunchtime.

The top slice of bread she'd just grabbed, raised like a bedsheet to peek at what, without noticing, she'd piled onto the slice below. Bologna, Swiss, mayo, lettuce, avocado, a few old shrimp. A few cookies stuck around the edge. She wanted everything. She carried the sandwich wrapped in a napkin up to bed. Onto the bed table, as she slipped her body fully clothed beneath the quilt.

Her crime. Or rather her sandwich, on the bed table. *She'd wanted everything.*

But how had she slipped during that session. Down down to those floating-in-the-water plants. Talking to these people as if her mother's approach to life had suddenly made sense to her, as if her mother's acceptance of the surface of things was truth. Because it was useful.

Just because it seems to be true, doesn't mean it isn't.

Her crime, or rather her sandwich. She'd wanted everything.

The door slammed downstairs. Somebody started up. "Who is it?" she cried. Disturbed in the middle of her secret ritual.

"It's me, Ma." Her elder daughter.

"I'm up here. Napping." She finished the sandwich. Fast before anybody bothered her or came in. Juices from whatever was inside it dripped on the quilt. Cookie crumbs brushed from the quilt. The napkin for her hands, tossed on the bed table. The decision. I will sleep right now. Having lied, she would carry it out. And this time, the rabbit hole she fell down on her way to sleep had some other woman's life that made her lose her cool this afternoon, some other mother perishing. A sandwich awaiting some other mother on the bed table. Avocado mayonnaise.

Mother, ma, mommy, Stella, she murmured, passionate as that little girl admiring her new shoes that afternoon in the office. Crying out her own mother's name. Before she lost everything, all words fell down the hole with her to darkness, blank. Then the real dreams began, the picture show.

There was somebody at the door in her dream. Then Henry in daylit life.

10

First Nana, then Henry

Henry and Nana jointly discover or uncover the magnitude of their wife and mother's drowning. Some running shoes get bought. Nana learns about the moral values of the real world. Henry starts to understand something about the times and his own situation. He ends where we found him in the last chapter, on a Wednesday, at Ros's door.

"I don't care about the clothes or the money, really. But I must know why you decided to pick on me? When there are other ways you could get cash." Her mom asked Nana.

Her mother's eyebrows were rising like some movie star with an important question. Here in this office where Nana had come like a prisoner, knocking on the prosecutor's door, going in. For Henry, whom Nana had told about selling her mother's clothes before Lila could tell him, had made her tell her mother. And now her mother was telling her things.

"Name one way," said Nana, "I could get money." Feeling excited, because arguing was how her mother played with her, like other people's mothers played tennis or hearts. "That would be quick enough. Besides, you have too much." Nana's fingers spread. "You're rich, we're poor, me, especially."

"So why not ask me for some clothes to sell, Nana?"

"You guys make me furious, all of you, you especially." She said loudly. Because her mother was so smart. She knew that her mother wouldn't have given her clothes, only she didn't know how she knew it. Or the reason she *knew* it, which her mother always insisted on.

So she decided not to stand here, but turned and grabbed and slammed the door and ran away downstairs to the basement, where too late she remembered that custody stuff on Henry's workbench in the corner. But it was gone now. She waited for a moment for her mother to have followed her, but no one. Then she went back to the back of the basement to where the old t.v. was and turned it on.

"I'm going to torture you," she'd told Sophie the other day as they sat here watching *Love Boat* reruns. But when? A few days, a few weeks, everything had run together.

Settling into the torn pillow couch. Left arm circling her neck until it touched her right shoulder.

If she'd asked her mother for clothes to sell, her mother wouldn't have been able to make up her mind what to give her. "I might get fatter or thinner or need that purse some time," she'd say. Or give her something, then want it back.

That was true. Even her mother would admit it. That was the reason she stole.

Snap, she turned the set on. Instead of going upstairs to tell the real reason to her mom.

Because admitting wrongness once in a while was a way her mother stayed in the right all the time.

I'm gonna sing when my spirit says sing, sang some pretty people in braids and curls and fancy hairdos on the smeary screen before her. She leaned forward. She concurred. She applauded.

～

In Cambridge, Nana sat on a red plastic chair in a special running shoe store, with her money in her blue jean pocket and a man kneeling before her to slip some sneakers on from the box beside his white hand, black hairs on the joints of his fingers.

Cinderella, she thought, squashing her wish to leave her bare foot in the hairy fingers now slipping the sneaker on, tying it.

"My fathers are both skinny. My mother is wide. I have wide toes and narrow heels," she told him with her head bent down. But her voice was too loud for the store.

"You're right." The man leaned back to pinch her big toe. Slipped the sneakers off and stuffed them back into boxes. "Try these." He brought another box. This time she wanted, as he drew laces through the holes, to stand on his bald head with her leg out like a ballerina.

Instead she stood up and jogged in place with these sneakers he'd put on her. "It jiggles. Back here." Pointing to the back of her ankle.

"It's not your last." He felt around her ankles. Last meant fit, she knew. "New Balance makes a kind, we're out of them now, but they have a seconds store in Brighton, you could try."

"Seconds?"

"They're less expensive than what we've got."

But Brighton had no subway to it, so she called Henry in the booth outside. Dropping her quarter and licking her dry lips, because last time Henry had said no to her and all this trouble came afterwards with her mother's clothes and maybe Lila's going home, because of Nana selling stuff at Coolidge Corner. At first, Nana said politely, "Are you too busy, Henry?" When he said no, she could tell from his voice that he wasn't irritated, so she said, "I would't bother you but. There's no subway to this place, where they have seconds. Which means cheaper stuff. But good."

Not adding, And anyway, I have the money.

This time, when she *knew* that she'd done something wrong, unlike the other time, when she'd only asked for money, Henry

said he'd drive her to the seconds store. "Only not now. On
Thursday. I'll pick you up at school, honey."

With that 'honey,' she stuck her hand into her jean jacket to
make sure her wallet was still in there and hit a square of paper. "I
don't believe this," she said out loud to the photograph that she
drew out. What was that? She guessed. She didn't guess. She
couldn't throw it out. Thump, thump, she could hear it like a
horror movie in the garbage can if she did. Now she knew: From
on top of the refrigerator the day she sold those clothes at
Coolidge Corner. She put the photo back into her pocket. Should
she give it to someone? Her mother, her dad, or who?

Henry

"Now you're certain your mother knows about this," Henry
had said to Nana after supper last night, who'd told him back,
"My mother doesn't want revenge or retribution," which must
have been from some spelling list. About the clothes. As he'd left
her room, his daughter had stared at him. As if he had intruded.
He hadn't believed her. As to what her mother did or didn't want.
For like her mother Nana had become a manipulator with a large
vocabulary. Still, if Ros didn't care enough about her daughter's
theft to discuss it with him, why should he, the stepfather, go on
and on?

Now he punched nine on the office phone, to get an outside
line.

"George Adelle, please, Henry Twist."

He'd said yes to Nana about the shopping trip Thursday. As he
waited for Adelle, his former partner, to pick the phone up, he
had the feeling that Adelle *had* to say yes to him about a job, to
balance out the universe.

"George. It's Henry." With Adelle on the line, he dropped seeds to form a path to his need for a full-time job with his firm. How pleased the guy at the DOE was with his work, he muttered. Did George remember, whatshisname? Seccombe. But now, funding and so on, tapping his pencil as George said, "Henry, you wouldn't believe how good the stuff we did together in the old days looks at the moment. You'd be bored silly by most of what we're doing."

He didn't believe it. Adelle had scores of interesting clients. Tapping his pencil and waiting for the man to say okay to a lunch at least, if he'd said yes to Nana's shopping trip.

The lunch got set. "At least I'll lay your options out as I see them, Henry."

Pleased by how well the call had gone, he called the lawyer he'd been avoiding.

"Legally speaking if your wife died, your stepdaughter should return to her biological father. But I assume you can work out something informal with the guy about custody. He doesn't actually want her, does he?"

"Not that I've noticed."

Adelle's secretary called back to change the date. Which meant he had to change his date with Nana. "Oh Dad, you always do that, put me at the bottom of your list."

But once upon a time, they had been pals for nature walks, buddies for chores, the newly minted stepfather he'd been and this daughter who'd barely known her so-called biological father.

What, he wondered, as he penciled "Running clothes for Nana" onto Friday in his date book, was George actually working on these days? Remembering that hospital ward with aspirin and television sets in a room at the end of the hall they'd done with some social psychologist. Proving that patients who had to walk to have their pain or their boredom relieved left for home days sooner than their sedentary sisters.

～

"Is that a song," asked Henry, "or a riddle?," although he knew it was a riddle-song, this bubble-gum rock thing that Nana had turned up loud in the Volvo. About some nobody, said Nana, who was really a somebody, a girlfriend.

"It's too loud, Nana. Turn it down." But Nana kept her hands in her lap. "It's as down as it's gonna be," she said. Then "Oh, oh," she said, ashe reached over and snapped the radio off. "Cut it out, Henry. I was just going to."

"No, you weren't." They rode in silence. She put her feet on the dashboard, which wasn't dangerous, but was annoying, as "Your Nobody Called Today" went on more softly. "What kind of race are you trying out for?" he asked her.

"I'm already in it."

"What kind of race are you already in?"

"How come you're so grouchy, Henry?"

He didn't know. "Tell me about the race."

"It's a team thing, the scores are cumulative, which means it's sort of a relay. I'm taking the place of some older girl."

"Why all this competition? When your mother and I were young . . ." But his voice trailed off, as he heard Ros murmuring in his ear that in youth, in fact, he'd competed ferociously, while she'd done merely well enough to find a man who would support her. Then all known history had changed and she'd helped change it and he'd slipped into some machine he didn't under-stand and come out as her dependent. The tone Adelle had taken on the phone. As if being brilliant in interesting times meant that you shouldn't, in dull ones, earn a living. As if Henry had ar-rived in Rome from years in Gaul to find that Latin was no longer spoken.

"Who's the nobody in that song?" he asked Nana, feeling closeness, her long body leaning towards him in the car, as they turned into a neighborhood of small two-family houses. Por-tuguese and Pakistanis lived here. People who meant the neigh-borhood was inexpensive, but on the margins of respectable. As Nana explained that this guy was living with his girlfriend, only he had another girlfriend, who called the real girlfriend up by mistake looking for the guy. But when the real girlfriend asked her boyfriend who the girl who called him up was, her boyfriend told her, 'Nobody.'

"I met a man upon the stair and when I looked he wasn't there," Henry chanted.

"You used to read those things to me."

But maybe this neighborhood, he thought, driving the Volvo into the New Balance parking lot, could be a solution to their problems. He'd sell the Brookline house and make a pile. Then he'd compromise and take a boring, badly paid job with Boston Rehabilitation which would pay for a lifestyle a little more knockabout than.

"Bye Dad." He turned the motor off. Nana's hand on the door handle.

But what about the schools around here? Rosalind crept into his mind to ask. What about the children?

"You want to come in, Dad?" Nana was out in the parking lot knocking on the window on his side.

"Sure. Wait for me."

A lot packed with Volvos and Saabs to cross before they reached a warehouse. None of the people who shopped here would live in this neighborhood, he thought. Why should we?

Inside, people were trying running shoes on and lifting polo shirts with witty sayings on them over their heads and zipping up sweatshirts.

"Hey, what do you think?"

His daughter, temporarily headless, was pulling a royal blue sweatshirt over her face. As her eyes, then mouth reappeared. "Just tell me. How you like it."

How had he missed noticing the blank this girl now faced where her mother had once been?

"Fine, great."

"I'm paying, Dad." She held up the running shoes, like prizes, a few minutes later.

"It's been rough, eh, having your mother in his kind of shape, the past few weeks," he muttered on their way across the parking lot back to the car. Feeling awkward as a father on some situation comedy.

"Oh, Dad, you don't have to talk about it." Waiting for him to unlock.

Driving home, he began rambling on about his youth again. About his grandfather Twist the coal miner. How after one generation in which his parents had paid for their extremely modest life with terrible boredom, and that mean little garage that his father made into a house for them, he'd gone off to Harvard and met Nana's mother and started hanging out with people who considered money contemptible. Or unimportant. It hadn't struck him until recently that their attitudes had trust funds behind them. "But I can't believe you want to hear about this sort of thing."

"But Ma makes all this money," said Nana as they drove up the gravel driveway into the garage. "Made all this money."

Hands in her jean jacket pocket as they walked together up the steps into the kitchen.

"Hey Dad. You ever look to see if Ma took any of those?" Nana pointed to the row of pill bottles lined up beneath the kitchen windowsill.

"Hey Dad," Nana asked him. "Did you ever look to see if those bottles got opened?" He'd heard it twice. Both times Henry caught some tremor in her voice, so he turned to look at what she'd pointed at. A row of bottles lined up on the windowsill. ROSALIND TWIST/DR. KRIEGEL. ROSALIND TWIST/DR. KRIEGEL. On the labels. For pain, infection, blood pressure.

None of these brown plastic bottles had been opened. None of this row on the still had been cracked. There were two names on the labels the pharmacy had glued on as if his wife had married the cardiologist in some ceremony Henry hadn't been invited to.

It was only a little row of bottles lined up on the kitchen windowsill, he wanted to tell Nana. Only he'd lost his voice, which had been capped, as they were, shut tight as that day he'd brought Ros from the hospital and listened, after he'd buttoned on that wedding shirt she was still wearing, to her request: "Would you take those pills downstairs? I'm less likely to forget them down there." All these reasons for you to do her unreasonable bidding.

"Now would you go see where your sister is?" In a calm voice to Nana. "And tell her to get ready for supper." As if he were in charge here.

He sat on a kitchen stool and waved his toe at her.

"What are you doing, Dad?"

"I'm calling the doctor to see what, if anything, your mother has done to herself. Now get out of here, would you please."

Punching buttons on the phone. Hard, as if they'd yield something. A doctor on the other end of the line.

"Kriegel says you have to take those pills and stop. Both kinds of smoking." Henry, by their bed, a half hour postpill, was deliberately, to keep from wanting to strangle Ros, looking out the window. Keeping cool. Away from a view of her with pillows plump and soft behind her head. He heard her say coolly:

"Apparently, you and Kriegel have conflated several different problems. The pills, which are easy enough for me to take, if you'd only left them by the bed, and smoking, which, as you know, I've never really been addicted to, and your own problems with your work and the children." Propped up against her pillows, the last time he saw her before he turned towards the window, she was prepared, he saw, to analyze his problems. As she had that night after the restaurant trip, when he'd tried more gently, to help her stop killing herself.

"No," he told the window.

"Who took the pills downstairs in the first place?"

"Ros, I can't handle this." Turning towards the bed.

She shrugged, lifting her hand to dismiss him. He smelled

dope, death, dissolution in her veiled eyes, her gestures. That manuscript on her lap. God knew what she could be working on in her state of mind.

"I can't believe you're still playing shrink when you can't swallow a pill that's a matter —look, listen. The kids are going quietly crazy, and I have to get my life together. Couldn't you go away somewhere. You'll have to go away somewhere where you can get well without all this — mess — around you. This is impossible. Have to start taking care of yourself." He walked out before she could start arguing with him. Proud of himself. Not biting when she'd been outrageous. Not arguing. Only telling.

11

Lila

Lila in New York. (Thank God.) An introduction to everybody's mother, whose name is Stella.

Banished, said her sister. (She'd said that, Ros had said that, just as Lila reached the apartment.) Phone rang, as she opened the door. What a relief it had been to get delivered by Amtrak to Penn Station, then carried by escalator into the arms of a taxicab where a driver awaited her: "I usually work in the Bronx where the animals are" — the man was the beginning of a world of other voices — "I give students a discount, because I like them. I don't like the people on Park Avenue, they think they own the world" — instead of that close, claustral, home in Brookline, Mass. Where nothing happened. And nobody but the people inside ever said anything to you.

("They do own the world," she had said in a matter-of-fact way from the backseat of the cab. Which surprised her. But she didn't say, "People aren't animals." Although she felt she should.)

Then she'd walked up her dark wooden tenement stairs and been home. Where she didn't have to say anything at all.

Here was her sister on the phone the minute she got inside

saying, 'Banished. Henry something, banished me.' As if she were a queen instead of a citizen. So something. Arrogant maybe.

She'd thought of her sister's heart. As a twisted plastic pretzel thing, rebuilt with Diet Coke bottles, that made noises like a video game as it plunked, plunked plunked, lighted, flashed, on its way to another twenty years of running fine. She'd thought of her own descent from that taxi, how she'd run up the tenement stairs (the light was different here, the paint on the stairs was thick and mottled, there were bikes chained to the banister) and seen her door, could have kicked it open.

Oh blessed is the silence, the darkness, the loneliness, the solitude inside. The chain to pull on the hall light, (it is mine), but then the phone had rung and it had been Ros and she'd been banished, Ros said in her dying-to-chat voice, could you believe it, Henry had banished her for bad behavior, mentioned Arden, that impossible raggy family summer home, as a possibility, and what do you think, Lila? Should she go?

"Call home," said Lila. "I mean Mom. I'll see her tomorrow, but you call her first. Maybe she'll go with you. Her store is finished. Rents too high. Now good-bye. I'm exhausted. I've got to go."

The silence on the other end meant Ros was interested. But a long discussion would follow, so instead, she repeated her message, dully. "Call Mom about the trip. The last time we talked, from your house in Boston, actually, she said she was closing up the shop and retiring." Which was true. But supposed to be a secret from Ros. Then she hung up.

A note before we meet Stella (Mom)

Stella Oliner had had three children. Or rather Stella had had two children. Her youngest two. And a firstborn child, who was Rosalind and whom she'd felt was not a child exactly, but an adult who'd lived in a child's body, which was something else (and hard for her). There were other ways to look at this problem, of course. Perhaps Ros had been an ordinary child, but Stella had not, with her firstborn, become an ordinary mother yet. By the time Lev had arrived four years after Rosalind, and Lila five years after Lev, Stella had acquired a feel for motherhood, which meant she had a feel for childhood and for the bargains children and their mothers strike.

Meanwhile, her temper had cooled from heat and noise to irony, and her despair at what was being asked from her was tempered by a knowledge of her limitations. For she had seen by the time the last two came along, the limits on the harm she could do, as well as the limits on the good.

And so what, she thought, if Lev was somewhat silly and Lila was peculiar or like the rest of the human race according to Stella, they were more likely to be foolish than be wise. She rested comfortably with her feeling that these two were dear to her, residing in that small backyard corner of the world where her loyalties were planted, like her husband, her sister or her store. For if Stella was fierce about what belonged to her, her younger children were equally fierce about their belief that family obligations were wrong, somehow. Or was it that any obligations were tacky? A belief that had flourished like roadside weeds along with other heresies in the sixties. So they'd struck a bargain among the three of them. That if her children could decide to sidestep her wishes for their lives or move to California to avoid them, she'd avoid acknowledging their conviction, acquired in the world outside, that people were related if they *felt* like it. For families, Stella felt, as anyone not blinded by ideas acknowledged, were made up of people who owned each other.

But Ros had been different. The first from the moment of birth. After a labor that had made Stella question how her own mother, so brutally honest in other respects, could have failed to tell her how brutal these pains would be, she had begun staying home with her baby, entrusting her beloved Downtown Casuals to her younger sister Julie. Two years later, on an afternoon's visit to Julie at the store, she remembered that she hadn't always felt uncertain, fragmented and bored. Two months after that, she'd returned, against the advice of her friends quoting child psychologists, to her place behind the counter. By then this creature who cried at three A.M. developed rashes, grabbed cookies, other children's toys or Stella's breasts had become a sweet-natured, plump, acquisitive child. With a strong streak of willfulness: they all had to play what Ros wanted them to, including Stella and Sidney. For if good-natured Sidney didn't mind stopping in the middle of "Geese and ducks and chicks gotta scurry" if Ros wanted him to, something, Stella felt, was being wrestled from her by this high-handed child, her motherhood, her adult authority, her God knew what.

Ros was a gangster of family life, Stella told Julie once. Bending rules, other people's wishes and life itself to her childish wishes, then revising the family history so that she won, not just the fealty of the household but their faith in the decisions she had made for them. Her gap-toothed sister Julie grinned, reminding Stella that they already had a gangster in the family. An uncle Nathan who'd sported a diamond on his pinkie and traded black-market sugar during the war and whiskey during Prohibition.

Stella was right as it turned out. For by the time Ros had reached age twelve, she ruled that uneducated Stella's contribution to her children was drudge work merely, serving lunches, nursing sicknesses, seeing to Sidney, who saw, in turn, to teeth. (He also made halfhearted forays during family fights into organizing truces that no one wanted.) It was Ros, the eldest and the wisest, who organized day trips, saw to education and offered her sister and brother spiritual guidance and advice. For who knew more about the world they were entering? Someone like Ros, who'd just come through these schools, piano lessons, romances? Or Stella, who'd spent her childhood in a grocery store upstate?

Now, in the midst of Ros's own crisis, Stella felt superfluous, dismissed again. For she'd called and called and called her daughter's home and reached evasion and excuses in Boston. Ros was fine, everybody assured her. Only no one but them could see her. Her latest call had been different. Now Ros, according to Lila, was well enough to deal with patients, but couldn't speak to her mother on the phone.

"Do you think she's mad at me?" Stella had asked Sidney. "That I've offended her again somehow."

"Not unless she's mad at both of us." Sidney, famous for his carpet sweeper approach to family dirt, was convincing for the moment. For Ros liked her amiable father, even if her liking had a streak of contempt in it.

"What if something dangerous is going on, only no one will have the decency to tell me?"

"You'll find out, dear. Soon enough."

'I can't,' she wanted to say, 'stand you sometimes.' It was Sidney's bargain with life she couldn't stand, not Sidney. For his good nature had been bought, she felt, by ignoring real dangers to his loved ones, had been paid for through passivity and at action's expense.

Stella at the Metropolitan Museum

Society woman. Stella Oliner fished the phrase up from her youth and pinned it on this woman who was standing, rich and unemployed, behind the Metropolitan Museum's information booth. "Thank you," for the brochure on rich paper she got handed by that ringed hand, pointing out that Japanese ceramics were on the balcony, French drawings to the left of the marble staircase, American furniture near the Temple of Dendur.

Waiting in this hall for Lila beneath a ceiling so vast it brought back that story from God knew when, she'd read the kids: 'and another little ant,' said Scheherazade, took another grain of sand away.'

How peculiar to be standing here with all these people/ants at noon, when in real life usually she was in the store. Or on her way to some garment manufacturer. Thaler and Magnus, yesterday, who now had their blouses sewn, she'd noticed yesterday, in Haiti. Her kids would complain: but those women stitching blouses in Haiti are going blind, Ma. Which might be true. Also it was true that maybe the money that came from selling those blouses had made her kids so compassionate and also late all the time. But there was Lila, coming down a marble staircase that some countries in Europe were smaller than. Her long-legged daughter, red-haired in a blue and white striped not exactly clean, as Lila came closer, fisherman's shirt, and wide-legged British walking shorts. Hello, pantomimed across the hall. She was gratified by the outfit, the care in choosing, if not in Laundromats.

After Lila bent to touch her cheek, they went on walking. Past Egyptian mummies with Lila chatting and Lila never chats, Stella thought. Was she nervous? Turning to touch Stella's arm, as they passed mummies, examining her large hands as they sat down, chairs scraping, in the cafeteria. "We ordered cappuccino. And two sandwiches. Has something happened?" Lila, who was getting tougher, asked the waiter, for they'd made it through some minutes without their orders being brought. Which wasn't bad, thought Stella. Her standing up for them. Then conversation, which was harder, fell apart.

She doesn't like me, Stella felt, getting up to go to the bathroom for a break from all this. Then remembering that Lila liked everyone a little, and it was Ros who didn't like her and that she was in this place to ask: Could you come with us? With me and Ros to Arden, so Lila could keep them from getting on each other's nervous systems. She stood before the ladies' room mirror beside her daughter, who'd followed her in. Peering into both their glass faces as steam heat, left over from winter, carried perfume and urine and hot water smells to her nose. Now she couldn't ask, for fear she'd be refused. Wiping her hands with towels brown and rough and wet, she asked instead what Lila was in this museum to see. Heard 'Romance portraits.' Which turned out to be Roman. "Like these towels," Lila said, wiping the wetness off her wrists. "Rough and true like bags of cloves. You know what I'm saying?" As if they smelled of something. Textures.

"No," said Stella firmly, leading them out again into the hall. Knowing exactly what Lila meant, but why confuse the universe worse by saying these things aloud? Then back to their table, which now that Lila had said these things, had coffee smells and something terrible about its white Formica top.

Lila at the Metropolitan Museum

Lila drowned her shyness in a glass of water, as her mother glancing around asked what besides Roman portraits she'd come to look at. Lila started, after all these years, to tell the truth. "Touch base. As Ros would say. Are you sure you're interested? I'll show you upstairs, if you want, where when I was like seven or eight I used to wander because I thought: if we live in an apartment, we need an attic, so this would be my attic, like. While Ros and Lev would go, I don't know, to get a soda or something. Though sometimes Lev liked to get a rise out of me by coming in and telling me the mummies would climb out of their coffins, if we didn't run quick through that hall. So we ran and he made mummy sounds anyway. But mostly, it was the pictures upstairs, like that Brueghel thing which reminded me of Grandma, with all these folk people and the village she came from, didn't they have an inn? So I'd pretend I lived inside the picture frame and could walk around the fields or lie around and fall asleep under the tree with the man with the beer mug. Like Lev and Ros did in the park."

"They did what? In Central Park?" said Stella.

"Of course, when I got to Music and Art, I found out that nobody else played living in the pictures. Or nobody talked about it. It isn't painterly, that's all, or sophisticated."

"You always were" — Stella lifted the top slice of bread, to examine the ham in her sandwich — "imaginative. But then this whole painting business, living alone like that and being so poor when you could do all kinds of things. I like paintings when I see them, but it's different" — she smoothed her skirt — "for a life. You know, I wouldn't say this ordinarily, and I don't want you to take it the wrong way or be too sensitive, but I've always felt this painting business was something like that crush you got on Anthony Whatshisname when you were twelve and never got over."

"I think the same thing," said Lila. "I've waited all my life to have it over, which means, I guess, that I'll be someone else. But I never do. But I don't. I feel drunk on this assertion or negative of an assertion," she said, she who never said in words what she was thinking. She got quiet and looked at the white pillar behind her mother's dark head, and the folds in the white blouse and something in her mother's face that was disquieting. Love. And the way the skin on her mother's arm was getting looser, but was still freckled, as if the language of language cut into things all the wrong way. No language of freckled flesh or even cotton blouses, Love. And Sunday boredom, she thought. No language of falling asleep on her velvet couch yesterday, drained of light the way the day was.

"What does Ros want from me?" her mother said suddenly. "And I was wondering also if you'd come up with us to Arden. I know how busy you are. But I can't imagine the two of us alone up there together."

Lila narrowed her eyes to fix the shoulders of her mother's black padded narrow-shouldered jacket. It was that those Roman portraits caught, how absolute the fit that spirit and matter made. No spirit floating disembodied, but cut to fit its body home. Which was the matter with death absolutely. "I can't come. I have to stay here." She let her eyes drop to the tablecloth with coffee spills. "Ros is screwing up, and I don't know if she wants you to know, but she's making everybody nuts, by hanging around . . ."

She didn't want to tell on her sister, even if they were grown-ups now. And Ros was preferring to die in despair in order not to live differently. And Ros was preferring to die in order not to have to pay attention to what was wrong with her, absolutely. Or to be killed anyway, say she took her life in her hands. This thread drawn through the light behind her mother and words, here and there, strung like Christmas lights to keep them sane enough to sit there. "She's better now. But she, oh I expect she just wanted to get away. What she wants" — looking at this woman so uneasy with her being, as if she'd come out wrong — "from you, I don't know." Stirring her cappuccino, sugar in the bottom thick. Seeing, as she stirred, those romance portraits, ordinary living dead people looking at her through eyes that might be Jewish from a thousand years ago, she looked at her mother's blue eyes and said, "I don't know how to say this. I mean, I told her to call you. But if I hadn't, she might have called anyway to, I don't know, keep up her quarrel with you, I mean, with life again. However you got mixed up with it. So things can be the same. Like before she got sick."

And things and people die. And other things go on and on. Had tumbled her over some edge now and made it legitimate, a life as real as any other, for her to spend her own time on earth trying to paint them all into living forever despite the way she knew it made everyone, herself included, nervous, uneasy, discomfortable, love.

She left the museum with her mother. Down the biggest front steps in the world she'd grown up with. Jugglers here on Sundays. Buses pulling up and stopping, and always wrong. To Thirty-fourth Street only. Or Eighth Street and Broadway. When they needed Eighth and Fifth. "Come on. Let's take that one." She did that. Took the not absolutely number thirty-three or whatever was the right one. Because it was fun, she told her mother, getting to walk from wherever the bus turned out to stop at the end.

A tree behind them with a tiny plot around it at the bus stop. She felt the tree behind her, the tiny plot, as if it were a grave. "I'll take the next one," Stella said, waving good-bye as she stepped up to reach the bus which bounced like gigantic dice on rubber wheels down Fifth Avenue.

Mansions on her left, where people had camped out in their marble igloos with excrescences, or whatever you called them, once. This would all come right in her head, turn over into whatever they were called in the art history books, if she wanted. Renaissance palazzi. But she didn't want. For her sister's dance with death had freed her into riding free for once from wishing she were someone else. Then she stepped off the bus, towards a pyramid of Granny Smiths and oranges and purple cabbages that rose, extravagant and welcoming as royalty or prose, from the Korean vegetable market and she was downtown, on the pavement, where she belonged.

12

Rosalind

*Ros, with a little help from her family, leaves home. Starting back
with Henry at her bedroom door. The pill scandal. Its consequences.*

Just as she'd suspected, in a subliminal sense, it had been
Henry. Giving her orders, before she could even wake up. He'd
walked out before she could discuss his orders. Then that goddamned family called pretending to thank her, but really to let
her know they wouldn't be coming back. For therapy, ever. (That
husband and his prissiness.) And her children were stealing her
or were hysterical about, what was it, dolls? And her sister had
fled from her.

She had pulled herself together and called someone to her side
by dialing. "Lila, I've been banished," she'd announced, settling
against the pillows, more comfortable now.

"Call me back," said Lila. "Tomorrow. Or the next day. I just
got home. And call Mom, she's feeling rotten, apparently she's
lost her lease on the store — it's not worth going on with. Maybe
you two could go to Arden. Now I'm off."

An interesting development, knocked off her perch, how sorry
she felt for Ros (she meant Stella).

"Of all the women in the world," she told Henry the next evening. Or was it the evening after that? She couldn't just say, "I'll do what you wanted," so the evenings slipped by, until she finally found the right one and the two of them lay in bed. "Stella is vain, ungenerous, ambivalent to say the least about me. But folding up that store, my God, I felt so bad I up and called her yesterday. Between one thing and another, we decided to spend a little time at Arden together. Starting, you may not like this, but I'm going, for reasons too complex to mention, tomorrow morning. You weren't home to discuss it with, but my stuff is all packed and the kids know. First I checked the idea out with Lev who said, 'I love it,' as if my life were a movie he was producing.

"Henry?"

"Yes." Henry was by her in bed, but faced the window.

"Anyway, I had this fantasy of lovely Stella, with her hand on my brow, not that she actually . . ."

Now he was getting out of bed. "I have to go to the bathroom." His huge feet flat on the floor, ready to run.

"Henry? Can I ask you something? How come you invariably decide you have to go to the bathroom the moment I start talking about what's important to me?"

"I can't tell you how irritating your bubbling over about this fucking trip to Arden is." He turned to face her. "When I brought the idea up in the first place, you tried your best to talk me out of it. Now you're off tomorrow."

"You didn't bring it up. Merely . . . did you even mention a vacation? It was, I'm sure, Lila."

He went. She began yearning for him. As if the space between them that would begin tomorrow morning had banished the fear and loathing she'd felt each time he'd come to touch her.

"Mom? It's us." At the door outside. Two girlish voices just as she'd reached down, tentatively, to touch herself and see if this woman still felt things, existed. In came this doll and two daughters. One dropped the doll on her bed, and as if startled by something (that doll that shut, like death, her bright blue eyes, smudgy lashes on her rosy cheeks) she got carried back inside her head to that hospital dream of the beach at Arden and her toes dipped in the water, drawn out.

I can't leave the children, she thought as if the thought were new.

"Here, Ma." Nana had her thumb covering the photo she handed over.

"Oh. Right." She turned it over. Stared angrily at all this bloody murk, placed it on the bed table where those pills had been. "Is that the outfit you bought with the money you stole from me?" Looking over at Nana's new little breasts pushing up and out beneath her running suit.

"I took some of your things, Ma, and sold them for money." Nana looked level-eyed at her. "That's not exactly 'stole.'" While Sophie nodded solemnly. "You take good care of that dolly, Mommy."

"Here. Put her there." Nodding at the bed table where the photo was. But with this pounding in her chest. Her heart. "Since when do you say dolly? I thought you were more grown-up than that."

"I say it to myself," said Sophie quietly.

"Where's your suitcase?" said Nana. "I'll pack them for you." She nodded at the canvas bag in the corner, watched her elder daughter scoop the photo up and slip it in the outside pocket, then grasp the doll around her waist and place her, feet first, inside.

Nana went on surprising her, by reaching over and pulling the sheets up to tuck her in. Saying, "Good night, Ma." As she kissed her mother's forehead. "Good night, Ma" from Sophie, whose piping voice she could hear from the door, although her eyes stayed mercifully shut as they trooped out. Feeling like a doll herself, eyes shut, legs together, laid out.

∾

Henry's hand on her shoulder was saying sex now. All her yearning turned to fear. Fury. "You have some nerve. Sending me off with my mother over some pills I didn't take. How did I know those pills wouldn't poison me? You know how I feel about those drug-pushing doctors." Her head turned away from him, towards the bed table.

When what she meant to say was this: 'You know nothing about me, in the bathroom while I'm talking about this thing with my mother. The kids came in. I'm afraid to make love. Who knows what might happen?' Also that she had known, from the beginning of their green courtship, when he'd appeared in her kitchen and she was holding Nana and stirring soup on the stove, that she was a lady like a bowl of soup for him to eat. Even now, she was only *sometimes* a person. Sometimes a thing.

As he was to her. As they all were to her. Startled by her own intensity, clarity and incoherence. Waiting for his hand to spread over her mouth.

Instead, his enormous hands covered his own face. His long fingers got peeled off one by one. "I move around you like an iceberg in the dark. I can't remember what it was like before. Did we ever have fun, fuck? Anything? What?

"As for those pills, I did research on them. Weeks ago. They're okay, more or less, better than nothing. At least they'll do more good than harm for most people."

"Thanks." She sat up. "How come you didn't tell me?"

"About the research? Are you kidding?"

"You know I'm always interested in that sort of thing." They had their ordinary voices on. But he shrugged and wouldn't tell her so she lay down again, willing something between them. "Are you interested? Do you want to?" She touched his chest, drew a cross by his nipples, let him kiss her cheek, her lips, her nose. But the moment he lay down beside so they could touch each other, her heart began to pound again. "Terrifying." The sounds, the pounding hearts, the winding sheets around them.

She spoke into the darkness. "Henry," wanting to object to

something, his touch, the way he'd lain down or hadn't lain down, his timing or something, but it was okay, because he said, "Never mind, Ros, not now," and moved away.

$\sim$

Henry dreamed, he told her the next morning, stuttering as he was telling her this, head turned on the pillow, of a baby in a red bonnet with a mango in its hands except its hands had been cut off. Who went into the jungle, while he, at home, ironed sheets.

"Don't tell me what it means," he groaned.

She didn't want to, couldn't, without his associations, she said. But felt, My God.

Then she got out of bed, ran downstairs to drink some coffee. While he went back to sleep.

'Love lifts us something something something.' The car radio was on as Henry drove her to the station. Love, in these songs, as Ros pointed out, was really romance and promised transcendence instead of meaning, or merely pain and pleasure in your life.

Then they reached the station, where flushed with pride at her own bravery in going off alone (she pointed that out to him) she kissed her children, they were his too, in the back good-bye. Then walked with Henry to the train behind this temporary outbuilding, built since they had torn the real station down. He should ask George about the plans for, but suddenly he couldn't remember the last name of his old partner and finished instead his own comment about the railroad station. That metropolitan caper, he said, of tearing the old building down and building something schlocky, but temporary, then stopping.

So, she said. It goes. Kissed his lips, stepped up, got on the train. Up some iron stairs. Helped. Almost lifted up. Like love. That taking care. Then down the long smelly corridor.

She had planned to read short stories on the train, but every one in the collection she'd chosen seemed weightless, self-pitying and depressed. So resettling herself (that raffia on her ass) she searched in her bag and found an article that Henry had written on windmills in *The Nation* and thought about Henry as she read.

For the Henry who'd written the article was a balanced, sane and reasonable man. And the Henry who'd touched her cheek last night was familiar as flesh, beloved or detestable depending. While the man she'd been living with since the operation was so uninterested in her that he'd slipped out of bed into the bathroom last night as she was finally really talking to him. A man who was so — but now she looked out the window before she thought the word and spotted a seesaw by a mobile home. A man who was so stupid.

What was so stupid about Henry? For the first time in months, her thoughts were interesting to her.

What was stupid about Henry — returning after passing a salt pond to not looking in order to think through this thing without distraction — was the way he went on writing articles, bad-mouthing trendy restaurants, renovating barns in Somerville, while she—glancing out the window at a green lacy willow tree — was in despair. While I am in despair, she thought, plunging through the window in her thoughts as if her body could leave this raffia seat and use that willow like a lacy parachute to break her fall to earth.

There were cigarette butts on the floor at her feet.

"That's interesting," to her thought.

A pleasantly conversational voice inside her said: 'Rosalind had an operation, but she's fine now. Such a serious operation in one so young, so fat, so fair, so fine, so far.'

Her body was the one who'd had the operation. While the rest of her stayed out of it.

She felt better here now on this raffia seat with discomfort pressing the bottom of her fat thighs and the train rocking for comfort. For she could think these thoughts, then whoosh went the train through a dark viewless tunnel and her thoughts got left behind.

Henry's article offered her, when she glanced at it, the politics of energy again. "There are no technological solutions that don't call for social control of blah blah blah", she read, amazed that anyone could be writing like this while she was dying. In the seat ahead, a man with a sweaty neck and dirty children. A politician riding up to Albany across the aisle. College kids. A secretarial type. And 'suicidal' came to her, because everyone on this train was luckier than she. And it was impossible to go on traveling towards her mother in Saratoga, who was guilty, no doubt, of not being able to force her own heart to fail before her daughter's did.

With this, she'd punched a hole in something and felt and felt. Her children behind her. Nana screaming into the tunnel she'd left Boston from: 'Look where you're going, Ma.' She stood reassured because the train knew where it was going, and got flung against a seat, some sailor boy. "Sorry." She patted the canvas pocketbook to make sure her pills were there, for sullenly she'd asked Henry to pack them. ('Pack them yourself,' he'd said.) That Sophie's doll. Nana's photo floated down onto her quilt last night. Why and how had Nana ended up with it? Or for that matter, given it back to her. Then flung against all kinds of raffia seats and with her strength employed opening doors between cars, she reached the snack bar. Where she could sit behind a beer and watch the world through a window on her left. On her right, a parade of hungry human beings going by.

There was train after that. Train and window viewing. And sleep (her head jerked down and back, saliva awakening her, that drib drib dribble). "Saratoga," said the train man. She put her shoes back on. She looked out the window. She felt the train stop.

Between the silver steel train tracks and the jerry-built railroad station stood her mother waving.

"Hi, Ma." She let the train man help her down. She peered into the empty sky behind her mother's body. She stepped towards her, bent to hug, felt her mother's soul fly off. Then her mother's head bent, and an empty broken body leaned against her.

Pietà reversed, she thought, straightening up. "My arms still hurt a little." Stepping back. There'd be hurt in her mother's eyes. "Stella," Rosalind held her hand out firmly. As if the name and formality might organize something between them. Shrink holding her hand out to the owner of a dress shop on Greenwich Avenue.

The hand she met was limp and cool, then grasping. For she'd forgotten about her shy and worried mother taking courage at the last moment. Forgotten pine smells, the heat and steel of the Saratoga tracks. Forgotten, as her mother started across the parking lot, unlocked the door of the car she'd rented, her mother's murmur. The small sounds that reverberated, when they were together alone. The door slammed. That murmur. "It's strange, this cruise control, I don't feel like I'm in charge of the car." This dreamy feeling and the smell of sickening new air-conditioned leatherette as they rode smoothly past a Diary Queen to Saratoga proper, where Pasta y Formaggio shops had joined the trotters and the grand hotel.

"How was your trip." Her mother's forehead wrinkled as she glanced in the mirror to find her daughter.

"Fine. I looked out the window and read an article by Henry in *The Nation* and thought about things. How was yours?"

"Okay. I drove." A crossroads. Where scruff pines hid cornfields and there were roadside stands selling cucumbers, sweet corn, a dozen for a dollar.

"I was looking forward to seeing you," said Stella shyly.

Why did everything this woman said sound like an accusation? How many months had it been? And why had she refused to see or talk to this woman, who made her feel weak unless she was strongest? "What ever happened to that guy, who did the work for Grandpa?"

"Luther is okay, but his wife died of something, it might be cancer, and Junior got in trouble in the Air Force, but I can't remember if he went to jail or not. If you want to know, ask your father."

Now they were driving into Arden where the usual order of

things was reversed and the men, Sidney and Lev, carried the gossip and mail and groceries from the village to their bungalow on the hill. Now they were passing the Hilltop Stand whose three neon signs: Schaefer, Genesee, Bud, announced that grown-ups could buy pleasures along with Tootsie Pops for the kids.

The pine smells got stronger and the bungalow her grandfather had built was standing tumbledown when she got out. In the mountain air was her knowledge of the lake nearby.

"Let's go in." The car door slammed behind her. The porch door slammed. A wooden summer sound. A sloping floor. They were inside.

~

Ros slept that first night in her grandmother's room which was full of knotholes, with a picture of Switzerland in a gold wooden frame above her white iron bed. The next morning, stumbling onto the uneven kitchen floor, she found her mother dressed and offering, "Coffee, tea, or cereal or English muffins?"

"What I want most at the moment is a newspaper. Does Luther's stand have *The Times* anymore?"

"I'll run over and see," said Stella.

What she wanted most was a cigarette. But if she asked her mother to pick up a pack, there'd be a silent or noisy storm of reproaches.

She hung her jeans, a Pakistani overblouse, a bathing suit on hooks in the tiny closet. Stuck her hand into the canvas bag. Stared at the sandy real hair, the thick black lashes, the long slender legs and arms. Nana had had this doll before Sophie. Or hadn't she? Was it Baumbach who'd given it to her one Christmas? Or Baumbach's parents, more likely, to make up for their son's abandoning his daughter. She stood on tiptoe to lay the doll, toothbrush, pills, makeup, and photo from the inside pocket of her bag on the warped pine shelf behind a faded curtain. Grandma had hung that curtain fifty years ago and she and Lev had played musical comedy behind it.

She'd open the curtain, he'd step out of the closet. "Guess what happened to me on the way to the theater?" By now she had forgotten what happened, or what the joke was. "Ma, do you remember?" As the porch door slammed. In the kitchen where her mother was laying *The Times* out, setting blueberry muffins onto chipped dime-store china, roses in the center, gold at the edges, she sat down.

13

Henry, alone, then Sophie

Henry's story

Henry, awakening the morning after Rosalind had left them, touched his penis, touched his balls. Took his hand, which was not hers, away. Lay cushioned, the pillow behind him, relieved that she was gone from him. Fond of her again or was it love, now that she was gone from him.

But what is love? Tis not hereafter. This was college-educated goose down moving around his head which felt stuffed with wispy half-understood pieces of what had passed for culture in his youth.

But what is love? (As if someone named Love might come dancing through the bedroom doorway.) For in youth he'd chosen this Rosalind to be his joy, his other soul, his alternate body. Now death had shown up on their doorstep and Rosalind had taken him, adulterous, for a lover.

Lying in his bed, inviting him closer. While her real husband lay useless, solitary as a fallen leaf, discarded beside her.

Still, solitary now he could afford to think: Why didn't she die if she was going to? The agony she'd caused him. Seducing her death. Daring him — come closer. This lingering, waiting to see, on his part, this not knowing.

The machine at the heart of this house that kept them breathing, moving, heedlessly busy with their lives, had stopped.

Henry listened for house noises: heard someone in the kitchen, and got reminded, swinging his feet from the bed to feel the floor, that Sophie had to get to day camp by nine thirty.

～

Downstairs, Sophie in her nightgown had her index finger in her mouth, while her other hand behind her head twisted a curl. Round and round. As she, head bent, peered into her cereal bowl. Reading Cheerios instead of entrails for her fate, Henry decided. Bare feet crossed at the ankles beneath the table. Sophie looked up. Gray eyes blinking and would they spill tears into the bowl? Like some glassy-eyed martyr or Catholic saint. "I miss Mom, Daddy."

"Already?" He bent to kiss her small-sized head. Nice Daddy. Kissing Sophie's head, he felt.

But he felt irritable also, mixing yogurt in the bowl with Sophie sitting at that island orchestrating missing mom, with hands and feet and cereal spoon and eyes. As if he weren't anything at all to her.

"What can I do for you, my little lady?" Bowing, ironic, when what he really wanted to do was slam his fist on the butcher block. But what about me? Your father?

"Nothing, Dad." She looked curious, though, her spoon poised, her head tilted towards him. "You know, Quinn has purple jellies at camp, and I'd like purple jellies, instead of yellow, only."

"Let's get ready. It's time. Lunchbox, bathing suit, towel, yellow jellies, you." Counting on his finger. Craftsmanlike, good, as Ros would say, parenting skills.

～

"Pick you up at four thirty?" Henry stopped the car before the Brookline Creative Arts Day Camp, where he'd been lucky, he'd told Ros, this late in the summer to find a spot for Sophie. "It's probably no worse than a sports camp," he'd reported although he thought it probably was. Based on the poems in the camp's yearbook: 'I am the wind, I am polluted' on page one.

Now leaning over Sophie, he reached the handle and opened the car door to let her out.

"Four o'clock, Daddy."

"You have a good memory for details."

That intelligent patient look in her eyes. Children had it and peasants in every climate. People who depended on what wasn't them — prices set in distant cities, wind, weather, other people's whims and rages. Then resignation died in her eyes, and Sophie eyed him shrewdly through the window from the dusty road, where she stood, one sneakered toe behind the heel of the other foot, looking for signs. Would he, wouldn't he, pick her up on time?

"I'll be here at ten of four," he promised before he drove off.

Well, four, anyway.

If all went well and he didn't get a call that rearranged everything this morning, he and George Adelle would have lunch at noon downtown. A date that had been changed twice, no three times, by his former partner. Something clicked where it shouldn't in the motor as he started up the Volvo. He thought, Oh no, just let this damn car carry me to lunch downtown. Adding silently (no words even to himself), And let something good happen there. Remembering that hospital ward he'd worked on with Adelle, that air-supported tennis court, those apartments. Feeling like a child or a peasant himself. Waiting for fate or someone to rescue him from what was.

∼

"You know the facts as well as I do, Henry," said George at twelve thirty. Decent restaurant. Not too chic. Downtown. His friendly ugly Khrushchev's face with its high forehead, snub nose and puffy pockmarked cheeks was presented across the table like a gift. Or a fact. "You can drive a cab at night and sit home days dreaming up schemes to market solar devices. Or become a solar consultant and get sixteen an hour because everybody wants to be a solar consultant or a movie star. Or" — cutting his knockwurst, as Henry watched the grease burst from the cut — "go to Boston Redevelopment" — spearing a piece for his mouth, chewing, swallowing, wiping his mouth — "and pick up twenty-five thousand to supervise younger guys and check on variances for developers." His fat hands unfolded the napkin he'd used on his mouth for his pillow lap, lifted it to wipe his sweating forehead, his mouth.

"I've been thinking about trying the engineering firms."

"They're better in the pay department, but are you sure you want to work for the Arabs?" Adelle, who'd played Mr. Straight to Henry's Mr. Alternative in their firm, spoke now as if the man across the table were a child. "These are *real* Arabs, Henry, not like the ones you met at Harvard. Everything they build is bulletproof, airports and hotels and palaces." His fork down so he could concentrate. "The other thing about the Arabs is, not to sound racist, but they have this crazy way of operating." He speared the greasy meat again, pushed it around, examined it, put it down, suddenly, without warning, popped it in his mouth. "They decide what day they're breaking ground on and the drawings are due six months before. Never mind that the date got picked from the sky. Or you might need a few days more to figure things out or to draw." His mouth wiped. "So you do a fifty-million-dollar building in fifty minutes and feel a little sick again." Wiped once more.

The waiter, whose bald head was gleaming beneath the overhead light, poured half the Beaujolais into Adelle's glass as Henry put his hand over his own. But what was he doing this afternoon that he needed all this sobriety on his side? Peering down at the spinach salad he'd been poking around in like a lawn.

The tablecloth was stained with wine and oil, and broken pieces of bread lay around the edge of his plate by the time Adelle mentioned that he was walking over to a site his firm was working on. "Come see what we've, so to speak, got going these days. If you feel up to it."

Leaving this air-conditioned restaurant, they hit the hot air outside, then wove down narrow curving Boston streets, past espresso shops, video game parlors, blue movies, until they reached a grimy stone building with a broken Hotel Raleigh sign. A tall toothless broken-nosed man in the sagging doorway was looking down the street, it seemed, by the way he nodded solemnly when they arrived, for them both.

"We hear you're the architect for the city and wish respectfully to make certain allegations. My name is Michaels." An enormous hand held out to Henry, who, staring at the scab on the man's bald head, saw two watery blue eyes that were locked to his. "That in relation to the proposal to — to turn this hotel into a so-called homeless shelter, we object to losing the chicken wire over our places. Because no damned homeless, if you'll excuse the expression, is going to steal our valuables, Mr. . . ."

"Twist" — nudged by Adelle's elbow into answering. As Michaels, who was the age and height of Henry, leaned back against the sagging door with narrow rickety stairs behind. "And furthermore we pay for our places. I'm not wishing to cast allegations on anyone, but we happen to know for an actuality that there'll be dope fiends and little murderers living at the expense of the city and pretending to be women and children." Michaels looked down at his big feet.

But the plan, Adelle pointed out, to turn these hotels into homeless shelters came from the commissioner of housing, not from them. The commissioner was the one to speak to. Would you like his number? Taking his address book from his jacket. Still, "We appreciate your concern, Mr. Michaels, and will take your feelings into consideration, particularly on the chicken wire question." Turning the pages of the book. Writing an address.

Ripping it out. Handing it to Michaels, who crumbled it in his hand.

Still, Michaels followed them up the narrow stairs, where they peeked into a cubicle the size of a coffin with plasterboard walls halfway to the ceiling. While eyes peeked from half-opened doorways. Eyes peeked from doorways. Pleading in silence for privacy and their valuables secured. Hopeless eyes that had, with Michaels's help, turned into pleadings. How terrible it must be, Henry felt, with all those eyes upon him, to have to plead for things. Instead of ask, demand, insist.

The bum population, said Adelle when they were out again, had declined. The homeless population had exploded. There were hundreds of these places. Adelle's firm had a contract for as many of these jobs as they could handle. "And even" — when they'd reached the end of the block — "even if it's better than building prisons, Henry, I can understand if you don't want to take it on. It can't exactly make your career or your reputation."

"Are you asking me to handle these places for you and Havikhan?" he asked.

Adelle's hand on Henry's arm, as he said thirty an hour for the duration, and let's see how things work out. "About Havikhan, Henry. We're still partners, but we don't speak." Rubbing his fat hands with pleasure at the messy situation. As if Havikhan were a knockwurst that he was about to eat. "This stuff is nothing like what we used to do together, Henry." Looking back at the sagging hotel.

"You'd be surprised at how little I — I want an office to go to and a paycheck to take home and not be working for Hitler or the oman of Saudi Arabia." But now that he'd said it, Henry saw that he had reserved the right at forty to do something impor-tant, revolutionary, breathtaking. Not something like this, useful and even necessary, if you accepted the premise of these times that being housed was a privilege, a reward for right living. A reverie developed. Of shelters with bedrooms, communal kitchens, recreation rooms for the children.

"You'd be surprised," said Adelle shrewdly, "at how quickly you get used to getting paychecks and how small they look when they're exchanged for all the daylight hours of your life. Come in to the office tomorrow. We'll talk some more." A handshake, firm and sweaty, that shut Henry's reverie down, and wide-hipped swaying Adelle began to move away from him down the crowded angled street.

Sophie's story

"But without the doll I can't walk the tightrope," Sophie had explained to her pretty brown counselor Aya from Israel. Who had big brown legs in tan shorts and big white teeth and purply black hair. And the reason she had to explain to Aya was because the day camp was having a circus and some kids would dance to *Flashdance* in spangled shirts and some kids would be lion tamers and some kids would say their poems about how the world shouldn't have wars anymore. And Sophie had to walk the tightrope with a parasol. "I have no balance."

"But darling" — Aya had showed her nice white teeth — "it isn't a *real* tightrope." Pointing with her big brown hand to the dusty ground where the line would be drawn that Sophie would walk on.

But even if the line was on the ground she would fall off it she *had* to do it. 'Sophie, I'm giving up on you,' her teacher had said at school about that papier-mâché world she'd made. After her teacher gave up, she could do it. Fix the Italian boot and take it home. But still not show her mommy, in case it had something wrong. And if she couldn't walk the tightrope in the circus, maybe they'd *have* to go to Arden and find her mommy. Smiling nicely at this nice counselor so she'd know that Sophie liked her even if she didn't like to walk the tightrope. Then Aya went to see some other kid, maybe someone who wanted to walk that tightrope, some boy.

Sophie smiled at him. Delighted to have said all this to Henry.

"Some mouthful," he said. Delighted too. "Okay. Let's call."

She wasn't home. He didn't call back. He stopped wanting to. Sophie didn't nag him. Maybe later, Henry thought, putting the laundry in that evening, in preparation for work tomorrow, after Nana's running and Sophie's camp, but he watched the water being churned instead of finishing his thought. Wash, turn, wash, turn, something pleasing and ordinary about the swish swash, the bubbles, the movement of water and clothes around this plastic maypole in the center of the machine. Something doable about this laundry, these routines, Nana's running and Sophie's camp stories. That dopey job he'd found. The quietness of noises in the house. The world without her.

14

Lev

More Lev. A leave-taking. A decision. What turns him towards the East.

"My wife was pregnant." Rosalind's brother Lev pulled up the microphone. "The baby was overdue. She was nervous. I was deranged, it was hot the way it's hardly ever hot out here and my wife had decided to iron curtains. Picture it: this ninth-month woman in a white slip waiting for her baby in a house that would have curtains if it killed her.

"Meanwhile the phone kept ringing, because every other caller had a recipe for late or overdue babies including castor oil and something herbal from our neighbor. Someone, I should add, who'd borrowed my wife's winter coat to wear to New York, then lost it at the airport. Then the psychological types weighed in. The baby's littleness was caused by my wife's reluctance, as I remember, to give something up to the world outside her. The last straw was this friend who'd never had a baby calling to say she could sense that something was wrong. 'Just meditate until you get to a level that's really low and clear. Then visualize your baby coming down the birth canal and there she'll be,' she said.

Lev's microphone readjusted. "My wife is pretty polite and really likes this woman. But she hung up and she looked across the room where the iron had burnt a scar on the curtains, and started crying and crying and crying.

"We left the phone off the hook. I bought her flowers. The baby came. I considered sending a bill for the flowers to my wife's friend, who is incidentally a psychic counselor. That's something between a yenta, a shrink and a fortune-teller. I realize that people have always hung around births and deaths and marriages to offer you a piece of their mind. But these days it seems that half the population of this country is employed dishing out advice to the other half. Shrinks, lawyers, body workers, makeup consultants, psychic counselors, dermatologists. How come every time I open a magazine and find some expert telling me how to improve my income, my health or my children's chances in life, I feel a little less sure of myself and my values?"

The phones lit up as Chuck, the engineer, lifted his hands above his head like a triumphant prizefighter. This was a topic the premidnight or middle-class part of his audience would move right in on.

"Let me level with you," said the first caller. "I wouldn't run my business without an accountant or a lawyer or my investments without a broker. I don't expect to raise my own children without the help of a competent pediatrician, private school staff, even a family therapist, if it comes to that. But when my wife left me last year in the middle of everything, I mean there was no warning, well I picked myself up, then I found myself at forty, feeling I had to check into a health club to get my body into shape, this preliminary to inviting anyone female to the movies for God's sake. I mean something has gotten out of hand around here. N'est-ce pas? Or what?"

"I've had doctors give me drugs that made me sicker," Ed from Marin City said softly. "Dentists who wrecked my teeth. 'You have Oreo dental problems,' my snappy new dentist told me last week. 'What's that?' I asked. 'Problems caused by dentists,' he said. Other dentists, he meant, for sure."

On they talked, until Lev and his listeners had formed a consensus: it was the proliferation of meaningless options, like seven different kinds of checking accounts and six kinds of airfares plus constant changes in the social, economic and technological environments that made them all feel that what they'd known the day before was valueless.

"I was looking forward to being a wise old guy. Or an old wise guy. Or a boring old fart. Now I'll be out of date and invisible when I get old. Or older."

Midnight struck with the news, and the postmidnight people — who worked shifts or didn't get up early, because they were older, unemployed or insomniac — began calling. These were always the same callers, night after night, with the same things to say.

"I've been thinking about what you said about the Libyans on Wednesday night. It's like that everywhere, Lev. People fighting people. Why yesterday, my brother-in-law had the nerve to tell me, when he brought the lawn mower back, that he'd taken over to his place six months ago . . ."

A young man renewed his vow to stay celibate until Castro held free elections and shaved his beard besides.

A sixty-year-old man from San Jose confided, "I have to say I still perform to the satisfaction of the ladies. The other night . . ."

"Do you have a question or a comment?"

"How come I perform so well at my age? Is that normal?"

"I have no idea. It's certainly not normal to talk this much about it."

But it was normal. His uncle talked that way. This collection of unvarying and eccentric nuts was normal at this hour, while on the other side of midnight they were all studying up on life so they could be nuttily reasonable in a world full of less expensive nuts. Also muscular, pleasantly assertive and forthrightly flexible.

Meanwhile, he was feeling nutty too. For he couldn't get himself to call Andrew to say yes to that offer that he knew he would say yes to. Soon, but not now. Someday, but not today, he thought each morning when the thought to call Andrew occurred to him.

Now this show on the experts had been a secret apology to all these people, whom he loved indiscriminately with the exceptions of the ones he hated, for abandoning them for that daytime bullshit with the experts that he knew he would begin this fall.

"It's not my fault," he'd told Murial. "I get used to things and then they're mine. I'm not even sure if I like them, but I love them. Because they're mine. I always envied those people in books who get so mad at so-and-so after he does such and such that they never speak to him again. I think of that as character, backbone. What you have. Whereas I just get to like people who are insulting. If I happen to know them for a while."

"I can tell," from a woman caller, "that we've both had a lot of pain, you know? And have a lot in common."

"Friends help, family. Actually I'm rather lucky," he said sharply. Rejecting her assumption of identity with him. For if in youth he'd wished to be a sacrificial hero, shrugging off privilege and struggling with reality, he hated now at thirty-four to be seen as a loser, victim, schlemiel. As she then rejected his suggestion that she should find friends or a relationship, for thousands of people, she told him, already loved her.

At six A.M. he took his earphones off, punched Chuck in the shoulder, walked beside him to the cafe, rhymed by both of them with *waif,* for breakfast.

Not the visionary type, he sat in this waterfront cafe that had been lifted lock, stock and counter from the old longshoremen's waterfront and dropped into this new touristy wharf development of restaurants and gift shops. Stirring his coffee and sitting on a torn plastic stool, he had a vision. Of his tall thin apologetic younger sister strolling past garbage cans on her block in Greenwich Village. Beautiful in her rush towards life and fearful too,

like those women who ran marathons with their arms crossed
over their breasts.

"I've heard rumors, are they true?" said Chuck. "About you at
the station."

Chuck's fingers tore Danish pastry, as Lev, sipping coffee, followed his sister past the parking garage, avoiding legs of the
garage attendant on his torn plastic chair. Nodding at stoop sitters in housedresses, knees apart, varicosities on their calves. But
no, that was his last visit. By now, everyone must be young and
carrying a briefcase except for Lila.

"Hello," said Chuck.

"Sorry. I was thinking about my sister. I bet her neighborhood
has changed since I've been home."

"The one who had the bypass."

"That's the other sister." If in his heart he went on cooing like a
mourning dove about the changes in one sister's neighborhood,
how racked up he'd be about the loss of the other.

"It's my check." Grabbing.

Did Chuck think about life all the time? Or just drink coffee,
eat fried eggs with ham and complain about the station and his
woman, without this shadow over his shoulder? Death was
mixed into this, like limestone in a rock. And life smelled like
New York fall to Lev at that moment, exquisite and meaningless
and moving towards loss.

What lay behind that obscured farewell show.

"Aha. I knew I'd catch you home." Andrew had called at eight
A.M. "Now what happened to that contract?"

"How come you mailed me the contract when I haven't said
yes to the job."

"I assumed, like the last time, that you'd go into hiding, then
sign on the bottom line when the time came around. Only this
time, if you don't climb aboard before Monday, there'll be somebody else at the helm."

"Well, sure, okay eventually, of course. If that's the story, I'll mail it back this afternoon." Carrying the phone into the bathroom with him. Still, he hadn't mailed it. Did the farewell show about the experts first, so that his spiritual life was straight. Then waited, for a day or two, just in case.

~

"Even historical accident is a series of many people's choices." He turned to face Murial from the sink, wiping his hands on the dish towel. He meant this: that farewell show last night. That call from Andrew the morning of the show. The towel was filthy. He'd forgotten the wash. "I'm talking about the zeitgeist," he muttered.

"I don't understand, if you know that you're taking that job, why you don't call Andrew and say so. And now would you go check on Ollie? He needs your help."

The towel tossed, like a basketball, onto the kitchen table, Lev walked backwards a step or two, turning to pound on Ollie's door which had a poster with a skull and DEAD ASHES written below.

Inside, Ollie handed him a notebook. "Take a look at this, Lev."

> Great green gobs of greasy grimy gopher guts
> Mutilated monkey meat
> Chopped up parrots' feet
> French fried eyeballs
> Simmering in a bowl of pus
> Eat without your spoon
> Regurgatate, regurgatate, ra, ra, ra,
> Vomit, vomit
> Yeah vomit,
> Everything tastes better with blue vomit on it.

"You spelled *regurgitate* wrong," said Lev. "Plus I've heard that poem a hundred times. Last Christmas at Tahoe, remember? With Andrew and whatshername staying with us. Now I want to check on your performance."

Ollie hated, he said, going to a year-round school so his

mother could work for those assholes at the Brothers Bagel. Plus, why should he do a skit for history? "I could just say what I know, instead of acting it out." Still he picked up a shiny red cape and a piece of poster board shaped like a sword and started wrapping tinfoil around it.

"Forget the sword," said Lev. "What are you going to tell them in that skit?"

"I," said Ollie in a high female voice, "am Queen Elizabeth, okay? I'm knighting thee Sir Francis Drake, for kicking the pirates off the coast and discovering Bodega Bay, here in California, prithee."

"Queen Elizabeth didn't live in California. There was no California at that time."

"I didn't say she did."

"You said 'here in California.' Which implies that Queen E was decked out in a ruff with an orb in her hand in Richmond, say, near the oil refinery."

"Give me a break, Lev. Nobody else's father . . ."

While Ollie with brown bath towel draped over his head to make long hair, sat on the bed and wrapped the silver foil tighter around the sword, Lev thought, Ollie is right, I should give him a break. Nobody else's father is so contentious. How can we have another baby, when I act as if my stepson is my younger brother?

"Watch your head," he added, as Ollie practiced being Francis Drake, swooning with delight, after Queen E, whom Oliver also played, knighted him.

"Look," said Murial, when he came out of Oliver's room into the kitchen, which was their sitting room and Dee's playroom and her study. "I don't want to keep pushing this at you. But if you call Andrew, you can be finished with this night program and we'll have the rest of the summer to do things. If you put it off, you'll just work right up until September on one show or the other."

"I'm swooning." He grabbed a dish towel to put on his head and fell on the linoleum. "If you kiss me, I'll get up." And got kissed and got up and sat at the table. "We'll get a cabin in the Sierras," he said. "I'd like some wine, please, to celebrate. There's some in the refrigerator."

"What I'm thinking is Detroit, not the Sierras. My sister is furious at me for leaving her to deal with my mom alone. Besides, don't you think you should go back east and see your folks?"

He lifted his glass to the light. "You're right again. 'Exeunt with a death march.'" He rose, carrying the phone into the bedroom to make his Andrew call in private. Popping out to say, "No, I haven't called. I wanted to say that's the right thing to do, the right gesture. For us to take a trip back where we came from, before I take this, whatever you call it, tacky job."

The call to Lila.

"I can see why you wouldn't want to tell Ros about the baby, Lev, when her life has taken such a turn. But congratulations. Your children are always wonderful. I can't wait to see who the baby turns out to be," said Lila when he called her to tell his news.

"And you? Glad to be home?"

"Of course. This is New York. It's fantastic, like outer space, only it's the world, which is, you know, better. I saw this guy yesterday selling squashed beer cans that he made mugs of. Everyone was kibbitzing, 'At least you know what you are paying for,' said this guy with ACTOR'S EQUITY on his shirt. 'Not like somebody at the museum riding a bicycle over wet paint that I saw yesterday.' And so on. About drinking beer from something somebody has already drunk beer out of. I loved that mug, it was so silly, and everybody wanted to talk about it." Having talked more to Lev than she'd talked to anyone for days, she felt uneasy, she said. As if, like a balloon, she would lose her shape by letting what was inside out.

"I feel even sillier," she said. "Having said that."

"How are the parents," said Lev.

"Okay, I guess. I'm going to Dad's office for lunch."

"I went to Dad's office the last time I was home," Lev said gloomily. "Dad got tears in his eyes. He was seeing people come back because his work had failed. 'That hurts,' he said. 'Although it shouldn't. It's been twenty years with some of them. People wear out too. Look at me.' He was bending over in that back corset, because years of bending over patients had racked him up. 'Still, it hurts and I don't want it to,' he said.

"But I don't want to talk about either of them, if you don't mind. Him especially. I've been going a little nutty about this job I am apparently taking, but I don't want to talk about that either. I really wanted to find out how you are."

"I'm fine."

"Do me a favor. Don't tell anybody else in the family about the baby or the job even."

"I can't say anything. I'm trying not to talk. I'm desperate to work and everyone keeps calling."

"Maybe I should call Ros. Make plans and things in case we come to Arden."

"I think I have to get off," she said, surprising him by hanging up.

She must have taken the phone off the hook, because he got a busy signal every time he called after that for the next couple of hours.

He signed the contract. He let Murial mail it on her way to the co-op store. He felt relief all over, as if he'd downed an aspirin for the soul and taken a bath for an hour. Anticipating a headache which never came, he took a long lovely walk into the dampness of the Oakland hills and looked at houses they might buy.

15

Rosalind

Ros and Stella in Arden. Death becomes a familiar.

"But I — "

"It's my refrigerator, Ros."

"It's both of our refrigerator, Mother. We're sharing this refrigerator even if the bungalow belongs to you." Stepping back, away from her mother, on the uneven kitchen linoleum. Glimpsing a bread knife on the counter.

"I feel it needs defrosting."

"Great. Good. Only the frozen food will be ruined by the time the ice melts," said Ros calmly.

"If I waited until all the frozen food, my God, got eaten" — Stella's white hands twisted, clasped each other — "I would never defrost at all."

My God, what are we arguing about? thought Ros, who'd disqualified herself as a housewife years ago to everybody's satisfaction. "There's ice cream in there, Ma. All kinds of things that will be ruined." Compassion in her voice for the food. "When the kids come up, we'll just have to run out and get more for them." Why was she reasoning with this crazy woman? "Why not wait until they eat us out of house and home? Then defrost." Joking, when the real joke was that she wanted to strangle this prissy critical managerial person.

"*You'll* eat the ice cream before they do, Ros," her mother said calmly. Her judgment absolute, but with a mournful and triumphant edge as if she'd been waiting all week to say this. "While we're on the subject, what I can't bear is your standing by the freezer peering in, as if God knows what were inside. You know how much that adds to the electric bill?"

Ros began to laugh. To hold her sides.

"I pretend not to notice that I see you in there," Stella went on. "Meanwhile, the ice is building up and the whole refrigerator will be lost because you're being so stubborn and irrational."

Ros was laughing. Holding her stomach, her chest, the scar on her throat, the oilcloth-covered table. As if her laughter had crippled her and she needed support. "I can't believe we're arguing about this." Then laughter got throttled in her throat. Because even if this was funny, there was anxiety, animus, killing instincts in the air. Something dawned about this competition. This almost to blows about this refrigerator that opened and closed with living stuff inside. "Is that what we're talking about?" Her hand on her mother's shoulder. "Who knows the most about my body? Who owns the goddamned thing?" Remembering her own children: early morning sucking, diapers, shit, exhaustion, love.

Her mother looked bewildered. Moved away. Dressed her face with her eyes lowered and her take-me-away-from-this-craziness look. "I haven't the faintest idea what you're talking about. Is this some psychological thing you learned at college?" Walking to the counter as if exhausted, and leaning with her hand near the knife.

"You always do that." A level accusation. "Bring up something or other intellectual you know will make no sense to me."

"Do I? It feels right, and also" — shaking her head — "forget the interpretations. I just can't stand bossing you around. I had meant" — trying to muster her dignity after that unpardonable slip — "being bossed. Never mind." Walking, to retrieve some dignity, from the table and that knife out where the pines were, then thinking (as the darkness and trees came into view): a friend and an enemy, like Freud had. Always a friend and an enemy. Only I haven't seen my friend since when? Before the operation loomed. And my enemy, always close to me: Henry, Stella, whoever's closest to my heart.

Darkness and the pines outside. Death in the air of summer's end. Death in the clear air of fall. No sleep after that or sleep that somebody ripped open with the dawn (birdsong).

One afternoon, seated in the Adirondack chair, she nodded, dreamed something she couldn't capture about her having been bred for certain purposes, and few of them were — do-able. Only a few were do-able. Or some of them were done.

Death in the air of summer's end. Death in the clear air of fall.

On her third sleepless night, she went with her flip-flops on and a raincoat over her nightgown to the beach. Why me, why not Lev or my mother? she thought, sand and pebbles hitting her unprotected toes on her way down to the water. Kneeling by the water to feel with her hand, how soft, how warm, how cold the lake was.

She went home again. Feeling better, enough to admit to something. "Well," she said to her mother at suppertime, "It's been a bitch this doing everything. I've wondered, off and on, could I have, scaled back? Lived with more love in our lives, more pleasure, more ease and even — more justly?" This was too general a remark for her mother, who disliked, feared, even hated abstractions. "Lived more simply. Worked less. Had a smaller house. Let Henry do more of the — take more responsibility, I guess."

"Do you think," asked her mother earnestly, "this has anything to do with your health?" The accusation beneath the question turned like a sword (Rosalind watched this) against herself and she began to weep. Gently. Inconsolable. Her mother was weep-ing, not Ros. "I should have . . . I always meant to say . . . but you, so sensitive . . . to criticism . . . the way you people live."

How trite. These wailings. She barely heard the words her mother said. But tears. Annoyed her until she joined them. She shook her head. "No," she said and took a walk and thought a thought she'd thought before, about the rain raining in the country and — Stop it, she thought. About fleeing from her experience. Before, behind, anywhere but where she was.

Death in all kinds of things. Not just ends of summer, ends of salami, ends of school terms, ends of childhood. Thinking of Nana.

Usually not so clear and like a mountain spring inside her, her thought moved on to her pushing her life like a shopping cart full of unworn and discarded clothes. But now it (the thought) was gone. Before the life could be picked up and held or worn.

A howl in her throat the next night, when she came back down to the lake. A little earlier than the night before, but still in the dark. Each time she opened her mouth to the darkness of the water, a salt pool would soak through her skin and roll down her cheeks to her salty lips which she licked.

This is stupid, she thought. She thought. Licking the snot. Walking closer to the water, toes in the cold lake sand.

Her heart drawn out of her body. It went on walking on the midnight water across the lake.

This is scary.

Like a dog baying at the moon or a child sucking at its own salty hand, she wept. I will never stop crying, she thought, scurrying back up the beach holding the sides of her flannel nightgown up to the steps, then the stone retaining wall, where she'd been first in a row of three children playing tightrope with their arms held out like poles. Her heart, thump, thump, now that she was away from the water came back to her. I'm home, she thought, reaching the bungalow's front porch. Letting the screen door slam, despite the hour.

But her mother didn't awaken. So she ate a few things, she couldn't remember what later on and didn't want to.

～

It was fun the next evening, after supper, sitting on this stone wall, looking at the roped off kiddie pond, white floats on a white plastic rope. Kicking her feet, happily in the water, letting go. Remembering: cherries, she'd eaten, one a rotten one. Then, 'I am going to die,' in her own unspoken voice. Quiet and screaming inside. A scream so impossibly quiet it could have been a scalpel cutting the 'I' and the 'going to' and 'die' out so that the scream passed through her body but no sound came out. Or even registered as head or body talk. (It was still quiet and fun, in the place within where the cherries had been eaten.) Dusk over in the sky around gathered into fading pinkish next to dark. The center of pink began to fall like fireworks into the water. Or floated in the blue-black sky like cotton candy.

So what, came the answer. (On the dying question.) Lots of people will live on. This was from the pool in the center of the lake. They would be different from her. They would go on.

The thought seemed quiet. And humorous. Wicked in a way. Not to be devastated.

At home, afterwards, in her iron bed, she dreamed that her scar had opened up and her intestines had fallen on the linoleum that her grandfather had glued down and were scurrying here and there like crabs for everyone to watch until they died.

Her mother was mending an ancient pair of jeans when she came out to the kitchen.

"Can I make you a cup of tea, Ma?"

Stella looked up, her blue eyes startled. Shyness and the offer had startled her. "No, thanks." Needle in her hand. The faded blue pants lifted. Stella's left hand within one leg, while with the right she sewed a patch on at the knee.

Stella still mended. Amazing. Who else did in this throwaway country?

"Do you remember, Ma?" As the teakettle's whistle blew. She went walking towards its summons. "The night I was born, by any chance?" Sitting backwards, legs straddling a white wire ice cream chair.

Clutching the back as if she were holding on to — a chair back, she told herself firmly.

"Of course." Stella put the jeans down, looking at her watch. "A little after four at the Astoria General Hospital. The war was just over and I was lying in the hallway there were no rooms. We couldn't wait for things to start up again. This is you we're discussing." Stella's face now young and flushed. "I was so excited. I'd been drugged of course. So I didn't see you born exactly. But then they brought you. In this raggy gown. I had to examine you everywhere to make sure you were all right. I had to get you home and dressed to see how pretty you were. Then I said this funny thing. When I saw you had all your toes and fingers on. 'I have waited so long for you to join us, Rosalind.'"

Her dream that night: My mother had sisters to sew with. I am alone and buy ice cream.

~

At noon the next day as the town whistle blew, Ros walked down the warm tar road in her flip-flops to the kiddie pond. Lay in the water, pushed off from the sand with her feet, swam a few strokes, came out of the water and walked up the road to the bungalow. An old lady in a large straw hat trudged ahead of her. Her legs and arms shook as she walked along. She turned as Ros passed her. Smiled. False teeth in a dark wrinkled face. Glittery eyes. A doughty Jewish trudger. At home, she and her mother ate cucumbers with sour cream for lunch. Greedily like girls.

Now, in the late afternoon, back in the kiddie pond, she lay sea monster style, head up, and hands and belly on the sand below the water, feet kicking.

"Are you okay?" Her mother at the water's edge. "It's not too soon to go in again?"

"How would I know?" Kicking with her feet. Like a child learning to swim. "Don't worry so much about me, Stella."

"But who will worry about you if I don't?" Her mother's dress blowing.

"I will. I'm used to it, Ma."

Her mother turned from her and was trudging up the beach, skirt blowing, hair blowing, bending, reaching, looking for Popsicle sticks for the kids to build rafts with when they arrived.

My mother had sisters to sew with. I am alone and buy ice cream. Her dream. Her feet kicking. Her body turned round, as she swam out.

～

They were coming from everywhere: sending postcards, making phone calls, we're coming: 'Hi this is Lev, we're in Buffalo now.' 'But only for the weekend,' that was Lila and Sidney from New York. And Henry for the weekend too, but the kids would stay for the duration. Everyone converging at different times and angles. We're coming, we're coming, to see you, to see you. Like the sound that train that brought her up here would have made if she'd been in the movies.

Coming up from the beach with her body slipped back on, thighs, cunt, sand between her toes, itching where the scar was, throat for her to lump in, forehead for her dead grandma to kiss a capella. Visions of her mother at the water's edge looking down at her. "Don't worry, Mom. I'll worry about myself," she'd said, kicking her feet in the water.

Walking freely as if the air had parted for her, stones roughing up the bottom of her flip-flops, she climbed the cinder-block steps to the porch and yelled, "I'm home. Anybody home? Are you there, Ma?" inside the screen door. Hoping for a second that her mother would be gone. So she wouldn't hope, be disappointed, like the day she lit that first cigarette on that first day home in bed with Sophie, ruining everything before somebody else could ruin it for her. Searching in this jumble of little rooms, like the altars in a tumbledown church, for Hello, her ma. Who oddly formal glanced at her daughter's terry robe swung open to show her bathing suit and tummy and said, "Glad to see you, Rosalind."

"Pish tush," she grumbled. "What was that phrase? We used as kids? It had something to do with how a bathing suit that was wet felt on your behind."

16

Everybody

Everybody arrives, in some fashion. Or starts to arrive.

Nana first, her race

As Nana hung her blue jean jacket in the locker, before the race, she expected no saw that picture thing tipped and ready to peek out of the pocket. Heart like in a science textbook. Weird as shit. She'd figured it out, the last time she'd peeked in at it. What it was, that it was her mother's. Now it was gone. Because she'd taken it out of the jacket and given it back to her mom. Take that, take care of it yourself. Emptiness, and light enough to run, she trotted out. Everyone on the field was doing warm-ups. Debra their coach was punching air, her arms raised, her arms dropped. Debra's shoulders were wide, her hips narrow, and her haircut was a punky flip.

Debra lived in her body, walked on her legs. Debra knew what she wanted from you and told you how to do it. Wasn't always promising things she didn't mean or expect to carry out. Wasn't stealing from you. Not stuff, but *things*, like the things you'd decided to do yourself or your ideas. Say you wanted to go running or something, her mom would call up her friends and get advice and some coach even and before you knew it, you didn't want to do it anymore. You were filled, the opposite of empty or light. She thought of her mom (really, say, in her bathrobe or no shoes, and the soul thief disappeared). And she was light again. Not dark.

Everyone was stretching, arms crossed, like a promise now before their chests, then leaning back.

"Let go." Debra came to touch the hairs on Nana's neck. "Don't hold your head so stiff, it won't fall off."

She did it. Leaned back and felt those hands behind to catch her. The trees behind came up before and she came up and someone's hand was on her forehead. As if she had fever. She reached for the photo as if it might be under her sweats, but nothing, so she started to run around the track. One, three, five, six times. Empty now. Light enough to leap.

"Enough," shouted Debra. Waving them down. Into the van that was sickening inside (the plastic seats, the windows closed, the air conditioning) and on to the race. Pound, pound, pound, her heart and her legs.

Stretching, stretching, then again. Then the race! She got touched by the girl who'd gone first, and took off, pacing herself down the Fresh Pond path, round the pond through a woods up a hill, which was harder. But she liked the hardness, even her mother, who looked at everyone as if she expected to be handed a big piece of chocolate cake, knew that about Nana.

More slowly down the hill, which was harder, because her knee could go out or she could trip on pebbles. Spotting the blue and yellow sweats of the rest of her team, she went around again, the path, the pond, the woods, and didn't look back.

A tap to Jessica's shoulder. Now she wasn't younger or older anymore, only sweating, with her heart going thump, being thumped by the others on her back, and her feet had known where they were going.

"I want to call Ma," she told Henry that night at Burger King.

Moving fries around the plate and soaking up ketchup. Salty smells, grease.

"Call at home, on Sprint, it's cheaper."

"Cumulative," she explained to her mother about their score. A word as heavy as those boxes from her mother's closet. "If you know what I mean."

"Not in this context precisely."

She thought of salty smells, grease. What hangs in the air. In the closet. But said the kind of thing her mother would understand from her. "Well, all the scores get added up and the team gets a cumulative score. There was a team better than us and a team worse. And a bunch of teams that were nowhere."

"Are you glad you did it?"

"Sure. You okay there with Grandma, Ma?"

"Fine. Congratulations. Now can you put your father on?"

Nana went to the bathroom mirror to fix her wave afterwards. Stared at her face and asked this question: what kind of question was 'Are you glad you did it?' from your mother? When you had called to tell her that you'd just run a race.

Hurrah, she should have said to me.

I can live without her, Nana thought. Burst into tears. Wiped them away.

She heard Sophie on the kitchen phone. "Hello? Is that you? Ma?"

It was. She could tell. Still there. She grabbed a barbecue chip from the kitchen and went to ask her dad if they could go up for a while. To Arden. He said maybe.

Sophie

"Don't burn her yet, Ma," Sophie breathed into the phone. "Because I can't walk the tightrope without the doll and you have the doll, I gave her to you."

"What doll, honey, what tightrope, oh," said Mommy. "You brought her to me the night before I left for Arden. You know, Sophie, dear, you and Nana feel more substantial to me from far away than you seemed to me that evening. Believe it or not."

All this rolled over Sophie, the sound of her mommy talking when she wasn't looking at you, wanting to know how you felt. Then Mom, in her talking-to-a-kid voice, said, "Fine, I promise, I won't do anything until you get here, Sophie. I am looking, at this selfsame moment," she said, in that other dreamy voice, "into our bungalow's fieldstone fireplace, which has ashes in it." Adding, "I've had a cold. But Grandma is bringing me cups of tea and things." The phone was in the Arden kitchen. Sophie remembered. By the cookie jar. On the wall.

"Cigarettes?"

"I can't. Grandma wouldn't let me. Besides I'm coughing too much."

"I brought you things, Ma."

"That's right, dear. Can you put your father on?"

She tugged on his shirt and said, "Mom wants to talk to you," but though he was only buttering bread for a snack, he said, "She can wait."

"He says he'll call you later, Mom," said Sophie, hanging up. Remembering how she had gotten those cigarettes that her mommy's mommy's said no to. But she was a child and they were all so old.

Henry

Henry gets some news.

"I did call the doctor about the cold, Henry. Also, if you must know, I asked him what my chances were."

"Was this Kriegel?"

"He said, 'Maybe you'll have another heart attack next week and maybe fifteen years from now. There's no way of knowing. No way of knowing what you'll survive. Most likely, if you take care of yourself, you'll probably see your kids grow up,' he told me. That was the clearest anyone's been so far. Outrageous, I felt, this drawing a line on my life. And a little, no, a lot better than I'd assumed.

The most interesting aspect, Henry, is that after that conversation, I went down to the village and in the middle of refilling my prescription at the drugstore I thought, 'I'm not that important.' As they handed me the bottle.

"As if I never believed before that the world would go on without me. It's needless to say bad enough to die, but if the world won't end when I do, well I had some notion that my death would be like a nuclear holocaust. Nothing but ashes afterwards."

"No," he said. "Yes." Sagging suddenly. Exhausted. As if he'd been carrying the burden of her mortality and with her lifting it, he felt what it had weighed. As for his job, he didn't feel like telling her. She was certain to dub him the Homeless Shelter King. Suggest he look for something better. When he actually liked what he was doing. "Good. Fine," he said briskly. Was it heartless to be glad that she knew what he had known about her? So they wouldn't be in separate countries, lying side by side in bed.

Nuclear holocaust, for Christ's sake. It was appalling. He hung up, wondering, as he took the wet paper bag of garbage out, whether other people secretly felt that way about their deaths. What, in other times and places that let them live beyond their lifetimes, had been buried in this country and this century? The garbage bag burst as he dropped it into the can out back. Country graveyards, he thought, as coffee grounds and plastic spoons fell out, families that went on forever. Plaques on the walls of churches, synagogues and mosques. The mind of God remembering.

Henry drives. They leave for Arden.

"She's a stupid brat," said Nana from the Volvo's back seat. "She's always been a stupid brat and now that she's older, she's an older stupid brat."

"What are you doing, Sophie?" Henry drove with an eye out for the sign which said TURNOFF FOR LEE. The map beside him on the front seat.

"She's held the magnet stick the whole trip," said Nana. "I could grab it, but the stick would break. Tell her, Dad."

"Nana doesn't need a turn. She's a teenager." Sophie's thin voice from behind his neck.

"Give Nana back the magnet stick," said Henry reading signs. Route 21 would also take them to Arden. He took the exit. He listened for noises in the back. Being a parent was a form of administrative work. As in: forget about justice when there's a fight, the best you can do is to restore the prewar order. Or create a new one that lasts a few moments.

"Thanks, Dad," from Nana.

"How come you didn't say 'see, Sophie,' try to make me feel bad?"

"I didn't have to make you feel bad. I got the magnet stick. Watch me do an amazing trick with it."

The amazing trick, Henry saw in the mirror, was to make the wave on Nana's forehead stand up. "You look so Dracula," said Sophie gasping. "*Now* for my amazing trick."

"Hey, Dad. Sophie is picking the scab off her knee."

"That's enough. Hand the stick up front now." Turning where it said Saratoga.

He'd had facts in his life since Ros had been away. Facts were what she had undone. Hours to be on the site or at the office. Kids to pick up and no one to say that he was failing, for not doing or being what?

Of course, as well, the dullness. Boredom at the supermarket and in the office. So many blueprints of the same crummy accommodations to draw. So much ruined Sheetrock to call the contractor about. *So* much chaos, despair to house inside these Sheetrocked walls and no one at home when he arrived back in Brookline, but they were driving past the state police in Arden now. He heard in the air around him Ros's accusation, not about this job — it was he who found it dull, though not dishonorable, he whose life had slipped away before her illness, but some emotional tune, some siren song he didn't know, that she wanted him to sing to her. Tenderness. (He whistled the word.) Could that be all?

Now they were up the hill down the dirt road where the bungalow was. Where no woman appeared in jeans at the sound of the car, hair loose to her shoulders, freckles across her nose, bangs above her bright blue eyes.

He'd missed her, like a missing tooth. Limbs. Lost. Mind. Or missing tune. Hello? He hollered into the empty house. Got out of the car, slammed the door, stepped onto pine needles, stared at the empty bungalow, listening for noises, feeling midday heat. Got back in the Volvo. "They're probably at the beach," he said. "Let's go down and try and find them."

Lev

Lev drives. They leave from Oakland for Arden.

"There's not just one answer," said the Brink's truck robber on KCPR as Lev and Murial and Oliver and Dee drove out of Oakland. "Not being able to see any light at the end of the tunnel, balanced by when something radical happens you give yourself a whole new scenario is another." The man was answering the interviewer's question: "Why did you rob your own truck of four million dollars, then spend it over the course of the next nine months?"

"At the time of the theft, you'd just split up with your lover, is that so?" asked the interviewer.

"I was in many respects much happier sleeping on a mattress on the floor with my dog Flopsie and having problems meeting the rent, but being loved and loving someone." said the robber.

"He bankrolled the people he met to take-out banquets, trips to Jamaica and so on," said Lev, as, beside them on the freeway, he saw yellow-brown hills with scrubby green plants.

"Dee is being a pain in the butt," said Oliver from the backseat.

"What I really want to know," said Lev, "is are those his words? My dog Flopsie. And so on. Or did they write them out for him. I've been thinking recently. About people's right to chose their own words and not be paraphrased. It's a little known form of civil liberty. Because what people say is as important to preserve for history as their furniture or their ideas. But maybe I feel this way because I grew up in an age of radios, televisions, telephones and so on."

"I told you, Oliver. Stop bothering your sister. She'll stop bothering you if you stop paying attention to her." Murial turned so her hand could threaten to slap, then she faced front again. "I'm listening, Lev." Touched the hairpins that held her hair rolled up on her head.

Lev kept the dial of the radio moving past "We are Pacifica Radio," the listener-supported station he'd started out on. "We are here because you are there. Once again, if you have musical announcements you want to share, there're a lot of delicious events in the area. Be that as it may, greetings."

"Also," said Lev, "when I think about the restrictions of the show I'll be doing, those experts and so on, I don't mind so much, if people can call in and say what they say in words that are their own. Or am I trying to justify myself?"

Meanwhile he was driving up a ramp that said LAKE TAHOE, turning the dial to the national public radio station where some of his friends had gone to work. "Minority women are especially impacted by this phenomenon, Evelyn. Let's pin down, because we're going to talk about it, what is 'poor'? As women become the single heads of households. Tell me, because I really want to know. Concretize it for me."

He couldn't do worse than that. This 'what is poor' and 'concretize it for me' and having worked the FM dial past the conclusion he'd feared most — that his past had been glorious, his future would be tawdry — he gave AM a try, deciding that maybe he deserved his good fortune after all, unlike people who asked what poor was.

"Other animals have brains," said an AM creationist, "as large as man's, but none of them have done what men can do. How do you explain that if man is merely mortal material matter?"

Lev snapped off the radio because Oliver thought he heard a sound behind that might be the bikes on the rack falling off onto the highway.

Lev retied the bikes, checked the trunk and found the grill and box of bathing suits and cocoa mix, then got back in.

"If you buy an annuity," asked the radio, "what if the insurance company goes bankrupt?"

"Good-bye, house," said Oliver, pretending they were starting out.

Which pissed Lev off because they'd gone seventy fucking miles, and what had Oliver done but beat up on his sister in the backseat?

They were driving past the sign for Sacramento now and levees and growing shoots of rice.

"Do you know, Lev, when my stepfather was stationed at Leavenworth, levees were where we used to, teenagers on dates went to them to — I wouldn't exactly call what we did making love, but you get the picture."

"I probably don't," he said. "Get the picture. All these things are different enough, person to person and state to state, to be essentially unrelated acts when you get up close." Driving a little faster, he went on to connect how radio allows you to tune in on different worlds, nothing you'd chose, but nothing you could conceive of not having touched, having touched it. As opposed, say, to the control having a tape deck gave you. "Actually, if you must know, I made this different-when-you-get-up-close bull-shit up, because I can't stand hearing about, even in retrospect, you doing anything with anyone but me. Also, I have to know that I'll be doing the best of all possible jobs this fall. Because what I'm terrified of is getting bonded not just to Andrew but to these yuppie radio types. The way I am to the night program and our slummy neighborhood and you, Murial, honey." There were tears in Lev's eyes towards the end. "Furthermore, I want you to promise me that all our kids will turn out to be wonderful."

"Everything doesn't have to come out right, Lev," said Murial seriously. "That's what the bonding, as you call it, is for."

"You mean love," he said gloomily as the car began to climb a pass through the mountains that had been blasted out of solid igneous rock.

~

"This is the place," said Lev the next morning, "where some peo-ple ate each other." They'd been driving round the mountain through switchbacks that Oliver insisted on calling 'switch-blades,' past the Donner Pass where Lev wanted to get out and walk around. Nobody else wanted to walk, so Lev *had*, Oliver said, to tell that repulso story. About how these guys on their way to California had nothing to eat, so they ate the first guy who'd dropped dead, then starting killing each other for supper. Oliver had already read that story in *The Encyclopedia of the West* that Lev gave him for Christmas on that ski trip. "We were in the cabin. Your friend Andrew and that stupid woman with the fat hair were fighting upstairs. I mean, I could hear them bopping each other, so I was reading that story to myself to drown them out."

"What were they fighting about?" Murial had her hands folded in her lap, to remind Lev, he felt, that the next incident with the kids would be his responsibility.

"They have pots of money." Lev was trying to reconstruct that scene as he drove around the mountain curve. "Maybe it was sex. Abandonment. Neglect. Frustration. Or Andrew forgetting their credit cards or her asthma medicine, which she believed was purposeful or unconscious. I remember scuffle noises and not knowing if I should go upstairs and separate them."

"Andrew is responsible for this trip," said Murial blandly.

"What are you getting at, Murie? That we shouldn't speak ill of a benefactor?"

By nightfall, they were in Reno. The old women playing slot machines reminded Murial of her nearly blind mother who'd stopped gambling when her eyes got bad as if luck had something to do with seeing. "This depresses me. I want to get out of here," Murial said. "I know, I know, you think it's interestingly tacky. But it's awful, in reality."

The next day in Elko, Lev made everyone wait in a diner while he played 'authentic country music' on the jukebox, which Oliver said was cornball. Lev said the music was a hundred times better than heavy metal. "We were into peace and love, so Oliver's into war and hate," he told Murial as he climbed back behind the wheel from the diner parking lot.

"It was boring, Lev. Waiting for you," she said seriously. "And hot."

Still, despite his family's scoffing, Lev went on driving through Platte, and Ogallala, through stops for bathrooms and greasy hamburgers and half-cooked frozen french fries, through nights in the motel rooms they all were crowded into, with a joyous sentence inside himself: This is me, Lev Oliner, driving through everywhere I walked through with my fingers on the atlas when I was a child. First in Floral Park, Borough of Queens, New York. Then in that apartment in Washington Square Village. His feeling: bliss and some child's country, some child's dream fulfilled.

He stood alone at the Mississippi one early morning, he stood alone at the Mississippi, full of barges full of gravel moving beneath a bridge. Looking down at brownish waters. Then turned away with tears in his eyes, because what he saw was a river, when what he had expected from *Huckleberry Finn* was freedom, a state of mind. Pretty, he thought, looking back at the flowing brownish waters, as if they might, while he'd looked away, have picked up some of the meanings he needed to see. It was there now. A real not so pretty brownish river, silt filled, laden with barges full of gravel, moving slowly down the river between the necessary banks.

What exactly were levees, he went back to the motel to ask Murial, anyway? You know, Murie, what you made not exactly love by when you were a teenager in Kansas.

~

Somewhere on Route 80 Lev decided: "We need our own room tonight, Murie." The kids got put next door. The two of them came clean and wet from separate showers to being naked beneath a sheet together. While the air conditioner humming dried them and a voice on the television with the sorghum, corn and wheat quotations drew the heat, boredom and excitement of the past days from their flesh. He tried explaining from on top of the clean white sheet. "It wasn't Paris or Peking I fell in love with as a kid. It was this country." Touching her foot with his toe. "Where there were levees and people like you, Murial, practical and matter-of-fact and loving, and violent peasants, like my Grandfather knew, or maybe was, in Russia. But what do real Americans do?" Facing her now, propped on his elbow, feeling the skin around her elbow. "I remember asking my mother. 'We *are* real Americans,' Stella said. Which I knew wasn't true. Because we were Jewish and lived in Queens and Greenwich Village. And my grandparents came from Riga instead of England or Scotland or Ireland, even."

"What do you think my folks are? What did you call it, violent peasants?"

"Not them, Murie. Other people. Other Americans." His penis stirring. He ran his fingertips up Murial's downy white arm.

"Hagibaba" he began to murmur, a tune his Russian grandmother had spoken on his skin, folding Murial into his arms as if she were his child, he lay on top. She was his aunt and a jungle gym, someone to play on. Then a person beloved again.

"That was nice," she hummed afterwards.

"That was spectacular." Noticing the air conditioner's hum.

They reach Detroit, Murial's hometown.

Nothing in East Detroit — which was, said Murial, respectable working class to redneck — was what Lev had expected. Not Charles R Street with its relentless row of brick houses behind the hurricane fences where Murial's sister lived or Freud Street, pronounced Frud, said Murial. Or Johnny, Murial's heavy-hauler brother-in-law, who was built like Ernest Borgnine and had a scrapbook full of clippings. About the trains wrecked and fallen in gullies that he'd picked up car by car with the crane he'd built or the safes he'd lowered on pulleys to the sidewalk, while engineers, incredulous, stood below watching.

"Go ahead," this gap-toothed, grinning, big-bellied, short-legged Johnny said in the kitchen. "Swing off the cabinets, Lev. They're built to hold you."

"You really want me to, Johnny?"

Lev would have giggled and swung, if Murial hadn't stopped him.

For Lev was giggling, high that first day, because everything was like the movies, or some ballad, with freight trains picked up and lifted over this working-class hero's head. Paul Bunyan or John Henry. A mechanical genius, Murial said. Only all this was real and therefore altogether different from what was mythic or what he'd expected. Plus these were Murial's relatives.

"It's getting a lot darker in this neighborhood the last couple of years," said Johnny companionably, after his wife closed the scrapbook on the coffee table. Coffee and cake got handed around. "There a lot of niggers in California?" His legs stretched in front of him, his feet in scuffed black dress shoes crossed over each other.

"I didn't come home to listen to racist bullshit," Murial hissed from the hassock, her knees drawn sharply together as she sat up straight.

Sweet-faced Johnny hiked up his pale blue pants and looked alarmed and uncomfortable. Reached for a toothpick from the glass on the shelf above his chair. "Janet?" The toothpick glass was empty.

Janet paused, hand to her throat, on her way through the swinging door to the kitchen. "Murie, you've been off playing in California while we've been living in this town and taking care of business. Johnny just asked you a questeion. You could answer him."

"I wasn't playing in California. I was working and going to school and having children. Anyway, thanks for the cake. But we've got to go downtown now. Mom's waiting for us." Murial standing, stared come on at Lev.

Janet came back to the dining room with a new box of tooth-picks. Handed one carefully picked out to Johnny. "Leave the kids here. We'll look after them. You'll have enough on your hands with Mom."

Murial hesitated, shrugged. "Okay, I will then. Thanks."

"Johnny's an essentially sweet guy," said Lev as they drove off of Charles R onto the throughway. "Even if the racism is a little startling."

"You know he took an ax to my car when I was a teenager? Because I wasn't taking care of it right, according to His Highness. He thought he was my father, because he'd married my older sister, and mine had split. I thought he was," she pointed, "there Lev," she pointed. "Not at the project further, there. I'm sure, from what Janet said, that my mom'll be at the bar at this hour."

He parked by the bar.

She grabbed his hand as they started towards the tavern. Clutched his fingers like a child.

"You're uptight," he said. "Upset, I mean. I never saw you this way before. Except before Dee was born. You remember? Hanna calling?"

"Be gentle," she said, tightening her fingers on his. "Be nice to me. This is my family. They drive me wild."

The bar was dark, woody, pale green, with beer smells and a greeting sprayed on the mirror behind the Four Roses bottle: HAPPY BIRTHDAY, ED.

In the middle of the bar sat Murial's mother, Alison. This tiny woman with thick glasses and thin legs, who must have been beautiful once, because even on a barstool she was behaving like a queen.

"Hi, Mom." Murial kissed her mother's pale cheek, then stepped back from the stool to make room for Lev.

"It's been such a long long time, since I've seen my baby girl." A ringed hand extended from Alison to Lev, who felt sure that this excessive length of time must be his fault. Should he kiss the ring? His hand got grasped by Alison who grasped Murial's hand on her other side. "This is my Lev and this is my Murial," said Alison, presenting them like nosegays to the tall thin red-brown man with the processed coppery hair who sat beside her.

"Nice mom you've got there." The hawk-faced man moved two stools down so they could sit.

"This is my Lev and this is my Murial," murmured Alison to the woman on her other side, who was white faced with dark circles beneath her eyes and red lipstick round her cigarette.

"This is Alison's stool," the woman said. "It's the stool Alison always sits on. Hey, Alison, how come you're here tonight? They let you out?" Laughing and coughing and making rings with her finger on the spilled beer on the wooden bar.

"We'll all have to go take a trip out to Flint tomorrow morning," said Alison. "Did you know, Lev, that there are Indians buried in Flint? That name is for the arrowheads. Lester here told me so." Her ringed hand on the bar cupped to make a peaked-roof arrowhead. "Is that true, Lev? About Flint and the arrowheads?"

Her stool got turned first to Lev, then away before he could answer. She reached her ringed hand down the bar to Lester. Joints enlarged in the stretched hand. Arthritis. "Is that what you told me, Lester?"

"More or less. That's what I told you. Don't know if it's true or not."

"You know if there's any music around here?" Lev asked Lester, then felt silly. As if this man should know about music because he was black or rather reddish brown and looked like somebody from the Basie Band and Detroit had been the home of God knew how many jazz musicians. He'd done a program on Detroit and jazz once.

"Lots of music around here," said the man softly.

"Anyone we should go see? Anyone you like?"

"I guess, I'd have to say: I like all of them is playing around here in the last couple of years." Luther's arm extended for his glass. Took a meditative sip. "All of them without exception. Can't tell 'em apart."

"I told you, Lev, he knew about the Indian graves."

"Finish your beer, Lev. I want to go home," said Murial, as an enormous woman with enormous arms wiped the bar in front of them. Swish with a white rag. The flesh on her upper arm shaking as she wiped, she looked up, gave their faces a quick but searching examination, smiled. "Evening," she said. "What's yours?"

"I'll have a Bud," said Lev.

"Murie always" — Alison patted Lev's arm — "understood me, when I was tired after work or sad. My baby, I called her. You know what the best thing about having kids was, Lev honey? Having them."

"Nothing for me," said Murial.

Alison's head was bending towards the bar, as if there was

something there she felt needed examining. She quivered, rested her head on the bar, covered her forehead with her hands.

"Having them," she murmured.

"Wrapped around a telephone pole," said someone further down the bar whom Lev failed to find in the darkness.

"Lev, let's go. She's had it."

"Let me pay for that," he said, spinning coins onto the bar for the mug of Bud he'd been brought.

The woman scooped up the money and wiped the bar with a rag in what looked like one motion.

"Good-bye, good-bye, nice to meet you." Lev gave a special nod for the black man. Walking with Alison hanging on his arm out to the dark street where the car was parked.

Alison fell asleep in the car. Woke up long enough to say "having them," then fell asleep again. The next morning Lev didn't know if saying "Your grandma" to Oliver was a betrayal of Alison or Murial, when Ollie complained that the backseat smelled like somebody had peed on it.

"I mean it, Lev. It's like a cat box back here."

At the motel.

"She gave me a bone." Murial held up a steak bone with felt pasted on the back and a safety pin through the felt. "She sits in her room when she's not at the tavern making brooches out of what's left over from dinner at my sister's. Otherwise, as far as I can tell, she lives on saltines and cans of vegetable soup. I can't stand it."

"Lila would love that pin. It's interesting."

"Or she puts a penny in the fishbowl for each beer she has instead of a whiskey. Now what's that supposed to do for her, I ask you? What's 'interesting' anyway? We don't know 'interesting' in Detroit. Does it mean 'different' or what?" Murial sounded truculent.

"Well, I can understand," said Lev, "how after raising all you kids with all those husbands deserting her or dying and hardly any money, I mean, why shouldn't she sag a little at the end of her life?"

"Nobody deserted her. She left my dad because he wouldn't stop screwing around. Or going off to Alaska on construction projects, instead of working in these rotten factories, here at home. With the four of us under six, can you believe it? She used to pin us together with safeties so we could come to the furniture store at lunchtime while she was working. Janet, then Mike, then Edwin, then me," in order by size. Or we'd go window shopping. Everybody got to pick out something. It took me years to figure out that other people actually bought things.

"Another thing. I wish you wouldn't understand everything, especially my relatives. It's fucking patronizing." Tears in her eyes now. "Janet is furious with me. Running off to California while she's stayed home and had Mom and the rest to take care of. I'm the family brat. I always have been."

"Brat?" said Lev. "You should see my family. Me, you know, the others — The weirdest thing I've got to tell you is, do you know who your mom reminds me of?"

"Maybe you shouldn't tell me."

"Well, it's all those fancy gestures, and all the royal seduction stuff, even if your mother lacks the pretensions of the person I'm thinking of. You get three questions."

"Who is it?"

"First I thought Hanna. Then, I thought no, not Hanna. Ros. Probably via some aunt. God knows who these women learned those tricks from. Some movie? But isn't it incredible that we should marry each other's relatives?"

"It's why, with each other, we feel at home," Murial said slowly.

~

"Order anything." Lev leaned on his elbows the next evening over the red and white checked tablecloth at a country French place outside of Buffalo. "Anything you want. Price is no object." Waving his arm, so happy to be away from the road and its bad food. From the Fritos and macaroni and cheese at his in-laws' house in East Detroit, although he'd have believed before he'd spent the week there that he loved bad food, Americana. Still, day after day it was depressing. *So* when the real loaves of bread, yellow and white beside the sweet butter crock, appeared on the red-checked cloth, tears came to his eyes.

"I can't believe it," said Murial. "You're crying over food."

"I'd like to believe it's the opposite, that it's impoverishment that brings these tears to my eyes. How would I know? I only live here."

But in the motel bathroom after dinner, he was on his knees before the toilet vomiting pâté, salmon, new potatoes, chocolate mousse and brandy, wine. Gazing at the octagonal tiles on the bathroom floor when he was through. As if to explain to some unseen audience that he'd lost something here, some diamond ring, and was on his knees running his fingers along the tiles to recover it.

"I guess I overdid it." Returning to the air-conditioned chill, the huge motel bed, the woman in the center of the headboard, reading *The Buffalo Inquirer.*

Lila

The City

Hitting the street and the garbage cans on her way east to her father's office, Lila turned her head down Greenwich Street to catch the two World Trade towers glittering in the downtown sun. World trade must be, she decided as she turned her head away, all those boats leaving Brooklyn in the early morning to carry rubber tires to India and bring back cardamom and cotton blouses.

She had, in her early twenties, hung plastic bags of spices on a gallery wall, and gotten a little famous as a result, without knowing why she had done what she'd done or why other people had liked it.

Now you see it, in this city. Now you see it. Only rarely do you not, she was whistling as she crossed Bleecker past positively Fourth Street near where she grew up to be this joyful hummer of tuneless tunes inside herself. Then inside a twenty-story multicolored building past the doorman to an office door that said: s. oliner, dds.

In the clove and disinfectant waiting room, childhood like a tent enveloped her as she positioned herself on the couch that she and Lev had named discomfortable, for the way it had sinking spots, then got hard again, like the lake upstate with spots of warm and cold. *People* flashed from the magazine rack where once there had been *Time*.

"Lila, how you doing?" Patricia, the receptionist, covered the phone with her hand. Whispered, "I'll get your father," but Lila shrugged. "Is it okay? If I just . . ." Pointing down the hall, walking to find her father in the lab. His fingers lifted from his work on the counter. His blue eyes filled with tears. His lined pale face with carrot-colored curly wisps over his pale forehead. "Lila, I told her you'd be here."

Her was Patricia maybe. Or maybe not. Her father made feeling tunes with his words instead of sentences. "I" — he turned from her embarrassed — "dreamed you'd come in here in a white dress."

Lila plucked at her orange-striped T-shirt for signs that it might fit his dream of her. Failed to remind him that she'd called the office and Patricia had put this date on his calendar. Which was maybe why he'd dreamed of her. "We're having lunch." There was a partial on the counter. Two teeth with hooks to fit the gap in somebody's mouth.

"Of course. I know you called me," said her father.

"Lila. How you doing?" Patricia's head in the doorway. "Dr.

Oliner, gosh, I really want to thank you. It's my cousin, she's like a sister, we were always very close" — the fingers of Patricia's left hand were twisting the fingers of her right — "is having an operation. I got your dad to call the hospital. He's such a nice guy. I figured they'd talk to a dentist better than just a relative. She's got these tumors from here to here and got so nervous about the enema that she wanted to wear her underpants to the operation. I said, Don't worry, Terry, you'll be asleep, it doesn't matter what comes out or what they think.

"But I just don't trust doctors. My mother died on the operating table from some nothing operation. That's just me, I guess. But thank you." Patricia's tiny back covered by its white nylon tunic and pants moved out into the hall on thick-soled shoes.

"Dr. Oliner." It was Patricia noiselessly coming back. "It's — Harry. The one you knew from way back when. Gee I'm sorry." She nodded at Lila. "You were . . ."

"Nothing," said Lila.

"I don't want to see him," said Sidney.

"Harry's arms" — Patricia held her own arm out for Lila — "are skinnier than my wrist."

"Let me go out and get him," Sidney said loudly. All I can do is keep pasting those old bridges in. He's got no saliva. Nothing I do will last on him."

"He's a very nice man, your father." Patricia sadly searched the laboratory shelf for something distracting to look at. Spotting a model of somebody's teeth, she said, "The ugliest teeth in the world," happily emphatic about something. "I swear to God, they look like toes."

~

"Harry, good to see you." Sidney appeared in the waiting room to walk his old friend and patient to the office. He put his hand on the fleshless shoulder of the toothpick man beside him. "Harry, good to see you," he repeated in a muffled tearful voice.

Harry's ancient fedora got lifted shakily partway to the clothes

tree. Sidney hooked it on a branch, where it sat like a crow awaiting Harry. Meanwhile, a young man with his head bent over a
magazine waited on the discomfortable couch, tossing his magazine away as he shifted his buttocks in preparation for conversation. Only who would he talk to?

"The patient is in dire pain," he began to Sidney. He had his
finger in his mouth to illustrate his sentence. "The patient feels
like a building that's been sandblasted. I'm glad I finished writing
my book before I had my teeth done."

He stood now, in T-shirt, shorts and flip-flops, as if he were
about to follow Dr. Oliner into the office. His shirt had a Picasso
dinner plate on it. JUAN-LES-PINS, it said below.

"Patricia will set you up," said Sidney.

The young man followed Sidney and his old friend into the office. "No shit," Lila heard him say. "I don't believe it."

What the young man didn't believe, according to Patricia later,
was that people swallow their bridges a lot. The advice of this office
when they swallowed them: watch what comes out of you for the
next few days and you'll find them. It's better than paying five hundred smackeroos to replace what replaced what once was yours.

Patricia, exhausted, returned to the waiting room rubbing her
eye shadow behind her glasses. "The Lord giveth and the Lord
taketh away," she murmured to Lila when the young man had
gone. Commenting on old men, young men, the teeth this office
pasted in and pulled and Patricia's exhaustion, irritation and be-
wilderment at life. Lila remembered Patricia's cousin, they were
like sisters really.

Why don't we have sayings like that? Lila thought, as Dr.
Oliner walked into the waiting room in that green scrub suit,
reddish hairs on his thick arms, rubbing his hands, prepared to
tell an anecdote.

⁓

"It's so nice to be back here." Lila sat in Washington Square beside her father, unwrapping her tuna sandwich. The wax paper

opened. She looked up. Caught a roller skater going backwards. Looked down again. At the white bread, pale tan and white fish paste at its edges. "Also, I'm excited about this picture that I'm working on," she said softly.

"Good. Good. I wish I could say the same. What I do is not a profession anymore, it's a business. The tax people come around every fifteenth like they do in your mother's store. The lab charges a mint for gold and once the price went up, they never brought it down from when it cost nine hundred dollars an ounce." Her father sucked on his soda through a straw. Put the empty bottle beside him on the bench. Arm around the back of the bench now, dropped to her shoulder. "If I did it myself, bought the gold and sent it to the lab to work on, they'd send me back a little less than what I gave them. A quarter ounce here, a quarter ounce there. It all adds up." He paused as if a question had been asked. "Do they do it purposely?" Looked into her face. "A quarter ounce here, a quarter ounce there. It all adds up." Looking helplessly down at his pale spotted hands, he turned his palms up, waiting for her to ask sympathetically what else he was having trouble with.

What was she doing here? Waiting for him to take an interest or ask a question about her work. Following a red Frisbee thrown by a small blonde boy at a thickset ponytailed man, who leaped to catch it. As she caught what she'd never acknowledged before: her jealousy of Ros. And this thought for its companion: that her sister had grasped what she'd wanted, not waited or asked for it.

"Is it true?" her father said finally. "That Lev has a job? Your mother told me. He didn't call me himself, you know the story?"

But the dream she'd heard about from childhood had landed on his face again. Lev would be rich and famous. "The name of Oliner," Sidney said chuckling, "will go down in history." And no wonder, she saw now, that Lev had done everything within his power to stay poor, on the margins.

"I have to go now." She unfolded the wax paper her tuna sandwich had come in. Placing the uneaten half inside. Stood up.

Waited for him to join her. Walked him back to his office. Feeling as if her father were an old man suddenly, someone who'd never change, no matter what, at twenty-eight, she told him. She walked briskly west across Christopher Street, with its pastry porny penises in the window of the Eat My Cookies Shoppe to Washington Street and home.

Dear Ros,

It seems weird to write to you. I was always afraid to write to you or to Lev, because I can't spell or punctuate. But this is my question. Do you know any books that would explain how things got to look the way they look to us? Meaning to people here and also in Europe. These would probably be books about western civilization, I guess. The Renaissance? I sort of know that. And then what.

In a way, I'm also wondering how come I got to be a little art star in my early twenties hanging plastic bags of cloves at that gallery and how eight years later, I'm still trying things. (In fact, the only things I did before this that I really liked were those mud houses, you remember, with people hanging out the windows, that all those gallery people said were craft, not art. And what did they mean by that? I now think they meant those houses were too soft, not in technique, but in feeling.)

This slowness of mine is not just because I have to teach to make a living or am a girl or am pathologically shy about pushing myself forward in the art world. But really, I didn't know until now what I wanted to make that wasn't disposable. What wasn't disposable, apart from people, when I was growing up, were things in churches or museums. Only the church paintings seemed so much less self-conscious about imagination than the museum ones. As if in the olden days you didn't have to be blessed by Freud or somebody before you were allowed to put what you saw around the edge of life in your paintings.

Also, I've never been an individual, as I now understand the word. Only a member of a family. This has something to do with what seems real to me by way of forms and contents.

So now I'm making this triptych thing. Like those ones of the Virgin, only the person in the middle looks like you, Ros, a little.

Which isn't because you're good or bad, but only mysterious. To me, I mean. Will you be mad, I wonder?

And weren't Jews forbidden to paint portraits? So only God could make a man or a woman.

I hope you and Ma are doing okay together.

I called Brookline on Saturday. What good kids you have, sister.

Love,
Lila

Lila and Sidney leave by train for Arden.

"What you love," said Lila, high on a balcony above Grand Central Station with a glass of blood red Dubonnet in her hand, "is what you brush your teeth for. What you do every day, because you've chosen it or been chosen by it, like painting which I go on doing for" — peering down at Saturday's people in the marble concourse in shorts and sandals with backpacks and suitcases — "no particular reason. This is a little like the Pantheon." Pointing to the dome with its painted constellations above them. "I never liked Rome when we studied it, but it must have been a lot like this country." Across the concourse, a thirty-foot Kodachrome ad with an eighteen-foot father, a fifteen-foot mother, and a ten-foot child walking hand and hand through a field of black-eyed Susans. "Militaristic and good at building highways with people from all over the empire coming in until it was no longer Roman."

"I like it that you talk to me. None of the other kids," said her father. "I don't know anything about what they think or do. And Lev's new job. Is it the same as the other, but in the daytime? The women in the office keep asking, but I can't get a word out of Lev on the phone."

They were quiet, peering over the balcony. As if he might deliver a speech to the crowd below, while she followed an old man in a wheelchair with her eyes, being pushed by a West Indian woman to the platform where his train would leave from. "You're a lucky woman," her father said, "to have all this to play with."

She leaned over the balcony, waving his words away with her hand. Dispersing them into the air beneath the dome, like incense or a benediction over the heads of the people it belonged to.

"That's true." Now she felt safe enough to acknowledge what he'd said to her.

"The Adirondack Voyager," announced a voice from somewhere in the dome, "due to arrive at this station at two twenty-five, has been delayed temporarily in Philadelphia. Please stand by for further announcements."

17

Rosalind

They arrive. They meet. They do what they do.

That there is nothing circumstantial in these visits means what to me? thought Ros, swinging on the thick slab of wood her grandfather had made into a swing. Creak went the rusty hooks above as the thick twisted braids of rope swung back and forth. Staring at her own fat feet which were bare and thinking, Put on your shoes, as if she were her own mother.

For she was offering nothing: no food, clothes and barely a shelter, no advice, no illness even, as a drawing card, she was solving no problems, making no problems, making no money, stirring no soup and ordering no take-out food, and, like a dream, all these people were appearing, merely to see her.

First Lev and Murial arriving last night, in a dirty car with dirty people piling out. Hugs, her back pounded, Lev looking frightened: Did that hurt you? Tea in the kitchen, Lev and she with their hands covering the cups to warm them up. "Tell me everything, Lev, if you're not exhausted, about your life." So he'd told her about his new job again. That he was really going to take it. "You were the only one who thought you might not," she said sharply, removing her hands from the cup. They were wet from the steam.

He'd seemed surprised. Said that all along, he too, etcetera. She'd laughed. He'd seemed startled. "What did you expect from me, unalloyed gloom?" she asked.

"This psychic told me," he muttered, "you remember Hanna, Murial's friend, that you were in trouble. Psychically speaking."

"How would I know? If I am, I mean. In trouble." This surprised her. That she knew that she didn't know.

This morning she'd had a discussion with her mother about the order to do things in: groceries, laundry, a swim, then surprised herself with her own outburst: "Who gives a shit what order we do them in, Ma?" This instead of lurking around her mother being sullen.

"I'm sorry. I didn't mean to ask. What kind of language is that, Ros?"

"I'd forgotten that sort of thing offends you. It's not the sort of thing I generally say, in any case. It'll be nicer when my kids get here. Don't you think?" Her face turned to see freckles, thick lashes, blue eyes, mirrors of her own.

"You don't have to patronize me. But yes." Stella shrugged, lifted her chin, narrowed those eyes and got her I'm-going-to-say-this-even-if-it-kills-me look. "I love your kids." Her dark head turned away, silk hair smoothed behind her ears. "I'm glad you asked me, the other day, about the day you were born. I was sure I must have told you that before."

"Never."

"I'm surprised. I would have thought."

This morning some maniac from next door came over with an ax to cut down a tree on their property that kept the sun from his lawn. No one could understand what he was shouting, but Lev kept trying to reason with him — "There are deeds in town. This is the property line" — as the skinny potbellied man in shorts stood with his ax blade resting in the pine needles. The man took a step towards Lev. 'I'll kill you,' he shouted, raising the ax to the level of his shoulder.

"You get the fuck off of here, or I'm calling the goddamned troopers," Murial stepped down the porch steps of the bungalow to scream.

"Fuck you," said a woman who'd quietly walked through the blueberry bushes that separated them from their neighbors, while everyone had been staring at Lev and her husband. Everyone stared at the woman.

"Double fuck you," said Murial with her legs spread wide on the steps.

"Triple fuck you." The woman was staring at her adversary's eyes.

"We could go on like this all day," said Murial, hand on her hips.

"Come on, Elsie." The man with the ax backed onto his property. They all stared at the varicosities on his legs as if they needed somewhere new to look. His wife, glaring, followed him home.

"Murial is terrific, n'est-ce pas?" Ros found her arm slipped through her mother's.

"It's not only axes that bring this out in her," said Lev. "You'd have to know my brother-in-law. And me maybe, pontificating."

"I've never heard of a woman who talked like that," her mother murmured, staring at Murial's polo-shirted back as her daughter-in-law climbed up the porch steps to go inside. "Not that it bothers me."

"What about Aunt Julie?" Her mother's arm grasped. As if they were lovers, friends. Walking up an aisle which was the cinder-block steps to the porch.

"Of course. How funny I forgot." Julie, her mother's sister, was irritating, fussy, anxious, profane, beloved.

Now they were on the beach. Lev was standing, thick legged, in the water washing sand out of Dee's bathing suit, and Murial was lying on her back on the blanket beside Stella, while Ros was on her stomach on a towel.

"Is this significant? Or even true?" Ros was writing in the margins of her article as Murial turned on her side to ask what she was working on. Her mother went on flipping the pages of *Vogue*.

"Something about families, mothers and motherhood, mostly. Your sister Julie would like it, Ma. It begins with the Nazis."

"What a thing to joke about, Ros. That's Julie's towel you're lying on." Stella sat up, her slim legs crossed Indian style.

Ros looked down at the towel she was lying on. HOTEL PARIS was written over the end nearest the lake. Her aunt had supplied them all with towels when she'd lived alone at the hotel. "My aunt was a career woman. Bohemian, radical, unbearably opinionated. She used to insist that the weather report was a capitalist plot. They deliberately didn't tell you if it would rain on the weekends, she'd say, so you'd go away anyway to the Catskills." The wind came along and she grabbed at sheets of manuscript paper that were about to blow away. Weighted them down with a small sand castle. As her mother surprised her by murmuring, "She still is, opinionated." About her beloved sister, whom she criticized constantly, but not in company.

"I don't know how you managed that car trip, Murial," Stella said. "All the way across the country for days and days. In our family, Ros and Lev were always arguing and Lila was always throwing up and the car rug was full of ground-up Wheat Thins and orange juice."

"I don't see why that couldn't be true," said Murial. "About the weather report."

"My kids," said Ros, "are invariably disgusting on trips." There, she'd done it. For the surface she'd presented to her mother's critical worried eye, apart from what was uncontrollable, like Baumbach's leaving her with Nana or this heart, had no flaws in it. No problems in her life, except for what was solved, solvable or not worth mentioning.

"The major insight of this article I'm writing," she said loudly, "in case anyone wants to know, is that the lives we live outside the family affect the ways we live within. Who makes the most money matters, not only at the bank but in the kitchen and the bedroom, par exemple. Furthermore, women are as different from each other as anyone else, but mothers, for some reason, are all supposed to have the same wonderful qualities. All this is obvious in any playground, but not many people have explored the implications of what they've noticed, for therapy or anything else."

Lifting a rock to place on her article still threatening to blow away, she said, "Fuck it," when nobody responded. "I can't work on this thing here. Does anybody want to go into the water?"

She watched the pages of *Vogue* blowing to keep from feeling bad, as everybody said, No, not yet, Ros, later, but go on ahead if you want to, alone into the water.

How many mothers, she thought standing, starting for the water's edge, did it take to make a discussion take off? But then Murial and Stella were alike, the opposite of her, great on details, silent or unresponsive when any statement more general than a grocery list or weather report came up. Henry would be coming soon. She'd read him what she'd written. They'd had that once, she thought, lifting her arms as she walked out to where the water covered her hips. Intellectual companionship.

A few strokes out, she turned to see them all; sitting on the beach, gesticulating, found the bottom with her toes and walked back. Stuck her toes into the sand, like Sophie might. Hung around the blanket.

"Lev was trying to reason with this asshole, who was waving an ax around."

"I'd really appreciate it, Murial, if you wouldn't repeat that story. Move over on the towel."

"But you're wet, Lev."

"Murial has experience with axes. Her brother-in-law."

"Don't drip on my article." Ros, who had already put the manuscript away, taken it out again, put it back into her canvas bag, and zipped the bag up, now turned to find it. It wasn't, she remembered, on the blanket anymore. She was ready to gossip. Sit down. "So who is this brother-in-law, Murial?" When a huge sandal foot with an enormous big toe was set on the sand beside her hand. Reddish brown hair around the bony white ankle. This was Henry. She was looking up at his calf. "Well, what do you know?" she said surprised.

"Not much." He bent over double, almost, to kiss the top of her dark shiny head.

"Why didn't you call to say what hour you'd be getting here, so I could be home?" Squinting, looking up, towards his belly, into the sun. Shy suddenly. Wishing not for rain but for anger or irritation to fall from the blue sky as if they might atone for something. How glad she'd been to be gone from him, how glad she was to see him now.

"I don't know. I didn't know, I guess, you'd want me to."

"I — " If she had a rejoinder, she'd lost it somewhere. "Come on. Sit down."

∼

Henry's face above her was getting bigger like the rising moon as she lay beneath him on the motel bed, and she thought idly, Will I smother, will the scar open up?

Let it go, arch your back and meet him.

A howl of pleasure salty as that howl by the lake that night. And why not weep, after all, for pleasure, for something lost and found again? Disentangling her legs from his. Semen on her thigh, wetness dripping from the hair around her vagina.

Henry lifted himself, bent like a bridge, collapsed beside her on the bed. "Nice." Turning to the motel lamp. "I feel human again." Then he didn't pull the lamp chain. Fondled her breast as if his hands weren't part of him.

"I hope the kids didn't mind us going off." She pulled away a little.

"Ros. I've been hanging around them for weeks."

Silence. Turning on her side to face him. "It's not that your love doesn't touch me, Henry. It's that it's generalized somehow. That you don't know me very well in a detailed sense." This because she couldn't say: Is there some less detached way you could fondle me?"

"Bullshit. Love is not your thing, Ros. It's too irrational. You'd rather I liked or admired or approved of you, which I'm sorry to say I often don't."

"Is it that simple?" His back to her now. Her hand on what the kids called wings, bony protuberances. Pleased by the aptness of what he'd said to her.

"You know I thought my life would be so much better than the one my parents lived. It's different, that's all." He switched the lamp off. "I can understand now why Adelle isn't speaking to Havikhan," he added.

"Don't change the subject," she said. "You think that, Henry, about your life?" She felt insulted. As if she had been supposed to provide him with a top-grade life and failed. In the darkness, after the lights went out, she hit a rock at the bottom of her soul. "I can't imagine what I've been waiting for, with you or me or anyone. As if we all had to become something before I could love us." Expelling air as if her breath had been choking her and was now fleeing from her mouth. "Do you think it's possible for me to live merely? Instead of pushing my life in front of me as if it were an obstacle?"

But an hour later, waking up, she shook him. "What was all the urgency for you to work? What did you think I'd be doing meanwhile? Stop seeing patients so I could concentrate better on being sick or dying?"

The light was weak but coming in the window. He was half awake, shaking his head, returning to the land of sleep, his long body a center of heat beside her. Her own body there. Imperfect, but breathing, small, large, breathing, desirous.

Her idea, the next morning, was to organize a shopping trip

for everyone. Oliver, Sophie, Nana, Dee at the Village Store for flip-flops, polo shirts, school clothes for fall. Can't we wait, said all the children, until it rains? First we'll go to the beach for a whole day, climb the mountain then the store, okay, all right?

All right, she said, mock tyrant. After the mountain, the store, the store.

18

Nana

Nana takes charge.

"No, I mean it, Ma. We all saw it. A huge black bear on the top of the mountain." Back on the beach Nana raised her hands to the blue sky then curled them to make bear paws. She went down on all fours. "The bear eating blueberries," she said, knees on the sand. Rising to her full height in sockless sneakers with her paws still on, she explained to Grandma as the beach wind whipped around her, how she'd made everyone walk slowly down the mountain after they saw *it*. Finger on her lips. Being oldest and tallest by six months, she had promised to supervise.

Her mom had made a fuss that morning. 'You go with them, Henry.' But he wouldn't. He wanted to read something. 'You go,' he told her mom. Who actually got up and started towards the road with them. 'This is insane,' she said. 'I'm in no shape to climb a mountain. You go alone. You're responsible here, Nana.'

According to Uncle Lev, coming right up from the lake dripping water on their blanket from his curly hair and his hairy chest and legs, this mountain was a "dinky, eastern hillock. Not hardly worth mentioning."

"Another party heard from." Her mother with her legs crossed, rolled her beach blanket weight from one buttock to the other like a reducing machine to avoid the dripping water from Uncle Lev and the towel he wore around his neck. Who was putting his two cents in about the mountain without even knowing what had happened to everyone up on top, Nana could see, which made her mad.

"But to Dee and Sophie," she said with the sandy wind in her teeth, "the mountain must have looked incredible. Like it looked to me at their age." Sunburn burning on her cheeks and forehead, hair whipping around her mouth. The air got cooler as she got braver, standing up to Uncle Lev.

"There on the mountaintop, while we all stood behind this big black rock to look down at the lake and find you guys, we saw *it* coming. Behind the trees, onto the bald spot. A huge black bear, Ma." Nana curled her fingers for claws. How tall like this, lifting her hand for height, it was, she said, sliding between the pine trees to the other side of the mountain, down on all fours to eat blueberries in the pine needles. "We stood still like Indians, as it finished its berries and walked over the mountain. Then it was gone. We turned and filed like Indians," she lowered her voice. And thank heaven Uncle Lev didn't give her his pointing finger — 'You get one more time to use that Indian cliché' — because she'd stood up to him about the mountain. "I put my hand over Dee's mouth so she wouldn't make noise, then we ran to the bottom and straight in a circle around the lake to where you guys are."

"It's hard to believe. A bear. In that dinky mountain." Her mother shook her head, squinting. But pretty Auntie Murial grabbed Dee and put her on her lap and said, "Thank you, Nana, for leading them back to safety." With her gray eyes wide between her freckles.

"That's all right." Nana looked down at her ragged old sneakers.

"I can't believe there wasn't an adult with them," said Grandma Stella.

"*Adirondicus boricanus.*" Uncle Lev was on his stomach snuffling on the blanket where Auntie Murial and Dee were. "I know the type."

"How could you, Lev?" her mother said. "I'm absolutely certain you've made that so-called species up, apart from getting everyone wet on the blanket."

"Out now." Auntie Murial pushed Lev's snout away with her big toe.

"A joke." Lev was groaning as he crawled away on all fours.

"But it wasn't made up." Sophie, practically crying, kneeled to get her head pressed against her mother's scar above her bathing suit top, rested there.

"I believe you." Her mother's half-closed eyes and hand on Sophie's silky bangs, gently smoothing the way the hair was growing, instead of ruffling in the opposite direction like Henry did.

Oliver, when Nana peeked at him, shrugged his neat tan shoulders to say: the littles get a lot. Then huge Henry coming from the lake had to hop on one foot to shake the water from both ears and grab a towel before he could sit still and bony with his knees up and listen to the story.

"Actually" — Henry was flicking at his long toes to get the sand out — "I'm fairly sure there is an Adirondack bear. Why don't I take the kids to the village library where we can look it up?" Folding the towel in fourths and standing up straight.

"Sophie, bend down. There's something on your face." Grandma Stella made Sophie's face perfect with a tissue, pushed her gently back towards their mom. "I have a suggestion. If you run, Nana darling, to the bungalow, there's an envelope with our address on it which you can use to get a library card. Everyone at home can see it too. I always like to support that little library." Taking money from her straw bag. "Here, as a donation."

"I'll pay, although I don't see that they actually need," began her own mom as Nana took off like a shot with the dollar in her sneaker laces across the beach because she hated this bickering her mom and grandmom did. Then turning saw the kids except for Dee running behind her and Lev and Henry walking up the road. The mothers were still sitting on the beach, though, oiling their legs.

She slowed. She stopped. She got up on the stone wall by the road. She was first in a single file with Oliver and Sophie behind her and their arms stretched out for better balance. Henry and Lev were walking beside them on the road talking in low men's voices.

"We're renovating flophouses," said Henry "The Palace, the Prince, and the Providence are the names of what, would you believe, I'm currently at work on. Taking four-by-six cubicles with a mattress on a plank of wood and making spaces for the homeless — they're families, children and women, this go-round. There are fifty or sixty of these places downtown, and the firm I'm working for got the contract for practically all of them."

"Is this the land I used to love?" sang Lev in a high female operatic voice. "You have any idea, Henry, what percentage of the population is involved in the homelessness business? I mean as real estate operative, flophouse owner, or someone like you, Henry."

"What does that mean? 'Someone like me'?"

"You're a kind of — you and I, people like us, we moderate, meliorate, make the messes of this country less offensive to the nose." Her uncle was dancing as he piled sentences on top of each other.

Henry once said to her after a phone call from Uncle Lev that it was easier and paid better to talk about things on the radio like Lev did than to try to do anything. But Lev looked so happy. Babbling on. "Ameliorating loneliness, distributing info. Everything superficial is my line, nothing profound."

Henry shook his head. "It may be *distasteful*," he said. "It may be unaesthetic, or even wrong to provide solutions that aren't what one knows *could* be provided, but for God's sake, Lev, that's what there's money for" — he was shouting now — "do you want these folks in the streets?" as they entered the village, a white clapboard house with ceramic gremlins on the lawn. Nana could see that Lev was gleeful, playful, silly, like these plaster elves. For unlike her mom, Lev didn't take himself so seriously. (She didn't know if she thought you should or not.) Now a brown and red mansion was in front of them. A mill owner's mansion with a cupola, a gazebo, said Henry. Down the next hill to the millworkers' street by the Hudson, where, Lev pointed out, wash hung on a line and porches tumbled into dandelion lawns and rusted things stood like dinosaurs: a truck, a motorcycle, an old car on a lawn strewn with old bones for the dog.

She liked them both. Both these men.

"My mother's brother had one of those. He sold sugar on the black market during the war," said Lev.

"You're talking about the Hudson? The Second World War?"

"Yes," said Lev.

"Do you happen to know — you're from around here, aren't you, Henry? — if Flint, Michigan, has Indian graves or arrowheads?"

"I'm from Minnesota."

They were in the center of the village now. "Early nineteenth century republican virtue stands before us," Lev said, in the form of the Arden public library with its white porch and three white pillars and three sagging steps to climb to reach the dark green library door with its brass knocker.

Nana remembered that that library card was still her responsibility and the address was at the bungalow and so without telling anyone where she was going, she ran back like a shot down the road to where the bungalow was only she couldn't find the envelope in her grandmother's room even if Grandma Stella was always right and perfect. But had to go into her mother's room and go poking in the musty closet behind the curtain under her father's big backpack and a pile of books and that doll on top of a pile of papers in her mother's handwriting: 'A patient tells the following story.' Which was enough, she didn't want to read anymore. The doll lifted by her ankle, then tossed on the iron sagging bed. Underneath the doll there was a letter addressed to her mother from Auntie Lila and next to that, that boring everywhere-she-looked — photograph.

Rosalind Twist
Box 723
Arden, New York

Lila Oliner
340 West 11th Street
New York, New York

"Dear Ros," said the letter she stuffed back inside the envelope.

She stuck the photo into the frame of the curved bureau mirror so her mother would see it when she looked at herself. Then ran with the envelope down the hill past the red hilltop stand and those pottery gremlins that Sophie thought were darling to the village.

Sophie, Henry, Oliver and Lev were sitting on the front steps of the library waiting for her to bring the envelope, so they could find the real bear's name in a book and get the facts on it right.

"Here I am," waving the envelope. Stopping on a dime, in front of them, her arms held up.

WE ARE CLOSED FOR THE DURATION WHILE REPAIRS ARE COMPLETED ON THE LIBRARY, said the black and white sign on the dark green door behind them. OUR HOURS WILL BE FROM NOON TO THREE P.M. MONDAY THROUGH THURSDAY WHEN WE REOPEN, DUE TO STATE AND FEDERAL BUDGET CUTS.

Everyone's face was lifted up to her, Nana. Because the library was CLOSED FOR THE DURATION . . . So "follow me." She waved the envelope like a signal to start a race, then halfway down Mill Street got her idea. They could go to the drugstore and find a paperback dictionary like Henry once bought her for spelling.

Inside the cool drugstore with its vitamin and candy smell, Sophie went straight to the postcard rack and turned it until she found a postcard. "See." Signaling the rest. "Here's the mountain where we saw *it*."

"Aerial View of Cobble Mountain," said the print when Nana turned the card over. Surprised that Sophie had really found their mountain, when all green postcard mountains under blue skies looked the same as all others on these cards. "Look, Henry." Nana's finger on the bald spot where they'd stood. But there was no bear on the postcard.

Henry took the card and Nana moved to the book rack where she found a red paper *Merriam-Webster's*. "Could I have the money?" Standing before him with the book before her.

"Take this." Henry gave her a bill from his shorts. "This." Some coins.

She turned it over. "It'll be more." Pointing to $3.50US/$4.25Can.

"I'm not convinced that you need to actually *own* that book." But he gave her more. She paid the blonde lady at the counter. They went back out to the sunshiny stoop and sat down. "Bear," she found under *B*, snuggling down next to Oliver, surprising herself by handing him the book.

"Bear, suffer, endure. Bear and suffer are very close, but bear suggests the power to sustain oneself under adverse conditions, while suffering is closer to the acceptance of affliction than patience or courage in bearing." Oliver, who was eleven, stumbled so badly over the words that Nana didn't think he'd understood them.

"I love it," Uncle Lev joked, lifting one hairy leg in shorts and sandals to the step above. "The power to sustain oneself under adverse, is it conditions? That you saw stumbling around on all fours eating blueberries on Cobble Mountain."

"I knew that 'bear' was wrong. I thought it would be funny to read it." Oliver, handing the book back to Nana, looked teary and pissed at Lev's joking.

"The bear," Nana read, "is a large heavy mammal with long shaggy hair, rudimentary tail and plantigrade feet."

"Go on." Sophie was picking at her knee scab again.

"As in: the European brown bear, the large creamy white polar bear, the American black bear, and the yellow grizzly bear of western North America, sometimes referred to as *U. horribilis.*" Nana giggled as she sounded out the word, handing the book to Uncle Lev, because the next part looked too hard for her to read.

" 'Go you the next way with your findings. I'll see if the bear be gone from the gentleman and how much he hath eaten.' Come on, Nana, I'm not performing Shakespeare on the stoop, ha ha, on my vacation."

"But nothing in this book," Sophie lisped, "is like what we saw. It was dark, but not black, and it must be American because we are." Looking troubled and intelligent, she'd put her lisp on to be the youngest. "Nana made us go slow so we got to see it, but wouldn't make noises."

Which made Nana remember that she'd been captain on the mountain then. "Follow me," she said standing up. She led them past the post office and the IGA to Sue's Donut Shop, where they lined up on stools at the counter and ate cinnamon donuts and lemon-filled donuts and blueberry donuts like the bear, she joked. And around them, country words thrown out like baseballs:

"Glens Falls, fart around."

"You want the snowblower?"

"A man can't have a good affair without someone telling his wife."

A big fat man in overalls to his pale fat wife and baby. "Kathy, if you can't keep that baby from crying, I'll have to go buy her a new mother."

Laughing to beat the band.

"Let's go," Nana said, although Lev complained when they were outside that she'd cut him off from his 'roots, these country copulatives.' "Don't be silly. I know you're from the city," she said. "I *feel* like these are my roots," he said in a whiny voice. "They were my grandfather's roots in Russia, so why can't I inherit them along with blue eyes?" as everyone walked behind her up the hill past the state police and the firehouse and Luther's Stand on the hill to the bungalow. Where she'd rock in the hammock and live that bear thing over with her eyes closed and the pines waving like an ocean on top of her.

Grandpa Sidney and tall Aunt Lila with her red frizzy hairdo, stooping together and both shy, smiling, were standing under the pine tree by the hammock when they got home.

She stuck her hand in her pocket, remembering that letter from Auntie Lila.

So Sophie was the one who got to run up shouting, "Auntie Lila, Grandpa Sidney, we saw a bear up on the mountain." And she got to follow.

19

Rosalind

The End

"We went to a concert there last summer." Ros, on the beach, clasped her ankles and gazed over her knees at the summer camp across the windy lake. As Stella talked. Once the camp had had an Indian name and a statue of the Virgin on the beach. Now it was for music students. But oh no, it wasn't enough," Stella said, "for us to hear the trumpet voluntarily, we had to listen to a lecture on horn music first from the director." Stella was wiggling her nail-polished toes. Her remark, apparently innocuous, had been aimed, Ros felt, scratching the bottom of her sandy foot, at her older daughter. For in this family only Ros studied up on what she was doing or seeing or being before she did or saw or became it. As if knowledge would protect her from unpleasantness, surprises. ('All surprises are unpleasant to you,' Lila said once, then put her hand over her mouth as if she were ashamed of having noticed.) All experience, too, thought Ros now, as she reached out for the bottle. "Can I have some oil, please?" Not to mention catastrophes from out of the blue, attacked by a heart she'd barely thought about.

A long odd-shaped cloud floated above.

"When I'm finished." Stella, oiling the space between her neck and her bathing suit top, took her sunglasses off to let her blinking eyes plead, before she handed the bottle over, for Ros to give her the benefit of the doubt. Don't assume the worst all the time. Her sunglasses got slipped back over her blue eyes with the heavy mascaraed lashes.

Ros rubbed white oil on her thighs, examined their jiggle, reached up to soothe the scar line showing red above her bathing suit. "You want some, Murial? This isn't the ultimate sunscreen like you'd use in the Caribbean, but it's certainly strong enough for this place." Offering the bottle to Murial now sitting with her legs stretched out and two large knuckled hands on two knees whose bones were prominent.

"I thought you loved this place," plaintively from her mother on her stomach.

"I do. It's just not the Caribbean." She'd heard herself complaining, Whatever you have to offer me is inferior, as strong a bass line as her mother's piping treble, which mixed a little girl's bossiness with timidity.

"Thanks." The oil bottle accepted into Murial's freckled hand, squeezed. The drops rubbed carefully in a circle by Murial's palm onto Murial's bony knees. "Would you believe the stitches from my Windsor, Ontario, high school basketball thing are still, you see this, white? This hem thing? Does anyone want to go swimming?" Rising, square shouldered, flat hipped, long legged, freckled, white.

"Okay. Why not?" Standing bravely before her mother's eyes, who'd see the flesh jiggling on her ass and thighs and note once more the outward visible sign of her elder daughter's shame and failure. Fat. Only fat. So what, she thought, wriggling her shoulders a little, trying to feel before she hit the water, some small-town miracle that went: Only fat. Unlike heroin, Hitler, murderousness, malice, terminal dissatisfaction or whining, even. Walking with Murial to the water's edge. Her mother stayed behind on the blanket. "I've put the oil on," Stella said from behind her sunglasses. "I'll sit for a minute and bake, if you don't mind."

⁓

First Ros (inside her head) had watched her mother Stella watch her and Murial enter the water, then swim to the raft. Jiggling thighs and ass, a frown. Still *she* must be ready to swim the distance, or she wouldn't be starting out, right? (That was her thought about her mother's thought about her. The *she* was her, Ros, of course.)

Then her mom had walked down the burning sand to the water. And until *she'd* put her toes in, her soles were burning up. Cold, cool, she'd sprinkled water on her slender wrists and arms and watched the minnows dart between her toes. Some child thing. Children on the beach behind her stroke. Stroke. A little tinge or twinge there below her own breast while back near the shoreline, her mother's shoulder twitched a sand fly off and her mother's long feet had the sand brushed off. Her feet from the ground and plants reaching up at her from underneath the water.

Then from behind, her mother came up to the raft. They were together. Wet, hair clinging, slender, all right. Fat, sort of famous, funny, not so right. They joined.

But Ros had gotten her, that is, gotten here, first. Her first. The heave had been uncomfortable, water spraying off her ass, belly flop, the big seal flopping on the rock, like near where Lev lived, that chilly San Francisco. Only this seal was her, wet beneath her breasts and belly.

Hello. Acknowledging there were three of them now. She turned over and lay flat on her back to listen to the lake water lap against the rusty oil barrels that kept the raft afloat. Closed her eyes and saw her elder daughter in the race, her own clothes stolen, her — somebody's children growing up. 'Let me worry for myself,' she'd told her own mother. As a taller, leaner Nana with new hair — or was it color or style only? — played before her eyes. Feeling cold and warm as the sun played with the odd-shaped clouds and her wet skin and her bathing suit and turning over thoughts of that bravery, standing before her mother, with that back of the bathing suit showing. That ping. Pang. Judgment. Her own elder daughter's judgment. As if both of them, Nana and Stella, were an outfit she'd worn for too long and had to turn over to let the sun dry from her back.

Lying cheek against the canvas raft, with two quiet women on either side, three wet but drying women and one her mother, from her body once, she wondered what exactly Nana had taken, and would she feel its loss — remember, identify any of those skirts or blouses, pocketbooks? Notice what she'd lost? Then she came up with that plan for all of them: today the mountain, tomorrow the Village Store. The only place, she leaned over to whisper to her almost sleeping mother, where she and Stella had enjoyed shopping together, a fact that Stella didn't remember at all.

～

"'Dear Ros,'" read Nana the next noon in the middle of the Village Store. "'It seems weird to write to you,'" Nana waved Lila's letter at the rafters, then read on. "Blah blah blah." Looking down the page. "Now I'll read you: 'Do you know any books that would explain how things got to look the way they look to us? These would probably be about Western civilization.' Blah, blah, blah."

Nana looked around the pine-paneled store full of flannel shirts and down vests and cowboy boots as if she'd never seen them before. Housedresses for the women and also jeans. Old lady dresses and old man sweaters, kid stuff, bathing suits. Pausing dramatically in front of Ros to bring the letter up towards her eyes:

"'It's not that you're bad or good, only mysterious.'"

"Lila said that about you, Ma," said Nana who was wearing the black corduroy jumper she'd tried on earlier behind the curtain in the dressing room, over her sweats.

"Do *you* think I'm mysterious?" asked Ros.

"Not really," said Nana shyly.

"Not even on the stoop?" She'd promised Nana that she'd buy her something, then overwhelmed by dizziness had to sit down right away instead of coming inside. "Here, take this" — she'd been waving cash around — "you go pick something out by yourself." It had been Stella who'd insisted that she go inside again the minute she felt better.

"That's only because," Nana paused, "you never know for sure, I mean you'll always *pay* for things, it's only you don't like watching other people getting stuff when you don't." Nana rushed ahead. "But why should Lila be afraid that you'd be mad at her in the letter?"

"She painted a picture of me." How much it meant to her, her elder daughter's finding her knowable. "Why don't you get the jumper? Black's fine. What do you think, Stella?" (There was a feeling here, like fall. Cool air and passionate colored leaves. I'm coming home from school and everything is ordinary, in the loveliest sense, and doomed.)

"Very nice." Stella nodded towards the jumper, although Ros knew that Stella would notice that the corduroy was thin and the seams badly stitched and the price worse than in New York or Boston.

"'What good kids you have, sister,'" read Nana from the letter. "Did you know that, Ma?" Then dragged the jumper over her head and turned from a judgmental schoolgirl into that long-legged runner again. Streaking to the counter before Ros could say, 'Not really.'

"Wait a second, Nana." Ros picked up a pair of navy blue sneakers. "I want to try these." Slipping off her flip-flops and lacing up the sneakers. "Not for running, God knows, but so Lev can resurrect his favorite stories about how I used to put my sneakers on to hail a cab to ride to Greenwich Avenue. To understand the joke, you need a context."

But Nana from the counter said she already knew the context. "You told me, Ma," said Nana, "you lived at the end of that block."

"I'll pay," said Stella who'd joined Nana and Ros at the counter. "I want to." Palm flat against the air. Pushing air and all of them, encountering in her hand resistance. Refusing it.

The children prepare a play.

"It was nobody's idea in particular," Ros told Lila on their way down the hill to the IGA store to buy franks, rolls, and marsh-mallows for the picnic. "Serendipitous, I'd call it. Sophie had her usual fit, dragging me into our bedroom to help her find that doll. 'I thought that doll was dead. I thought you had burned her.' So I took her hand and she dragged the doll by its foot to where Dee was playing outside with that stuffed turtle. Did Lev get that in the Village Store? It's nice.

"Well, that's that, I thought, prepared to watch for develop-ments. Now Sophie will immolate the doll or get Nana to help her. But no, she squatted down and made it walk.

"'Say the doll is a bear,' she told Dee. 'This is a friendly turtle with red and white spots.'

"Oliver came by. 'I'll be a dog,' he said. 'Who grunts and sniffs.' And went grunt, grunt, sniff, sniff, rooting around in the pine needles for something. Then he ran into the house and came back with this bizarre piece of jewelry pinned onto his chest, like a dog bone or a steak bone, and that photo from my operation which he wanted the turtle and the bear to sit on like a flying Per-sian carpet. Only it was too small, of course. I found myself totally and irrationally offended and asked him rather sharply, I suspect, to take it back to the bedroom and put it on the dresser mirror by the view of Lake Arden and that old photograph of Grandma.

"'For sure, I only meant to hold it,' he said. Then he went down on all fours to grunt, grunt, sniff, sniff in the pine needles.

"'Maybe,' Sophie said, 'Oliver is a pig.'

"'What is that a picture of, anyway?' said Oliver.

"'Now somebody is lonely,' said Sophie. 'And somebody opens a door.'

" 'That's the script?' I said. Then felt bad for being ironic at the kids' expense. That happens too frequently in this family." They neared the donut shoppe. "Anyway I didn't see why we shouldn't make a production of this thing, despite its brevity and whatever problems it may have, dramatically speaking. You remember Dad saying that? 'Don't make a production out of things.' I'd also like to get a lot to eat this time. Despite your and Mom's tendency to underdo things on the supply side. Marshmallows, which I insist we burn to a crisp on the outside. I recall being fond of the mush when you get in."

"Ros, for God's sake. Everybody likes those marshmallows," said Lila.

They bought marshmallows. They found Lev and the children by the river.

~

"A pine needle bear?" asked Lev, when Sophie showed him the doll with the pine needles glued on to be fur. "That's insane. Bears aren't green even in the Adirondacks." Sophie's little girl eyes were waiting, willing, wanting him to see what she saw in the pine-covered body she held out.

"Lila made it for me," Sophie said patiently.

"Don't listen to Lev," said Nana. "He said I had to take my running suit off to be queen."

"I pointed out that queens in the past didn't wear running suits, not that you couldn't." The kids were pissed. Ros could tell by the back of Lev's neck that he was in a stubborn fit. "You need a director," he shouted. "Go ahead, ruin it. Do it however you want to." Which they were going to anyway, Ros pointed out. Then stopped. Why did she always have to take this tone, this pedagogical — as he left them by the river feeling silly, she felt sure, mortified, losing his cool, getting chased from the woods by some children.

She caught up to him where he hit the street by the river where the Hudson stood in that yard beneath the flapping wash, by pieces of this truck and that motorcycle. A permanent exhibition of some bygone civilization. In Detroit, he said, Murial's family had stood around his Datsun like an object from outer space. "You drove all the way from California in that sardine can?" they asked.

"I can get a real car that goes where and when I want it to, now" he said. "Excuse me, but I have to run, that makes me so — uneasy." Jogging up the hill past the stand, hitting the dirt road, the stones and the dust that flew around him. He ran back. "How was Detroit?" she asked.

"Detroit was well." He sat cross-legged on the spot she'd brushed clean. "Everyone has troubles, but money helps. With money troubles especially, that's my startling conclusion from being with Murial's family, who don't lack money at the moment, but have lived so close to the bone so recently, you feel everything beyond survival is like a wall-to-wall carpet on a concrete floor. Otherwise, everything's well, families are pretty much alike, I guess." Remembering that flirtatious woman with her ringed hand raised above the bar in benediction, as she went on about some Indian burial mounds, who was now floating like a ghost above the gestures of his sister. "Murial's brother-in-law asked me to swing off his kitchen cabinets. 'Go ahead. They're built to hold you.' It reminded me of Grandpa building things to last forever, then smashing them up when he got mad. This guy took an ax to Murial's car, for reasons I forget. I guess it shouldn't be surprising that Murial and I would marry each other's relatives.

"How are you, Ros?"

"Wondering how come I thought life would be so easy. Was that money, do you think?" Her heart pounding as they reached the top of the hill, that stand, that corner, the bungalow. Her mother sitting. Wandering over to them. "But definitely." Ros's hand swept the pine needles, let the dirt she'd picked up with the needles rain down through her fingers. "Ordinary," she said. "I think that's the concept I'm after." She made for the hammock exhausted.

Stella perched on the painted blue ice cream chair by the hammock, as if she weren't sure she were invited.

"We're talking about how come we thought it would work out okay," said Ros. "My life, I mean."

Nobody said anything for a moment. Ros listened to bees, a motorboat in the distance, wires humming. Dragged her hand in the pine needles as she rocked.

"That was my fault," said Stella. "I can't tell you how unpleasant my childhood was, working in the store with my parents fighting all the time after we lost it. I wanted to give you kids a normal life. Still, your expectations always surprised me."

"I, for one, can't tell you how sick I am of everything being the mother's fault," said Ros. "A whole country believes in nineteen forty-nine that it's arrived at the golden age for good world historical reasons, like a war we won, and when it turns out it hasn't, it's the mother's fault. What about Dad, besides?"

"I was working." Sidney puffed on a pipe from the tree stump.

"So was I. Or don't you remember?" Stella turned around on the ice cream chair to face him, exasperated.

"For some reason, the night of your operation, Ros," said Lev, "this schoolteacher person from Berkeley called the station. She was talking about her father. 'I started yelling,' she said. 'That he'd always run out on us, and so on,' I liked that, 'and so on.' I should tell you about that show sometime."

The children trooped into the yard.

"Here come the wars and alarums," Lev muttered before he could explain to Ros, who leaned over the side of the hammock to ask what 'and so on' had meant to him or what that show had been about. Nana jumped out in front of them with her legs wide, bowing.

"Everything will be revealed tonight," she said. "Down by the riverside. Grown-ups bring the picnic, please."

"Okay, okay," Lev said. "I'll go to the village this afternoon."

"Lila and I have already picked it up," said Ros.

~

"Down by the riverside," Lev sang along with his guitar as Ros listened from her corner of the blanket at the edge of the cliff before the Hudson. On the other side of the river, a pile of stony rubble, once a paper mill, by a rusty railroad bridge. "How picturesque." Ros waved her hand through the air, trying to encompass what lay before her.

"I forget why we live in California" — Lev slapped his hand against his banjo strings to stop the chord he'd begun and turned to Murial — "when it's so lovely here."

That was gratifying. Ros grasped the chicken breast that Nana had volunteered to skin for her. Lev was insufferable about the Bay Area, like everyone else she knew there.

"I admire your leaving the skin off, Ma. It's the best part of the chicken," said Nana.

"Thanks."

"I bet you hate the picturesque." Lev leaned over to Lila.

"I just don't care about it. It's been seen and organized by somebody, I guess."

"Plus, this way I get to eat the stuff." Nana, giggling, stuffed skin into her mouth, as Oliver, also giggling, waved the tinfoil sword he'd made for the play and said he had no intention, Lev, of laying his sword and shield down.

"Who asked you to? Not on the blanket, Ollie."

"He's got your number, Lev," said Ros. "Our number, should I say. The peace and love one." Looking for Henry to nod knowingly at, she found him by long-legged Murial, which gave her a pang.

"Go on." Murial handed Dee a pot with a spoon to bang. "Announcement," she said. "But you say it, Lev, it's your family."

Bang went Dee's spoon against the bottom of the pot.

"There will be a baby born to us. In — what month is it now, August? — something like March."

"April," said Murial. "That was lovely, Dee sweetheart."

"Congratulations." Ros felt another pang. "To life" with her Saratoga Vichy water. She felt jealous.

"How marvelous," said Stella from the blanket's edge.

"May I?" Sidney knelt beside Stella, pulled his slacks up, dropped himself onto the blanket, arms hugging his folded knees, reached with one hand towards Stella's.

"Play's about to begin," shouted Nana, standing up.

The children disappeared for a moment on their way down the cliff, then showed up once more on the sand dunes below. They started into the Hudson, walking on the row of small dark rocks that led out into the river towards a big black boulder.

"Be careful, Ol," from Lev. "I want you holding on to Dee at all times."

"Sophie," said Ros. "Hang on to Nana."

"Close your eyes, Ma," shouted Nana. "What you don't see won't bother you."

She obeyed. She heard Sidney telling Henry some moldy joke about Moses and Jesus walking on the water at Coney Island. She winced as Moses yelled, "On the rocks, you schmuck," when Jesus started sinking. She laughed and opened her eyes. Still it bothered her, the children out there on that boulder.

Nana sat cross-legged on the boulder in running clothes and a ruff made out of Queen Anne's lace, while everyone else stood waving and squinting in the flashing setting rosy sun.

Nana said something unintelligible and Dee and Sophie and Oliver ran around behind her and squatted down. "What was that she said?" Ros elbowed Sidney as Sophie, from behind, dangled some small green thing on a string to below her older sister's shoulder.

"A falcon," said Lev.

"A bear! A bear!" shrieked Nana as Dee peeked from behind

Sophie, then made a dash for the front of the boulder. This tiny girl on the front of the boulder preparing to slide — down down — into the water. Dee, Dee. Ros felt her legs picked up beneath her and she began to run. Down the path to the sand point by the river, breathing, stumbling, across the narrow bridge of rocks out to where the children were. By the time she got there, Oliver had come around the rock and grabbed Dee with his free hand, while in his other he waved the stick he'd wrapped in tinfoil. "Don't worry, Ros," he said loudly as she arrived. "I've got her."

All the grown-ups were standing at the edge of the cliff. "Come on in," shouted Lev. "All of you. Now."

Her breath was running ahead of her as she turned to reach for Sophie now that Dee was safe. Her hand prepared for anything, holding or slapping or falling useless to her side, which it did. She looked down at her feet in sneakers that had carried her out here. Back out at that grown-up audience across the water that had watched her run. ("They're all all right, Lev," from Murial. "Let them finish the play.") Felt this stitch in her side, but went on breathing. Found the breath that ran before her inside her now, her lungs catching on, catching up.

"You okay, Ma?" Sophie pressed against her side.

"Fine." Inexplicable tears in her eyes, that stitch in her side.

"Take that, you dirty bear," shouted Oliver. Poking the air with his sword and trying to hit the doll that Sophie had dangled and now held against her chest.

"It's not a bear." Sophie held the doll up. "It's my doll. Stop."

Oliver's next blow, another attempt to hit the doll, landed on Ros's arm.

"Let her have the doll. I'll be the bear if you want, Oliver," said Ros. She crouched down, heard something, was it her knees or ankles crack, began on all fours to nip at Oliver's leg. She rolled over on her back and played dead, waving her arms and legs like a spider.

"You're not the bear, you're my mommy," said Sophie.

Ros's head lifted.

"My sister," shouted Lev from the cliff.

She sat back on her heels.

"My daughter," from Stella beside him almost too softly to her.

Her hand on the boulder helped her stand as Henry, who'd followed her down to the riverbank when she'd dashed across the rocks, cupped his hands around his mouth and mouthed, "My Rosalind."

"Good-bye," she told the children. She walked slowly with her arms held out back across the rocks to where he stood. Teeter tottering, looking down at the wet uneven bridge of rocks, certain she would slip and fall, she stopped.

How tiny jagged were the rocks. How cold must be the water.

"Don't look, run," shouted Nana from behind her.

She ran. She got one sneaker wet as she neared the shore, dipping it in shallow weedy water. Henry's hand reached towards her from the bank. "You came down," she said accusingly as they stood together on the narrow strip of sand. "You followed me."

"You first." He pointed to the overgrown path that would lead them back to the cliff and the others. "Watch out for prickers. They're all over."

"Why didn't you shout before?" she called from behind him. "When I got stuck?"

"Why should I have shouted at you? You did okay with Nana's help." They reached the blanket. He knelt, removed her wet sneaker, dried her foot with a paper napkin.

"Sit." He pointed to the blanket. "I'd like to say," he said, "that I wanted to see what you'd do yourself. But you know me, I never shout, no matter what."

On the boulder, Oliver knelt before Nana, tore off his paper towel cape and said he'd come around the world to protect her, dear Queen. Rising with his hand to his heart to add, "By Datsun."

"The end." Dee stepped out from behind Sophie and curtsied, holding out the legs of her shorts.

"Wait, it's not over." Nana knighted Oliver by bopping him over the head with her wallet.

"Now." Nana raised her arms and flexed her muscles.

Everybody but Ros bowed. She could see the tops of different colored heads. "Go on, Mom," Nana shouted. Ros from the blanket bowed too, hands crossed over her chest like an acrobat. Bowing, smiling, giggling, as Henry's hand grasped hers to lift it like that of a prizefighter.

Silence for a moment from the grown-ups, as if they'd fallen into some dream. Cheers from Lev, clapping from Lila, and Ros's own voice surprising her. "If this be magic" — waving towards everything: the crumbling mill, the setting sun, the children's play, the men and women on the blanket, the revelation of the ordinary, the mysteries that remained, the picnic supper and her wet feet in sneakers which would carry her out of these woods — "let it be an art lawful as eating."

Everybody clapped before settling down to stick marshmallows into the fire, set them aflame, wave them in the air until, charred but fireless, they could be popped into other people's mouths. "Thanks." Ros ate the one that Nana climbed over Henry to offer her from the end of her green stick.

"Hum Six," Ros told Henry, extracting marshmallow from her molar. "You remember? Freshman year. The class we met in and that quote, for the record, can you remember where it came from? Although what I wanted to say was benedictory, but I'm not eloquent tonight. In fact, I feel sad and even silly. Plus my feet are wet." Reaching to lift up the peeled stick Nana had dropped, lifting it, dropping it, as Henry said, "Not really. That class yes. That sentence no. You, of course, I remember. But not with your finger in your mouth."

She took her finger from her mouth and stretched for paper plates, napkins, old bones, watermelon rinds. Met Stella's ringed hand reaching for the plastic forks. Three black cherries and a pile of cherry stones, plastic bags to put the garbage in. As Lev brought out his banjo and Murial poured brandy into waxy paper cups:

> All I want in this creation,
> Two little girls and a big plantation
> Hot corn, cold corn
> Bring along the demijohn.

A song, Lev confessed to them afterwards, whose verse and chorus had two entirely separate origins. Then darkness fell from the sky onto their shoulders and the ground where they were sitting, leaned against each other. As Henry and Lev stomped the red and yellow fire dead with Nana's and Oliver's help, Ros rose with Sophie to walk back through the woods to where the road began, then started up the hill to where their bungalow was.